WAKE

S. C. M. REID

Published by

MELROSE BOOKS

An Imprint of Melrose Press Limited
St Thomas Place, Ely
Cambridgeshire
CB7 4GG, UK
www.melrosebooks.co.uk

FIRST EDITION

Cover designed by Jeremy Kay

ISBN 978-1-907732-66-9

Printed and bound in Great Britain by:
TJ International Ltd, Padstow, Cornwall

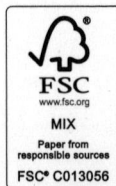

FSC
www.fsc.org
MIX
Paper from
responsible sources
FSC® C013056

I hugged my knees, curled in the corner of this dank room. The cold bricks scratched at my back through my top. I watched water trickle down the walls. Where it hit the concrete floor there were circles of green moss – testament to how long this old warehouse had been deserted. The bare bulb gave off a weak flickering light as it swung on a chain from the ceiling, throwing shadows around the room.

I tried not to look at my friend in the room. His eyes scared me. They were hungry.

This was a fine joke of my captors. I was unsupervised in a room with my friend, but couldn't even think of going near him in case he couldn't control himself.

There was no chance of escape by myself. They were too quick. If they had been human I might have had a chance, but no. I was surrounded by hungry vampires and I was beginning to look a lot more like lunch with every passing hour.

How the hell did I end up here?

Chapter One

I stood with my suitcase in one hand and a pile of papers in the other, peering across the road, trying to read the street sign. I was pretty sure I had the right street but I just wanted to check.

Yep, Kelvin Grove.

I turned and looked down the street, wondering which of these buildings would be my new halls. They all looked pretty similar. An almost orange roughcast finish covered the front of the buildings. Identical windows in rows, with larger windows every fifth one along. Dull silver railings at the front to give the appearance of balconies when, in fact, you would be lucky if you could fit a foot between the railing and the window ledge.

I walked along the street, pulling my suitcase over the uneven paving where the tree roots had pushed up the slabs. I crammed the papers into my handbag, able to recite the details by heart now anyway, and carried on walking to the next building, squinting into the recessed doorways for the numbers. This was it – the start of my new life.

Using my new key, I walked into the echoey main stairwell. It smelled of disinfectant, and the light bulb at the foot of the stairs gave everything a yellow cast even with daylight coming through the glass door. To the side of the door was a row of pigeon holes with flat numbers on them. Directly opposite the door was the start of the stairs. I moved to the side and could see someone's bike was stored underneath the first of the stairs. Beyond the bike was a lift.

Cool.

That would make it easier when my sister visited. I probably could lift her up and down the stairs but I didn't want to try it if I could avoid it. She would much rather stay in her chair anyway: she wasn't a fan of people seeing her lifted out of it.

I shifted my grip on the suitcase and started up the stairs, deciding to test the lift later on. I got to the flat and used the new key again to let myself in. There was an open space inside the door, with a small window opposite looking out onto some trees. An open door was next to the window. I nudged it further open and saw a toilet and basic shower cubicle. To my right was a narrow corridor floored with a hard brown carpet, which I guessed had many stains on it, but the colour hid them well. I stopped when I reached my room number – the one furthest away from the main door – and dropped the suitcase to the floor.

Opening the door on my room for the next year, I wasn't really too surprised. I'd been warned that most halls base their design on prisons but hadn't put much belief in it. Now I was beginning to wonder. Still, it had everything I needed: a bed, a desk, a wardrobe and a chest of drawers, and nothing else. The walls were whitewash and the curtains some crazy colour design you knew was the cheapest fabric available.

Dumping my suitcase on the bed, I had it unpacked pretty quick and then shoved it underneath the bed. I went back out of the room to see the rest of the flat. My room was next door to the living room, which opened into the kitchen at the back. As I walked in a girl looked up from where she was sitting in the low pink padded chairs in the living room area.

"Fit, like?" she asked.

I only knew it was a question as she went up at the end.

Shit. What do I say?

"Hi. I'm Stephanie, or just Steph," I replied.

"I'm Eilidh. Far aboots you from?"

I got most of that one.

"Just outside Perth. Yourself?"

"Aberdeen."

That explains the accent, then.

"How long you been here?" I asked. Now that I realised I could understand most of what she was saying I was able to look at her and not just panic about words. She looked to be tall and fairly well built, with short dark hair spiked up at the back.

"Got here on Wednesday. Other lassie Lauren got here yesterday, and you today. Just got one more person to arrive, then we're all here!" She grinned at me.

"What course are you studying?" I asked, keen to get to know my new flatmate.

"I'm doing politics and sociology. Like a good argument!" She grinned again, and looked like she was going to be full of energy. "So what about you?"

"I'm doing physics. Have to take maths as well, though I'd rather not." I pulled a face.

"Yikes, that sounds like my nightmare. Was shit at science at school. Didn't even take any science Highers. Couldn't wait to drop it."

"Well, politics sounds a bit like my nightmare too!" I laughed and she joined in.

"So what's the kitchen like?" I got up and walked through.

"Nuhen exciting. Usual stuff. We got a decent-sized fridge and freezer; that's something to be thankful for. Got a pal who's in a flat with five other girls and they all got to share a tiny little thing. She's ended up buying her own and keeping it in her room."

I nodded, more 'cause I felt I should than anything else.

"So the other girl, Lauren; what's she like?" I asked.

"Aye, she seems fine. Up for a good laugh. Should have seen the amount of clothes she brought, though. Thought her parents were gonna collapse running up and down the stairs!" She laughed, thinking about it. "You just arrived yourself?"

"Yeh. My mum and sister are coming down tomorrow. My mum's working today so I loaded the car up for her then came ahead on the train to get keys and stuff sorted."

It wasn't my only reason to come early, though. My sister probably realised I was avoiding the car but I think I managed to fool my mum.

"So are there any shops round here that I can get some food in from?" I asked.

"Yep. There's one round the block. I'll show you where it is."

She bounced up from the seat and went to her room. Definitely going to be full of energy.

She came back out, slipping some shoes on, and we headed out the flat. There was a convenience store just around the next block, where I was able to stock up on everything I'd need for the next few days: milk, bread, juice, a few pot noodles, and chocolate. Eilidh was easy to chat to on the way. Seemed she had an opinion on everything, though. When we got back our other flatmate, Lauren, was in the kitchen making herself a cup of tea. She was taller than both Eilidh and myself, with long straight dark hair, and a slim body shown off by her figure-hugging clothes.

The introductions were made and we sat in the living room chatting. Lauren was studying medicine. She was from the outskirts of Glasgow but had wanted to stay in halls for the first year at least, just to try it.

None of us wanted to cook for our dinner so we trooped out to try the nearest chippy. The smell of fat and chips greeted us in the street before we even entered the shop with its brown tiled walls. As we walked up to the silver counter Lauren was complaining, "We shouldn't be eating this stuff, you know. Heart attack on a plate. It's probably a whole day's calories in one meal."

Eilidh wasn't convinced. "It's not that bad, as long as you dinnae eat it every day. Besides, ye cannae beat a good chippy." She grinned back at Lauren.

I was pretty sure Eilidh wasn't bothered about the calories, and would burn off whatever she ate, with her energy.

We tucked into the contents of the paper wrappers as we walked back to the flat.

"I can't believe you actually like that." Lauren nodded to the bag in Eilidh's hand which contained her desert: deep-fried Mars bar.

"Yeh! It's a local delicacy! It was Stonehaven where they first started doing it. Like I said – isn't any harm as long as ye dinnae have it every day."

Lauren just shook her head. She was currently trying to pick her bit of fish out of the batter which covered it.

We sat in the living room, finishing off our food and watching Lauren's TV, which she had brought with her. We swapped stories about school and previous nights out. Mine were pretty tame compared to the other two. Seemed they had had a few boyfriends at school and quite a few drunken nights out.

Eilidh's phone went at the back of nine. She answered it with, "Fit likey quine!"

I couldn't follow the conversation, but could guess that it was friends from home. I was struggling to understand her at all now. Once she came off the phone she was smiling ear to ear.

"That's lassies fae town moved in and wanten to go and check out the clubs. You up for a night out?"

She pretty quickly managed to convince Lauren to go along. I claimed I didn't have anything to wear as I'd only brought one suitcase with me, plus I couldn't be hung over tomorrow as my mum was arriving early. Lauren offered me some of her clothes, but I passed.

They headed out at the back of ten, and I phoned home to check in with my mum and sister.

"Steph! Why didn't you call earlier? I've been worried whether you were all right." Mum's voice was almost in a panic.

"I'm fine, Mum. Got the keys and got my bag unpacked; even been food shopping. You been over the map with Ailsa?" Neither of them were particularly good with directions, that was normally my job.

"Yes, yes. I'm sure we'll manage." She went on for a bit, asking if I needed anything extra brought down despite the fact that I'd already packed the car with everything.

"It's fine, Mum. I've packed everything that I could possibly need. Besides, I can easily come back home to pick anything up. Not as though I'm in another country."

We chatted for a bit more, and then we hung up. I crashed on my bed, but lay awake thinking about the next few weeks, worrying about the course.

Wonder what it's going to be like.

The next morning I sat in the living room with my phone in front of me. I was waiting on my mum and sister arriving. Both Lauren and Eilidh were still in bed. They hadn't come in until about three. We now had a traffic cone sitting in our kitchen – the spoils of their night out. I had to smile at it – the obligatory student traffic cone.

Wonder if they pinched it off the statue.

They were late. My hands were starting to get sweaty. I tried to distract myself by watching the TV.

Eventually I saw their car pull up outside. I jumped up and trotted down the stairs to open the main door. As I walked outside my mum was helping Ailsa out of the car.

"Hey, was beginning to wonder where you guys were," I called.

Ailsa looked over, a frown on her face as she sorted herself. "We took a diversion." Her eyes flickered towards Mum and I figured she hadn't been listening to Ailsa's directions.

"Oh well, you're here now," I said, quickly cutting in to head off any arguments. I walked over and grabbed the handles on Ailsa's chair as my mum got a box from the back of the car.

The lift was just big enough for both of us to fit in. It worked, thankfully. I hadn't got round to testing it before they arrived. Ailsa had a quick look round the room once we arrived.

"Well, it's nice and cosy."

I snorted. "It'll maybe be cosy once I've got all my stuff in."

Ailsa stayed in my room and unpacked the boxes and bags that Mum and I brought upstairs. Once it was done we had some lunch and sat chatting in the living room. Eilidh and Lauren surfaced about one. They came through and got some water, then disappeared off again, giving us some privacy.

Eventually it was time for them to go home. I saw Ailsa down to the car.

"You know you can come and visit any time. Can easy fit a sleeping bag in the room."

She laughed. "Maybe."

I paused. I felt bad leaving her, but I knew that I'd have to leave home at some point. She should have been the one to leave home first: she was three years older than me.

"I'll be fine. Got Mum to keep me company." She rolled her eyes.

I laughed this time. "Give me a phone call when you get in."

"Will do. Keep me up to date with everything."

"See ya." I gave her a hug, then moved round to put her chair in the boot.

I went back upstairs. Mum was hovering in the room, sorting a couple of boxes on the bed.

"Ailsa's ready to go," I said.

She turned and smiled. "She's going to have to get used to me helping her instead of you." I frowned. My mum wasn't that strong. "You know she's got the frame to lean on if she has to."

She waved her hand. "Yeh."

She looked at me then, her face serious. "Your dad would be proud, Steph. You're doing so well."

Tears pricked the back of my eyes, but I didn't want to cry in front of her. I blinked them back.

"Thanks." I gave her a hug. It couldn't have been easy for her either.

We walked down to the car. I gave them some directions for the easy way out onto the dual carriageway. My mum waved them off, saying she knew where she was going. Ailsa's face looked exasperated already.

I stood underneath one of the trees and waved them off as they drove away. I tried to keep a smile on my face but I was worried about them. They were soon out of view. I turned to go back inside, rubbing my arms as a breeze picked up.

Later that afternoon our last flatmate arrived. Natasha was from Oban and was studying French. Her parents were helping her move into the room next to mine. She had just about the same amount of stuff going into her room as she had cooking equipment crammed into her cupboard in the kitchen.

By evening time her parents had left and we all sat in the living room again, chatting and planning what we were going to do in the freshers' week. It all kicked off tomorrow with matriculation. Most of the departments had introductions, and there were tours of the whole university in the next few days. Then there were all the social nights organised, with the two different unions putting on parties and special offers to bring people in.

We talked until late into the night, eventually going to bed when we had run out of steam.

Freshers' week passed in a blur. I did the tours round uni, visited the physics department, and went to a poster fair in the union to get some decoration for the bare walls in my room. The evenings out started to blur into one, and after the fifth I called a halt as I didn't think my bank balance and liver could handle much more. We went to loads of different pubs and a few different clubs. Most of them were quite good – friendly atmospheres – but very crowded with all the students returning at roughly the same time for freshers' week. I had vague memories of different coloured shots, karaoke, and kissing some guy I'd only met that night.

Definitely time to stop.

I knew I couldn't afford to get into the habit of going out lots, both for the sake of money and the university work. I'd always had to work hard to get my grades. They had never come easily and I couldn't muck it up now.

I'd been phoning home regularly. So far Ailsa hadn't strangled Mum yet for fussing too much. They seemed to be in good spirits. I hoped it would last.

We all got on well in the flat. Lauren and Eilidh were the social ones. They went out every night and stayed out the longest. Eilidh got lucky one night and Lauren stayed out a few different nights. Natasha and I enjoyed our evenings out but weren't really interested in staying over with guys we'd just met.

On the Sunday night we were all sitting in the living room again, talking over the last week and wondering what the next one would hold with the lectures. I had lectures every morning at nine, but the other girls' lectures varied from late morning to middle afternoon. Some didn't even have stuff on every day. They were sympathetic at my early start, and relieved for themselves.

I went to bed early, not wanting to sleep in the next morning, but ended up staying awake for ages, listening to the rain outside and struggling to get to sleep.

Chapter Two

I was late. I hated being late: it always put you on the back foot. It was all the more infuriating because I had originally been early. At least I wasn't lost – that was something to be thankful for.

This wasn't how I'd seen my first proper day at uni going. I got up early after having a crap sleep; rushed a shower; grabbed some breakfast; then left our flat. The weather wasn't too bad, for Glasgow. It wasn't raining and there was actually some sunshine coming through the clouds.

Realising how early I was, I decided to sit out in the rare sunshine and flip through some fresher pamphlets that had been shoved at me. Too busy daydreaming and not really reading the flyers for 50p vodkas, time had slipped by. Now I had two minutes to get to the physics building, find the right lecture theatre inside that building, and get a seat near the front, where I could make out the screens.

There it was: my building. Now please let there be signs.

Yes!

My luck was in: signs for the exact lecture theatre I was after. I hurried through the corridors until I came to a set of tall double doors. I paused outside, quickly running my fingers through my hair and trying to catch my breath, then pushed them open.

Shit.

I was late. There was already some old guy in a tweed jacket with leather elbow patches, talking at the front.

Glad to see the stereotypes are being kept alive.

Mr Stuffy scowled at me as I walked past his desk.

What? Do you expect everyone to be on time on the first day?

And now that he had turned to stare, so did the rest of the lecture theatre – easily all two hundred of them.

Great! At least things can't get any worse.

Mr Stuffy continued on talking whilst I tried to scan the rows of seats for an empty one. Without actually making eye contact with anyone, I could almost feel the pressure from their eyes. None of the aisle ones were free so instead of extending my mortification, I chose to sit on one of the steps next to the front row.

Now that I was out of sight of most students, my cheeks started to return to their normal colour. I rummaged around in my bag, dug out a pad and pen, and tried to focus on what Mr Stuffy was saying.

"This is the mainstream Physics course for those wishing to graduate with single or joint honours Physics. Those who have an interest in physics but are not planning to specialise in it, I would advise the Beginners course, which will be enrolling here today at 3.00pm, and a talk with your advisor about your choices." His tone made it clear that he didn't think much of those people. Whether that was the Beginners course or the advisors, was unclear.

There were a few shuffles, and chairs folding towards the back. I guessed a few people had second thoughts. I didn't blame them: this guy didn't inspire much.

"For those of you who do know what they're here for, I'll pass round some forms, and then we may as well get started."

Paper was passed along each row, and the usual details were filled in on forms. There was a steady stream of questions, and people getting out of seats to return the forms.

With all the movement a seat had become available in the row behind, and I gratefully took it. The guy next to me smiled as I sat down.

"Hi." He smiled at me.

"Hey."

"My name's Kevin. Most folk call me Kev."

"Stephanie, tho' most people call me Steph."

"Cool." He leaned back, relaxed now that I'd responded to him. He ran his hand over his hair with what looked like a practised gesture.

"So," he continued, "I'd ask what course you're doing, but that would be fairly obvious, so how about you tell me where you are from?"

I laughed. "Yeh, the introductions get a bit repetitive after a while, don't they? I'm from a wee town near Perth. Yourself?"

"Just outside Glasgow, though I'm staying in halls for this year. Wanted to get the full uni experience, you know?"

"Yeh, I didn't fancy late nights whilst living at home either."

"Definitely not." He laughed, just as I realised that what I had said could've been implying something different.

We turned back to the front as Mr Stuffy coughed and then started his lecture. The rest of the hour was spent scribbling notes and trying to figure out what I actually needed to copy down. I figured that anything on the board was a must, anything spoken was a maybe, and if he walked away from the board to speak about it – it was an aside and not that important. Hoping that I wasn't mistaken, I scribbled and tried to keep up. At the end of the hour I looked over my notes as everyone started moving again. I was going to have to rewrite them: after a day I wouldn't remember what all my little stars and arrows meant. Sighing, I started to put stuff away in my bag.

"So… Steph…"

I winced, not liking that tone. I'd been too friendly. A week at uni and you would think that I would have recognised the look of the guys who seemed to think every conversation led to one thing. Obviously not.

Kev must have caught some of my look 'cause he seemed to change what he was about to say.

"I should introduce you to these folks." He half turned and gestured behind him. At his words a few heads further along the row turned round.

"We've got Cathy closest to us; then Rachel; Alistair, or Ali as he's known; and then Matthew." In an undertone he added, "Definitely Matthew, not Matt." Each one looked up as they were introduced. Got a brief wave and smile from Cathy, a cool once-over from Rachel, a "S'up" from Ali, and a curt nod from Matthew.

I tried hard just to smile and not laugh. It had to be the most diverse row of people in the lecture theatre. Sure, at school a whole bunch of different people took physics, but not that many of them would consider taking it any further. I was the only one in my whole year group to even consider taking it at uni. But here in front of me was a selection from the majority of the social groups.

Kev was the front man, the charmer. He was just a bit too clean cut with his perfectly styled hair that you know he spent longer on than I did on my own hair. I was just waiting on him taking off his casual shirt to find a rugby top underneath, and then his transformation to American teen movie would be complete, except for the accent. Cathy seemed normal enough – a bit shy maybe. Rachel was definitely not in the same league as the rest of us. Everything was perfect: hair, make-up, figure, clothes and – wait for it – there was the designer handbag for her notes. Ali had baggy clothes, fake gold chain, and jeans falling off his backside, though only in the process of falling off. It wasn't like some guys where the jeans were actually below their bum and held on by a worn belt which then insisted on some bizarre walks to keep the last dignity. Matthew had his shirt buttoned right up, collar overlapping his jumper. Combined with his beige cords, he couldn't have been a more perfect image of most folks' ideas of a physics student.

"So, we were probably going to head over to the union and grab something to eat. You wanna join us?" Kev continued.

"Actually, I've got my first maths class in ten minutes."

"Oh, good! So have I," Cathy interrupted. "I haven't got a clue where I'm going. You got any idea?"

"Pretty much," I replied.

"That's a relief. I always get lost." She turned to the others as we started down the stairs. "Well, how about we meet you guys at the union after maths? You can warn us about any horrible food by then."

"OK. We'll be waiting on you," Kev replied as he walked away with Rachel.

Is it just me, or did he seem to be looking at me when he said that?

As I turned to ask Cathy about Kev's behaviour I found that Ali was standing next to us.

"He just doesn't stop, does he?" His breath exploded out. "No offence, girl, but he has been hitting on anything that could pull off a skirt."

Phew. It wasn't just me then.

"None taken," I replied with relief.

"Honestly, some of them during freshers' week – I wasn't even sure if they should be wearing skirts."

Cathy laughed. "He is a bit enthusiastic about the whole uni thing.

Maybe he'll get it out his system after a while."

"All right for you to be so understanding, but you don't have to share a flat with him. I mean, sure, there's gonna be girls coming in and out, but he doesn't have to be so – "

"Point taken," Cathy interrupted again. Seemed she was keen to move on, so I started with my own questions.

"So you guys are all in the same halls and flats?"

"Different blocks but the same site," Cathy provided. As we walked out the main doors of the building I took the lead, heading for the maths building and pointing out the way whenever we got to a corner. Cathy continued to explain that Kev and Ali shared a flat. Matthew was the floor below them. Rachel was in the top floor of her block, in the apartments with en suites for each room, and Cathy was a couple of floors below. They'd all met up during freshers' week, as having one big party outside on one of the rare sunny afternoons seemed like the logical thing to do, naturally. I was then filled in on a few of their exploits during the last week. Despite the fact that they were from very different groups, they had stuck together, with physics being their common ground. I wondered how long this would last as they made more friends.

We were outside our next lecture now. As it turned out we were in the beginners class. Kev, Rachel and Matthew were in the advanced class, so their first lecture was tomorrow. I didn't really mind. I knew maths wasn't my strong point and I was only taking this class as it was a requirement for doing physics.

This lecture followed pretty much the same format as the last. More forms, and then we started on notes. Difference with this guy's lecture was he didn't write nearly as much on the board, which meant we had to write our notes much faster to keep up with his speech. Whereas the last lecture had an air of bored indifference, this one was intense concentration as everyone was listening for each word.

As it finished and Prof. Drosson gathered up his notes, Ali stretched out his hand in front of him. "Might invest in one of those recorder thingies. No way I'm scribblin' like that each day," he moaned.

"You'll never learn it all. You'll just end up with a pile of tapes in your room, and no idea what is where," Cathy predicted. She then turned to me.

"So, you still wanna grab some lunch, or have you arranged to meet up with others?" she asked. That was decent of her; she'd given me an out if I wanted to escape. Unlike Kev. Think I was gonna get on fine with Cathy.

"Lunch would be good." I smiled. "So which union we going to?"

We headed out of maths, with Ali still massaging his hand and Cathy and I chatting.

Lunch turned out to be quite a long affair. We went to the GU union, grabbed some sandwiches and drinks, and then ended up in the bar downstairs. As it got busier over the lunch period more and more people came in that knew some members of our original group, whether from school, halls or parties, and in the end there were about twenty people where earlier there had been six.

Nobody from my school had come to Glasgow and my flatmates had their own plans for today, so I just listened in to the conversations around me. Debates on which was the better union – GU or QM; favourite music; clubs; how drunk we'd all been during freshers' week, filled most of the time. There was a definite split, with some people admitting freshers' week mistakes, whilst others were boasting of what they had done.

Eventually I figured it was time to leave. I had things to do this afternoon, or what was left of it, and the rest of them were settling in to make a day of it. Cathy and I had swapped numbers, and arranged to meet up the next morning before our lectures. I headed out, leaving behind debates on whose round it was.

Walking down the steps, I pulled the collar on my coat up around my neck. It had turned colder and a drizzle had started. The previous sunny spots had disappeared behind grey clouds. I stopped first at the student shop near the main building – the Hub. This building contained just about everything you needed for student life: a stationery shop, café, bank. The only thing it didn't sell was alcohol. I picked up some pads of paper and pens, thinking that if today was anything to go by I was going to use a lot this year.

Registering at the library, I observed that the librarians weren't any exception to ones I'd met before. Their contact with students hadn't made them more lively or flexible. If anything, it'd made them even more serious, with practically no patience. I started to look around, trying to find the areas that I would most likely use.

Yikes, this place is huge! Should have taken the lift.

Physics and Maths had a floor to themselves – a whole floor! There were already students sitting at desks, with piles of books around them and lots of notes spread out. It was the first week. What were they working on already? Feeling slightly overwhelmed by all the knowledge and seriousness of it all, I made a beeline for the exit.

Once I was in the sports building I started to feel a bit more comfortable. In these surroundings I felt more at home. I paid my membership for the year, got a programme of what was available, and then went for a nosy round. The swimming pool was a good size. I might use it at some point but I definitely wasn't joining any teams, so I moved on up the building. The gym looked well equipped, but I wasn't really a gym goer; the treadmill was a lot of time going nowhere, in my view. Further up were the multipurpose rooms. These were the ones I was more interested in. Peering through the window in the door, there wasn't much to see: wooden floors, hooks on the ceilings for punch-bags, and a mirrored wall. It looked a decent-sized room, big enough for the classes I was hoping to join. I hadn't trained in weeks and my muscles were starting to get stiff. I was restless, needing some proper exercise and not just lots of walking. There were a lot of martial arts clubs at the uni I only knew one style of karate well and had dabbled in some tae kwon do, so I was looking forward to learning some new moves.

As I turned to leave, some movement caught my eye. The side of the room had been hidden from view until I turned, and that was where someone was practising kata. I froze watching, feeling bad. Practising on your own needed a lot of focus and I knew from experience that you ended up being oblivious to your surroundings as you focussed on your moves, stances and breathing. Watching someone, I felt as though I was taking advantage, especially as they had stuck to the side of the room and hadn't even put the lights on, trying not to draw attention.

However, I was transfixed. I'd never seen a kata like this. The stances were very different. It wasn't until I tried to imagine doing them that I realised how strange they were. I was good at the style of karate I knew, but I would never have been able to hold these stances for so long. The strength needed to balance and hold still, then move to the next stance without a flinch as muscles trying to hold still suddenly moved again, was beyond me. I looked at the person now: a guy with his back to me. He had dark hair that wasn't long but was back off his face. He didn't have it spiked up like so many guys did. He was broad in the shoulders but not bulked up – a fairly slim build. As I continued to take stock my mind started to wonder what his body looked like.

The way that T-shirt sits certainly suggests enough muscles across his shoulders.

I suddenly realised I was looking into pale blue eyes. I froze.

Shit! When did he turn round?

I could feel my face start to get warm. Mortified, I managed to pull my eyes from his gaze.

Nightmare! You stupid girl, daydreaming! Great! He's probably gonna be at one of the clubs I'll join, and he'll think he's got a regular stalker!

I managed a tiny nod – there was no point denying I'd been watching – then walked quickly away. My footsteps kept speeding up till I reached the stairs and had clattered down a flight.

Once outside the building I gave a laugh of relief, the cold air calming my almost burning face. I continued to walk quickly, heading back to my flat. I tried to reason with myself that it wasn't really that bad. He probably didn't see me properly; I could barely see him as the lights hadn't been on. But I then groaned as I realised that the lights had been on in the hall where I was standing, meaning I would have been as clear as day to him.

Great.

Oh well. Judging by that kata he would be in an advanced class anyway. I'd never see him again. Now why would I feel disappointed at that?

Walking through Kelvin Grove Park, I tried to put it out my mind and just enjoy this bit of green in the middle of a city. I was used to living in the country and although the city didn't bother me too much, it was nice to have this bit of space. I stopped on the bridge to watch the ducks, envying their simple life.

Following a hunch, I kept going through the park until I came out the other side. Looking around, I got my bearings and smiled. I'd been right: it was a short cut. This would save me ten minutes in the morning at least. In a better mood, I headed back to our flat.

After rewriting my notes so they were legible, I left my room and headed to the kitchen. Some of my flatmates were already in and watching the TV in the living room. As I microwaved my frozen lasagne we swapped stories of our first days. Natasha had signed up for her first year French and Gaelic courses. Lauren had her first lectures for medicine. Eilidh wasn't back yet. They had had similar days to mine: lots of forms, meeting new folk and arranging to meet up again. Lauren was going out again tonight. She was grabbing some food just now, then getting changed to head for the pub.

"Hey Steph, you know that pub we went to last week – the one where you had to go downstairs to get in and there were all those mirrors on the wall?" Lauren asked.

"Yeh, think so. Was that the one where you got off with that Greek guy?" I asked.

"Oh yeh, I'd forgotten about that!" She paused with a smile, then shook her head. "Anyway, how do I get there from here? I just remember we went by taxi last time and I've no idea how to walk there."

I gave her directions. My flatmates had realised during freshers' week that I was quite handy to have around on a night out as I never got lost and always knew which way to go. I hadn't spent that much time in Glasgow before but I'd always been quick to get my bearings anywhere I went. Friends and family would joke that I had an internal compass like a pigeon, and was tuned into the Earth's magnetic field.

When Lauren went to get changed Natasha started cooking. I looked on enviously as she got loads of different ingredients out of the cupboards and fresh veg out of the fridge. For the rest of us, our shelves contained milk, eggs, and that was about it. Natasha's shelf was packed. I chewed endlessly on a rubbery bit of pasta as she cooked.

"So how come you can cook so well?" I asked, trying to keep the longing out of my voice.

"Cooking's always been big in our family. My aunt owns a restaurant, and I used to work summers there. Think my mum asked her to give me cooking lessons. It was quite cool really. I experimented with new dishes with my aunt in the afternoon, and then when evening came I was waitressing, or if it was really busy I was put on starters." She laughed. "I was the only person in the kitchen who didn't get their ass hauled when they mucked up a dish!"

"Wow, that's pretty impressive. A trained chef."

"Don't let my aunt hear you say that. I'm nowhere near trained!"

"Damn sight closer than I am," I pointed out.

God, what does she think about my frozen meal plan from Farmfoods?

She sat down at that point, with a big bowl of some curried dish. It smelt good. I pushed away the plastic carton with the remains of my lasagne.

"I've made too much, and it's not enough to do another meal." She paused and then looked at me. "You want some?"

My grin almost split my face. "Cheers!"

Natasha laughed. "That's stuff didn't look that great!" she pointed to the remains of my tea.

I tucked into her curry dish. It tasted as good as it smelled. We sat in silence for a bit, enjoying the food.

After we had finished we sat chatting, and I dug out a tub of ice cream to share. A few minutes later Eilidh came in. She dropped her bag to the kitchen floor and flopped into one of the chairs.

"I hate walking," she complained, "especially in the rain."

"You're on the west coast now. You'll have to get used to it. Give it a month and you'll have even more midges to contend with as well," I replied, laughing.

Lauren came in and joined us then. She was all done up for her night out: short skirt, thin leggings underneath, and sparkling blue halter neck top. She knew how to show off her figure to perfection.

"Why didn't I just go to Aberdeen Uni like most of my mates?" Eilidh asked. "At least it's not as wet there."

"Now you see, if we were being snobby we'd say 'cause you wanted to go to a *real* uni, where people talk properly, and away from the stink of fish from the harbour!" Lauren joked.

"Talk properly?" Eilidh almost choked. "Glasgow's full of Weegies! None of them can talk properly!" She paused, thinking, "Well if I ain't gonna git any sympathy fae you lot, I'm awa tae dry ma hair!" We all laughed at the emphasised accent as she flounced out with mock indignation.

"Right then, I'm off. Think I'll manage to brave the rain. Don't wait up now, girlies!" Lauren grinned as she headed out the door.

The rest of the evening we watched reruns of *Friends* on the TV, and chatted. Ailsa sent a few texts asking how the lectures had been. I replied telling her she would have loved them, to which she replied, "Probably as much as a snail loving a tub of salt!"

Later I fell into bed. The nerves of the first day had left me knackered. I only woke once – when Lauren came in about two in the morning with the theatrical whispers of someone who is drunk. She didn't sound alone. Rolling my eyes, I turned over and tried to get back to the dream I'd been having about a lone figure in a dark room.

Chapter Three

I checked my phone again as I pretended to be interested in the board covered in flyers for second-hand books, band nights and different student groups in front of me. I was early, waiting on Cathy and Ali. Thursday of the second week and we had our first maths tutorial today. I wasn't looking forward to it.

Maths had gone pretty much as I'd predicted – crap. I could follow most of the sequences when there were clear examples, but if the questions varied from the examples then I was screwed, and I had no understanding of why you would want to do the things in the first place. At least with physics there was a reason, a purpose for doing the questions.

As I contemplated one of the questions I was supposed to have done for today Cathy and Ali came up the stairs. I smiled.

"Boy, am I relieved to see you guys. Thought you were gonna make me go through this on my own!" I laughed.

"Nah, don't think anyone deserves that," Ali sympathised.

He had pretty much the same view of maths as I did. Only Cathy seemed to remotely know what she was doing. There wasn't even any point in asking Kev, Rachel or Matthew, as Ali and I had discovered when we were complaining about partial fractions and integration by parts. They had looked at us as though we were thick. At that point we'd decided to just keep picking Cathy's brains and leave the others out of it.

We went into the tutorial room and Cathy persuaded us to sit in the middle as Ali and I looked longingly at the seats at the back of the room. There was no chance of going unnoticed in the middle. As we got our assignments out some guy we hadn't seen before walked in.

"Morning folks. I'm Chris Taylor, a PhD student here, and I'll be taking your tutorial sessions."

Well, this was a turn for the better. I'd been expecting one of our lecturers that we had in the mornings, and so far they had all been pretty unapproachable, whereas this guy had potential to be normal.

"First, we'll go over the questions that were set for this week. Then I'll give you some more stuff to work on, and go over any problems. Let's get started."

The hour passed pretty quick. I'd been right in the fact that most of the stuff I'd done so far was wrong. Ali was trying to put a positive spin on it by saying that at least we already knew we had it wrong and hadn't thought we'd been doing it the right way. I had to laugh at that.

I'd decided to bite the bullet and ask for help.

Never gonna get it sorted by just staring at it.

Whilst it was mortifying to finally admit how stuck I'd been with things that this guy could probably do in his sleep, it was a relief to finally get some of it sorted. Focusing on his explanations, I had to remind myself to not just tune out when I didn't understand. After he explained something once I mulled it over in my head, five other questions immediately springing to mind. As time went on a frown was developing on Chris's face.

Time to give the guy a break. Well, at least it wasn't as bad as I thought it would be. He answers my questions, for a start.

After the hour was over we packed up and went for lunch.

"So that wasn't so bad. You weren't shy in asking that guy questions, Steph. Think some of the others were wanting a shot," Ali commented.

I frowned, looking at him. "Thought I might as well get some of the problems fixed, especially if the whole course is going to be like this. And it's a damn sight easier asking him than interrupting the middle of a lecture to ask then." I felt a bit annoyed at explaining myself to him. He was supposed to be just as stuck as I was.

"Yeh, I suppose. At least I got some of the stuff I was stuck on cleared up as well."

I looked at Cathy for some support.

"I think it was very brave of you asking for all that help," Cathy supplied.

I wasn't sure if that was a compliment or not. "What?" I asked of them, almost stopping in the corridor.

"Oh come on, Steph; he's easily the best looking lecture tutorial person we've had. As time went on I thought you were in some physical danger from the girls in the row behind. *They* certainly didn't get any work done in the last hour," Cathy accused.

"I can honestly say I wasn't thinking about his looks." But now that they mentioned it I supposed he wasn't too bad looking. He was easily over six foot, with dark blonde hair and blue eyes. "I was just thinking someone was going to finally explain this stupid subject to me."

"Yeh, sure," Cathy said vaguely. "Come on. I'm wanting lunch."

We sat in the big cafeteria in the QM union, having come to an unspoken agreement that they had better food.

"So, what clubs you trying out today then, Steph?" Ali asked, smiling.

I'd become a bit of a joke with trying out the different sports clubs at uni. So far I'd got Rachel and Natasha into yoga, though for different reasons. Think Rachel thought she would get a body like Madonna if she kept it up – not that she wasn't already slim – and Natasha liked the chill-out factor. Ali was now into boxing after I persuaded him to go along with me as none of the girls would try it out. It had been a good session but I wanted a martial art that didn't just rely on my arms, as they weren't exactly strong. So I kept looking for some other club. Kev had come along to the judo with me, but it wasn't his scene. He'd been keen for the whole contact thing but his expression quickly changed from a grin to shock when I managed to throw him over my shoulder the first time. At least now he wasn't trying to hit on me every time he saw me.

I'd felt confident enough to try out the karate clubs myself. Although I'd enjoyed them I didn't think I was going to learn many new things. The style of karate I knew had already taught me a lot.

"Well today is the turn of the kick boxing club. You wanna come?" I asked.

"Kick boxing, eh? Might try that. What time?"

"Starts at seven. You gonna come, Cathy? You've got to try at least one of these things. I've got everyone else doing them now!"

"I'll think about it," she replied, avoiding any eye contact.

"Oh come on; you're woosing out! It's good for you. Keeps you fit.

Give you a bit of self-defence. Just try it, one session," I wheedled. I felt a bit mean pestering her but she hadn't tried anything out so far; she just spent her time studying.

"OK, OK, I give in. I'll try it once, but I tell you I'm rubbish at sports. At school the PE staff gave up on me and let me do theory work all the time."

"You'll like it, honest. It's not like netball or anything – way better," I tried to convince her.

She gave a half-hearted smile and changed the topic.

It was late afternoon as I walked back through the park again towards our flat. The trees were starting to change colour, the leaves turning yellow at the edges. It was weird to think that it was already autumn. I had to remind myself that the university term started much later than the school term.

I'd spent the start of the afternoon talking with Cathy and Ali, and we arranged to meet up later to go to the kick boxing. I was wondering if the guy that I'd seen on the first day would be at the club. I hadn't seen him since that afternoon. In some ways I was relieved as I'd made a bit of an ass of myself watching like that, but at the same time he intrigued me. I wanted to know what style of martial art he was doing, wanted to know the person who could do those stances with such ease. I was a bit in awe of him, stupid though that may be.

If only I could meet him without him realising that I'd been the one watching.

Shaking my head, I tried to bring myself out of my daydream. Right now I had to go and do some maths problems whilst the explanations were still fairly fresh in my mind.

Sitting on the bench, tying my shoes, I looked up as I heard the door to the changing rooms going again. Cathy walked in, looking round nervously.

"Cathy! You made it! Over here," I called.

She looked relieved to see me as she walked over.

"Ali refused to come on his own. He stood at my doorway shouting on me till I agreed to come! I shouldn't be here; I'm no use at this," she rattled on.

I interrupted her. "How do you know you're no use if you haven't tried it? Just give it a shot. Promise, it will be a laugh. I'll show you how to do it all."

We finished getting changed and walked to the hall whilst I was giving Cathy some pointers on the way.

"The main thing is to keep your thumb on the outside when you punch. Don't tuck it in. You'll break it that way."

Cathy looked at me worriedly. I didn't know if she believed me or not, but I could always hope.

There were about thirty people in the hall, with at least twenty in the proper gear, showing that they were regulars. Some punch-bags were hanging at the back, and stacks of hand targets and mitts were piled against the mirrored wall. There was no one resembling the guy who had trained in here over a week ago.

Both relieved and disappointed, I waved to Ali, who was swinging his arms around, trying to warm up. He jogged over to join us.

"You've to give your name to that bloke over there, and he'll sort you out."

Turned out 'that bloke' was the coach, and wanted us in groups according to our experience. So for all my promise to Cathy, she ended up with Ali, which wasn't the worst situation. I, however, didn't get the best end of a bargain. The group I was in everyone knew each other and quickly paired up after the warm-up. I was left with a guy who could have been mistaken for a wrestling pro: he easily had seven stone on me. He didn't look too impressed either at having been left with the runt of the group. For all I'd done martial arts for years, I was by no means big and muscled. My main strengths were balance, flexibility and speed. Brute strength wasn't part of my make-up.

I reluctantly picked up the pads. Cathy and Ali's group were working on some basics. We were doing different combination routines. As I looked down the line to try and see if there was anyone closer to my size I noticed that just about everyone was smaller than this guy. I got the feeling he'd been deliberately left unpaired. Whether that was for me, as a cruel trick for the new-be, or just because no one wanted to partner him, I had yet to discover.

Holding the pads up, I was about to nod to say I was ready to start, when a jab landed.

Fuck!

My arm had gone flying back.

Jeez, give me a chance to get ready!

He continued working on the routine, swapping stance and starting anew. I gave up trying to offer any resistance through the pads. My arm was going to move back whether I resisted or not, and I would rather save my energy. For all he had strength, his technique wasn't that good and he was tiring quickly. After the two minutes were up, we swapped over and he held the pads. He held them up for someone his height.

I just looked at him.

He smiled.

Jerk!

I grabbed the pads and pulled them down so I could hit them properly. His smile reduced as he realised that I wasn't completely overawed by him. I started punching. There was no way I could punch as hard as he could so I just worked on my technique and speed. I kept going, trying not to slow down as I got tired. The coach was walking up and down, giving advice and pointers.

"Good work," he said, at my side.

It wasn't much of a compliment but it was enough to put a frown on Hulk's face as he hadn't received any comments on his turn. I tried not to smile too much.

We worked through other combinations with the small pads, then stopped for a breather and to swap over to the large kick pads. I took the chance to check on Cathy and Ali.

"So, what do you think? You coping?" I asked.

"It's not as bad as I thought it would be actually," Cathy replied, with a small grin on her face.

"She's got a mean cross!" Ali was almost sulking. "Seriously, there is no way she's not done this before!"

"Howz your group?" Cathy asked, looking over the people at the other end of the hall.

"I got paired with an ape, but I'm hoping to get even when we start kicking."

Cathy's mouth dropped. "You got paired with *that* guy?" her head nodding in Hulk's direction.

"Yep."

"You should see if you can swap." Ali sounded concerned. "He's twice your size."

"What, and let him think I'm running away? I've faced scarier than him," I replied, laughing.

If not quite so inconsiderate.

Cathy and Ali looked at me doubtfully.

"Anyway, I'd better get back. Catch you in a bit. Enjoy!"

I trotted back to Hulk. He tossed me the bag and I struggled to get my arms around it before it hit the floor. We were to work on power punches to start, then change to kicks later.

As I started to get ready I noticed someone new in the room leaning over to put their bag down at the side. I could just see the dark hair and the shape of the body, and I realised who it was.

Shit!

He turned round, his eyes meeting mine.

Now why did he have to look straight at me?

He kept turning, as though it was one motion, his eyes sweeping round the room, a small frown on his face.

Maybe he doesn't recognise me. Please let that be the case! But he definitely looked at me.

Wham!

My breath whooshed out of my lungs.

Hulk had decided to start whilst I was distracted. I quickly changed my stance and pulled the bag closer, to stop it banging into me.

Wham!

Asshole!

I almost screamed it at him. I certainly was inside my head. Most blokes held back if they were partnered with a woman, especially when punching the chest. Not this one. For all I knew, this was his full strength.

Prick!

With each punch I yelled an insult inside. I should really stop and ask for a chest guard if I was going to be partnered up with this stupid knuckle-dragger.

Dickhead!

How would he like it if I started doing this on his groin? Think he might have some complaint there!

I continued raging in my head, focussing all my anger at monkey boy's face. It took me a while to realise there was someone standing behind Hulk's shoulder.

Great! You again.

For some reason he had a small smile on his face. Maybe he thought this is what I deserved for spying on him.

He lifted his hand and put it on Hulk's shoulder. Hulk stopped immediately and looked round. Walking towards me, my unlikely rescuer held out his arms for the bag. I could barely move my arms to give it to him as they were cramped up from holding it so tight. Pulling the bag out my clasp, he turned. Just then the whistle blew to swap over. With a broader smile he tossed the bag to Hulk now. It knocked into his chest, making a whooshing sound much like I had.

I moved to the side to watch. This could be interesting. They were very different shapes but my money was on the new guy. Although Hulk had broader shoulders with obvious arm strength, he was smaller in height. He didn't have the smooth, controlled movement of the new guy, and for all that the new guy's shoulders weren't as broad, that didn't mean he wasn't stronger when proper technique was used. Hulk's bravado was fading. There wasn't any sign of his smirking now. In fact, he almost seemed paler.

I smiled and prepared to watch. If I couldn't serve just deserts, then the next best thing was watching someone else do it.

I wasn't disappointed. Monkey boy was pushed back almost two steps with each punch that landed. The new guy didn't give him a chance to recover and kept pushing him back, making it obvious to everyone else in the room that Hulk couldn't hold the bag for him. Hulk's face got redder and redder as the two minutes went on. Instead of controlling his breathing he started to hold his breath.

Wrong move!

I knew that as soon as you held your breath the landing punch hurt more and you got weaker quicker. By the end of the two minutes I almost felt sorry for him. Almost.

Turning around and walking away from Hulk, the new guy walked past me.

"I'll hold for you." His voice was deeper than I thought it'd be. It made it clear that it wasn't a question, just a statement. I started to feel annoyed at his presumption.

Don't be stupid, Steph. You didn't come here to be beat on by that asshole.

I nodded gratefully but he was already passed.

After a minute's breather we started on the kicks. I kicked first. I was much better at my turning kicks than my punches. With the right technique you got your whole body behind it. Hulk's face was a bit more serious as he held the bag for me now. There was something deeply satisfying about the sound of the kick when it landed properly.

Whack!

When it came to my turn to hold, the new guy stepped in and took the bag. As this continued Hulk grew more and more tired as he had double the workout that I had, as I got a break when I wasn't holding the bag.

When the paired work finished I moved away from the brute as quickly as I could. The rest of the session worked out quite good. At the end we were given half an hour to do what we wanted, whether that was work on the bags, skipping, strength exercises – it was up to us. I homed in on Cathy and Ali.

"How'd it go then? Persuade you to come back?" I quizzed.

"Maybe. It's certainly different to anything I've done before!" Cathy sounded a bit surprised with that herself.

Shooting a surprised look at Cathy, Ali responded, "Yeh, I'll be back. Think I like this better than the boxing."

"Cool. You wanna work on some bags?" I asked.

We moved over to one side, out of the way of people free-sparring, and grabbed some mitts. I was helping Cathy out with some punches she was doing, when we were interrupted.

"Hey, my name's Sarah. Sorry I didn't get a chance to chat earlier. So did you enjoy the session?" She must have been spokesperson for the group, all full of enthusiasm and almost bouncing where she stood. Her blonde hair was pulled back in a high ponytail and swishing back and forth, without a strand out of place.

"Yeh, it was pretty good. Think we'll be coming back," I replied.

"Cool." She hesitated. "So how do you know Fraser?" she asked. It sounded like she was trying to be casual but her glance towards my saviour from Hulk was painfully obvious.

"Who's Fraser?" I tried to sound uninterested. I didn't want to be stepping on any toes here. A martial arts club isn't really the place to annoy people, at least not until you know how good they are.

"The guy that took the bag off of you." She sounded irritated at my lack of knowledge. Evidently I was supposed to know Fraser.

"Oh, him. I don't know him. Maybe he just realised that I wasn't an ideal match for holding the bag for that brute." I nodded towards the hulk, who was currently doing press-ups in the corner.

I didn't appreciate the way it was my fault for not knowing someone's name, and the fact that she had to have seen that I was stuck with someone the complete opposite to my size.

"Oh, oh well." She looked at me. "It's just he's never bothered to join in our sessions before. He normally works on his own till we're done, and then the rest join him." Again she looked at me as though I was supposed to know something about this.

"Oh, right." I kept it vague. Looked like I wasn't the one he would be thinking was a stalker after all.

Weirdo.

"Well, hope you guys come back next week then." She was suddenly cheery again: I must have passed some test. With a wave, she bounced off out the room.

I turned back to Cathy and Ali. They were looking at me with the same bemused expression that I knew was on my face.

"Maybe this isn't such a good club. She must be trippin' or something," Ali wondered out loud.

"That was a bit weird." Cathy looked at me. "What do you think?"

"Truly random," I replied. I looked round the room. It was getting quieter: just a few people talking to the coach and, of course, Fraser leaning against the back wall behind the bags, frowning off into space.

"I wanna do some stretches, then suppose we'd better head off," I said.

Cathy headed for the door. "I'll get you back in the changing rooms."

"I'll pass on the stretches," Ali quickly commented. "You're freakily bendy and there is no way I'm trying to touch my toes again any time soon."

I laughed. "You'll suffer all the more tomorrow if you don't loosen off now!"

"I'll suffer!" he called back as he headed out the door.

I picked up the mitts and headed over to dump them in the pile.

As I did my stretches I mulled over the earlier session. I decided that it hadn't been a trick on the new-be to leave me with Hulk; it must have been that everyone was trying to avoid him. I also realised I hadn't said thanks to Fraser. This bugged me: I wasn't used to having to say thanks to people for rescuing me in a martial arts situation. I normally wouldn't have given up, but the guy had clearly no limit as to where he was going to stop, and he was way stronger than me. If only it had been sparring I would have beaten him there, but any activity based on brute strength, I was no match. Whilst I was thinking, lost in routine movements, more people came into the room. It was their movement that caught my eye and brought me back to the present. They all moved so smoothly, so confidently. Looking up, I spotted one of them was my maths tutor that I'd met earlier today. Odd: I hadn't pictured him as a martial arts person, but I suppose I'd been focussed on the stupid maths problems.

I got up and looked round for Fraser. Spotting him at the back, I walked over. It was quieter now; only the new guys were here. They must have booked the hall after us. Fraser looked up as I approached. His blue eyes narrowed slightly as they met mine.

"Just wanted to say thanks for earlier." My throat closed over. For some reason, I couldn't seem to get any more out.

"No problem."

It was his eyes. I couldn't pull mine away.

He wasn't side-on to me now. It wasn't dark, and I could see why the girl Sarah would be so interested. I'd already checked out the body, but now it was his face that held me: strong features, his blue eyes and dark hair contrasting with his smooth pale skin.

Focus, Steph! He already thinks you're stupid.

"Yeh," I blurted. "That guy was being a real asshole."

Someone joined us, but I couldn't take my eyes away to see who.

Fraser laughed. "Yeh, so I… saw."

Why had there been a hesitation?

"Anyway, I'll let you guys get on." I turned. It was Chris the maths tutor who was standing next to us. He looked from Fraser to me.

"Hi," I managed, not wanting to appear rude, especially after all his help today, but not really having anything to say. I started to take a step.

"You got partnered with Sean?" he asked.

"If that's the hulk wannabe, then yeh," I replied.

They both laughed.

"Yeh, he's a bit of an ass," Chris conceded.

More of a complete ass rather than a bit, I thought.

Fraser laughed again. Chris was frowning.

"Anyway, thanks again." I turned and walked towards the door. There were three other guys leaning against the mirrors. As I walked past they didn't speak, and I could feel their eyes on me.

Weirdos.

With my back prickling, I left and went to the changing rooms.

I walked Cathy and Ali back to their halls. Cathy would have found her way back OK with Ali, but I was too wired after training to think of going to sleep, so we headed back to theirs. When we arrived there was a bit of a party going on in Ali's flat. The flats in the two immediate floors had come round and the music was up and the alcohol was flowing. I even saw Matthew at one point, but I don't think he stayed for long. Although I wasn't in the mood for a proper session, it was good to have a laugh and a few drinks. As the evening wore on the more enthusiastic partiers were playing drinking games and daring each other. Ali was showing off the new moves he'd been learning, and provided some entertainment when he drunkenly tried to kick an empty bottle off the counter and ended up straddled over the top of it, clutching himself.

Eventually I figured it was time to leave. I did have lectures the next morning, and if I left at this point I would still be able to make them without too much of a hangover. Humming to myself, I headed along the streets and into the park for my short cut. I knew people were recommended to stay away from the parks at night but I figured I could handle anything that came along. It was only about a twelve-minute walk to the other side anyway.

As I walked I peered about into the darkness, keeping a lookout for any movement. I could see some people walking on other paths but none of them were on mine, so I wasn't too concerned. Humming to myself, I kept on going.

"You shouldn't walk through the park at night."

Shit!

I spun round, feet spreading, my arms up, ready to defend.

Where is he?

The voice had been close. Very close, hence my reaction. I couldn't see anyone here.

I started to turn again. No point in hanging around.

Fraser moved out of the shadow of a tree, just off the path.

Jesus Christ, man! You trying to scare me?

"You shouldn't be hanging around parks at night," I retorted.

"I was just passing through," he replied.

"So, not following your own advice?" Getting a fright didn't make me friendly. I started to move again. Even if it was someone I kinda knew, I still didn't want to hang around here. Images of him punching the hulk came back to mind.

"The advice wasn't for me."

He started to walk with me, keeping to the other side of the path, and out of my personal space. Confused by his sudden appearance and his decision to walk with me, I kept quiet, trying to think of why he could be here and why he was talking to me.

He seemed content to continue walking my way. Now that I could see the gate for the exit, and the streetlights started to light us up, I stopped.

"What way you going?" I asked.

"Whatever way you are."

I froze. My thoughts spun too fast to catch any of them. I'd always been paranoid about my personal safety, but no matter what I knew to defend myself I knew that none of it would count against this guy, and there were not that many people that could be said about.

Shit!

"You shouldn't be walking on your own at night. I'll see you home. There are plenty of weirdos around," he explained.

That didn't really help. It could still mean lots of things.

"Think I could see most of them off," I replied.

"Really?" He sounded sarcastic. "What if it had been Mr Hulk and not me that stopped you?" he asked.

"I would have heard him coming for one, and I sure as hell could shift faster than him," I responded. I still wasn't comfortable, but the more he talked the less threatening he seemed.

"Maybe," he muttered.

I started walking again.

Might as well get onto the street.

He followed me out of the park and fell in beside me, closer this time as the pavement was narrower than the path in the park.

I was less on edge now. If he had been going to try anything, the park would have been the place. The street was too well lit with cars going past.

I walked past the turn-off for my block. Watching Fraser from the corner of my eye, I could see him glance at me and then look down the street I should have gone.

Did he know I was supposed to go down there? I'm being paranoid. Maybe he knows the student halls in this area.

Maybe he had once stayed there, as an undergraduate. I assumed he was a postgrad. He looked about twenty-five.

He didn't say anything though, and followed half a step behind me. It felt like having a huge dog walking beside me, keeping to heel. I turned down the next block – the one that I knew had a 24-hour shop on it – and went in there. This place survived on the nearby students and their nocturnal habits. As I walked in I looked up at the security camera, making sure it got a clear shot of my face. I grabbed some fresh milk and paid at the desk. The whole time, Fraser didn't say anything. He sighed when we went in, laughed once, and then became serious again. Once outside, I turned to face him. "Thanks for the escort but I'm sure I'll make it from here."

"I don't mean you any harm. God, haven't you been around anyone with manners?" He was beginning to sound frustrated.

"Well, you saw a prime example earlier of me ending up with the asshole rather than the gentleman." I felt bad. Maybe I had got this wrong. Maybe he had been going somewhere else entirely and was now late because I was being awkward. He was looking at me expectantly

"Fine. It's this way," I gave in.

I didn't double back but kept going round the block in a circle to end up back at my street. I could see our living room from the street. The glow from the TV screen was lighting up two of my flatmates. I stopped across the road from my flat and turned to Fraser. "That's me home." I gestured across the street. "Thanks… again."

"No problem." He then added, "at least, not much."

I laughed, realising now that he really had just intended to walk me home – nothing more sinister. Just my alcohol-fuelled paranoia in the park made it seem otherwise.

"If only you had used that self-preservation to not walk through the park in the first place," he said.

"Yeh, yeh. Whatever. Most people, I could have seen off."

I had the sudden awkward feeling of standing at a doorstep saying goodbye when I didn't want to.

"Most," he said quietly, "but that's not everyone."

Pulling my eyes away from his was more difficult than it should have been. I was all too aware of his body opposite mine.

"So, I'll see you next week?" That came out more like a question than the statement I intended.

"Should do," he replied.

I broke away, getting my keys out as I walked across the street so I didn't hover at the door. I knew that if I stopped, I would just want to go back to him.

Once inside our flat I went to the living room area and flopped onto the comfy chairs. It was Eilidh and Lauren who were watching the TV. They both turned towards me expectantly when I sat down.

"So, who's the hunk?" Lauren asked.

I looked at her in disbelief.

"What? You were right under the streetlamp! You didn't expect me to not notice him walking up the street?" Lauren asked. "Come on; you know me better than that by now!"

"I'm going to bed," I replied, avoiding an answer.

"No way! You *so* can't do that! You know we'll just make up our own stories until you tell us!" she shouted at my back as I left the room.

"Feel free!" I shouted back.

Chapter Four

The second week passed similar to the first. I was finding my feet round the uni and getting into a routine. Lectures in the morning, lunch with friends, afternoons spent either rewriting notes, doing tutorial questions, or normal housework stuff in the flat. The Physics course was going well. The thermal and optics topics were good, but mechanics was a bit of a bore. I managed to keep up with the work though, and that was the main thing.

Maths was a different story, however. The lectures continued to confuse both myself and Ali, whilst Cathy tried her best to explain it all to us. I was truly grateful for the tutorials with Chris twice a week. After the first session I tried not to monopolise his time, but he always made a point of spending at least a quarter of the hour explaining things to Ali and me, probably 'cause he realised how hopeless we were at maths, though some girls in our class clearly didn't think this was a valid use of his time.

After our third maths tutorial we went to lunch, joined by Kev, Rachel and a few of their friends from other courses.

"So howz the maths going for you guys?" Kev asked with a grin on his face.

"Rubbish," Ali responded.

"I'm sure we'll get there though," I added.

"Yeh, you might. I'm pretty sure Chris wouldn't let *you* fail," Ali joked.

I glared at him and whacked his arm. His drink nearly sloshing over his hand.

"Hey, watch it!" Ali complained.

"Who's this?" Rachel asked.

Cathy jumped in. "He's a PhD student who's taking our tutorial sessions. He's got all the girls and even some of the guys watching his every move. He seems to have taken it as his mission to get Steph through the course."

"That doesn't sound too bad." Rachel looked at me, wondering, "What's the problem?"

"Apart from the fact that everyone is imagining his interest in me, nothing!" I protested. "Seriously, there are no signals; he's just helping me out with the maths," I continued, looking round at them.

"Don't think it will be that long before he asks you out though," Cathy added.

I stared at her. "You're meant to stick up for me!" I accused.

Their banter continued as we ate our lunch. Once we finished, a few people headed off for other lectures.

"So, you going back to that kick boxing club tonight, Steph?" Ali asked.

"Yeh, think so. What about you, Cathy?" I turned to her.

She hesitated and then nodded. "Yeh, why not? It was a fun last week. You gonna try and get a better partner this time?"

"Definitely," I replied.

My thoughts turned to Fraser. I wondered if he would be there. Would he speak to me? After walking me home I hadn't seen him again. I wanted to see him, but I didn't know what I'd say to him. I'd probably just stand there looking goofy, useless, much like I had at the club when I wasn't holding the bag. I was embarrassed that I'd thought he'd meant harm in the park, but then it was an odd situation.

Just have to wait and see.

Cathy looked a bit harassed when she walked into the changing rooms this week, looking round anxiously, trying to find me.

"Over here!" I called.

She smiled and walked over.

"Hey. You're always on time!" she said.

"Yeh, usually. Helps when you know where you're going."

Cathy looked embarrassed. "I couldn't remember if it was the second or third floor. I was looking round the changing rooms downstairs and trying to find the room, when I remembered it was up here."

I laughed. "Ah, you'll maybe find your way around by the time you're in third year!"

"I was hoping for second year, actually," she admitted.

Once we were in the hall I looked round for Fraser, but there was no sign of him. Trying not to be disappointed, I smiled as Ali came to join us. As we chatted, Sarah skipped over to us.

"You came back!" she enthused.

"Yeh," Ali replied, the sarcasm washing over Sarah.

"It's great to see you guys. A few of the other first timers haven't come back this week." She sounded genuinely disappointed. "I should introduce you to the others." She started walking over to some other regulars and we trailed behind like puppies.

"I'm afraid I didn't get your names last week, but these guys are Paula, Kerry, Scott…" she went on.

The names started to merge into one as she proceeded to introduce us to at least fifteen people at once. I started to feel like the object at some 'show and tell' – Sarah's shiny new bauble. Once we had been round everyone it was time to start. We warmed up, and then split into groups again to try different routines. This time Hulk was nowhere to be seen, and I gladly teamed up with someone of more normal proportions.

"So it's Steph, right?" my partner asked as I was pulling the targets onto my hands.

"Yeh that's right. Sorry, I didn't catch your name earlier," I replied.

"Greg. Don't worry about it. Sarah is Miss Social Organiser. We're not all as hyper as she is," he joked, looking over to where Sarah was enthusiastically hitting a pad with not much technique. We worked through our routines, chatting as we went.

Definitely a change for the better from last week.

After a break we started work on some self-defence moves. The coach showed us some attacks and how to counter them. Most of the stuff I'd seen before, but some of the defence had a different twist to it. It wasn't what would come naturally to me but it might work.

I partnered up with Kerry and we had a laugh as we tried to put together the self-defence moves, following through the different steps till we had it, and then the challenging part of swapping roles and figuring out the reverse of what we'd just learned. Having good spatial awareness was a definite advantage for these routines.

I noticed Fraser come in this time, as I wasn't so distracted by my partner. He walked round the hall, watching our self-defence routines as we worked, then chatted with the coach for a while. I didn't stop to look at him, not trusting myself to stop working entirely. He didn't acknowledge me either. Stupidly I started to feel a bit annoyed.

What's with him? Walk me home one night then ignore me the next time he sees me? A nod in my direction would suffice.

Time was up. Kerry and I smiled and nodded at each other. We'd been ideal partners for each other. Her background was kick boxing anyway but with my previous experience I'd picked it up quick. As I turned round to find Cathy I just about walked into Fraser's chest. I jumped back and looked up at him.

"You haven't got that lock right," was his opening to the conversation.

"Really?" I asked, with some bite in my tone.

So no acknowledgment, and now criticism?

"Really," he said. "I'll show you how it's done." He looked at me for my acceptance.

I nodded. If there's one thing that I will always agree to, it would be learning a new move. I threw the punch that started the routine. He blocked my wrist and twisted it, locking up my arm and the rest of my body incredibly quickly.

I gasped.

He'd got the lock spot on, trapping the nerve. Few people were able to do that to me due to my flexibility. It'd had caused no end of frustration to previous training buddies. He released straightaway and stepped back.

"You see how it's done?"

"Think so," I replied, rotating my wrist to ease the nerve.

He glanced at my hand. "You ready to try it?"

"Yep."

He stepped in. I blocked and twisted. He barely moved, never mind making any gasp like me. I looked at his arm. It was definitely locked, and even his shoulder was lifted, but it felt like he was resisting. One tug from him and he would be out of it. He just watched me to see what I'd do. I dropped it.

"Again," he said.

Oh really? Fine.

He punched again. I blocked, twisted and threw in an extra strike seeing as my lock wasn't doing much to his arm. He blocked my strike with his other arm and retaliated. I dodged that, then stepped in under his arm and lifted. There was a moment's resistance, and then he went sailing over my shoulder.

Of course he went into a smooth roll and stood up, looking completely unruffled, but I felt quite pleased with myself anyway.

"Not bad," I heard the coach say from behind me.

I turned and realised most of the club were watching. Cathy and Ali were at the side, with big grins on their faces. Sarah was opposite me, wearing a scowl. Even Chris and his friends had arrived for their training.

I felt my face go red. I hadn't realised everyone was watching.

"Thanks," I muttered, dropping my eyes and walking quickly towards Cathy and Ali.

Great! Now everyone thinks I'm a show-off.

We headed for the door. Sarah caught up with us before we made it.

"So." Her voice was chirpy but her eyes held daggers. "If you guys are going to be regulars, you should come to our night out this Saturday. We're meeting at Molokos on Regent Street at seven, then I've managed to organise free passes for Club Visage. We're all going. Got two passes for each person, so you can bring some other friends." The last part seemed to be emphasised.

"That would be good, wouldn't it, guys?" Cathy spoke.

"Yeh," I managed.

"Of course, I don't think Fraser will be there. His group keep to themselves." She looked at me, waiting.

"Well, guess we'll see ya at the weekend then," Ali spoke, obviously uncomfortable.

We left at that point, leaving Sarah behind.

"I've got a new name for her," Ali said. "Psycho Sarah!"

Cathy and I laughed.

"She is a bit unpredictable," I agreed.

In the changing rooms the other girls invited us to the pub for an after-training drink. It sounded a good chance to get to know more of them, and you were always too wired after a training session to go home. Ali had the same invite we did, so we all trooped out to the GU bar.

It wasn't too busy in the bar seeing as there were no special offers on tonight. We took over a group of tables and got the orders in. It was good: most of the group seemed to get on well and had known each other for a while. Sarah was definitely the social person, going round spending time with everyone. I got a few more questions about Fraser that I honestly couldn't answer as I just didn't really know him. I decided not to tell her that he'd walked me home. Only my flatmates knew about that. She seemed to get bored after a while, and moved on.

As time went on the bar started to fill up and Sarah now spent her time dotting between the new people. It seemed she knew everyone. Maybe that was why she was so obsessed with Fraser; she didn't know anything about him and that annoyed her. She was at the bar now with some girls who looked dressed up for a proper night out.

"Looks like Sarah's managed to catch up with some of her friends." Kerry nodded towards the bar.

"Are they always done up to the nines?" I asked.

"Yeh, that's her crowd. This is her night off. She's going for the hard-workout-slash-gym look tonight," Kerry replied, laughing. It was hard to imagine but despite the two-hour workout, Sarah's make-up was still perfect and the hair was chic.

"I'm going up for some water. Get you guys anything?"

After I took their order I headed for the bar. I stood next to Sarah's friends but wasn't expecting a conversation. Whilst the barman was sorting my drinks I had a look around. As I turned, my eyes caught Sarah's and her face lit up.

"Steph!" she yelled, even though she was only a few steps away from me. Judging by her voice and body language, she was drunk.

"Just the person!" She grabbed my arm and pulled me into the middle of her group. I felt distinctly out of place amongst these tall, dressed-up girls.

"Yeh, what is it?" I asked warily.

"Well, it seems you're the only person who can get Fraser to talk! And my friends here didn't believe me when I said that although you didn't know him, you had actually spoken to him twice!" she gushed out. Her friends were looking at me sceptically. I could almost hear them criticising my clothes.

"So I'll guess we'll just have to show them!" She grinned and grabbed my arm, pulling me towards her, and then sidestepped so I went beyond her. I felt a shove in my back as I passed her and I ended up bumping into the middle of a group of tall guys.

Angry and completely mortified at how easily she had managed to work me into doing exactly what she wanted, I looked up.

Oh crap!

Fraser and Chris looked back at me, surprised. I glanced behind me and saw the three other guys from his club that I'd just stumbled past.

"Sorry. Bar is more crowded than I thought," I managed to say, looking at Fraser, trying to convey what had happened through my eyes.

I didn't mean to stand here. That bitch!

"'Scuse me." I turned and went back my original spot at the bar, collected my drinks, and headed back to our table.

"You all right?" Cathy asked.

"You saw?"

Everyone at the table nodded.

Great; a whole audience to my ridicule.

"I'm fine. Can't believe she did that though," I replied.

"That was way out of line. Never seen her do anything like that," Kerry mused.

"Seems she's got a thing about Fraser. She doesn't like the fact that he knows Steph's alive," Ali explained.

A few people frowned and stared at Sarah, who was busy laughing at the bar with her friends. This wasn't good. I hadn't come here to split up a group: things ended up bitchy when that happened and that wasn't my scene. Once conversation started up again I said my goodbyes to Cathy and Ali, and headed out the bar.

Stopping at the top of the steps outside I sorted my coat, giving my eyes a chance to adjust to the dark. I took a deep breath and blew out, the cold air cleaning out the foul taste I had left in my mouth. I was walking down the steps when I heard the door open behind me. My stomach dropped. I turned, hoping that Sarah didn't have that big a grudge, as I would end up gladly whooping her ass and be in more trouble as a result.

"You're not planning on walking home alone again, are you?" Fraser asked as he came out.

"That was the plan." I smiled with relief. No bitch fights tonight then.

"Well, I suppose I could see you back again." He sighed with mock resignation, as he buttoned up his long coat.

"Thanks." I could do with some company. I didn't want to stew over the evening, not that I thought I would get much conversation anyway.

We headed along the street.

Again, I felt very aware of him at my side. We must have looked like Little and Large as I was barely up to his shoulder. I started thinking about just before I had thrown him, my back to his body, his arm over my shoulder.

Wakey, wakey, Steph. Stop daydreaming.

"So, you've made some new friends." He sounded like he was trying not to laugh.

"Hmm, and some enemies by the looks of things," I replied.

He just smiled. "Enemies would imply they were some threat to you." I considered that.

Laughing, I realised that she wasn't much of an enemy. Her tactics were the standard high school bitch routines: snide comments, dirty looks, and only making a move when surrounded by her friends.

I smiled, glad that the situation had been put into perspective. When I phoned home next, Ailsa would get a laugh at the story of how the girl with the high school mentality tried to make me look stupid in front of a guy, but it ended up that he walked me home instead.

We entered the park and I started to look around, checking the other paths for people. We walked along together, Fraser closer than he had been last time. He only gave a quick glance around, and then just looked ahead. It was quiet, so I stopped looking round and started thinking again.

"So, is this not a pain walking me home? Are you going in the complete opposite direction to where you want?" I asked, not expecting too much of an answer.

"Not really. Our flat is just up the hill." He nodded up towards the top of the park. Surprised, I looked towards him. I hadn't expected him to tell me where he stayed.

"I thought that it was just business offices up at Park Circus."

"No. There are some private flats," he said.

Hmm, *our* flat, he had said. Might as well ask now, seeing as he was talkative.

"So who do you share with?"

"Chris, and the three other guys you fell into tonight: Jonathon, Craig and Ross. I'll introduce you properly some time."

Embarrassed again, I looked forward, hoping the darkness concealed my red face. We carried on walking for a bit. We were nearly at the other side of the park. I could see the streetlights through the silhouette of the trees.

"So you all train together and live together?" I asked when I realised that I'd stopped asking questions.

"Yes." There was a pause. "Shared interests, I suppose you could say."

We walked out onto the street. This time I didn't bother leading him round the block. We headed to my flat by the normal route. We stopped across the street. I had that awkward feeling again of not wanting to say goodbye, so I just looked beyond him, watching a couple further down the street going into a flat. Fraser just stood and waited.

I jumped when my phone went off in my pocket. It seemed too loud in the quiet between us. Laughing, I dug it out to read the text.

"Who's it from?" Fraser asked, glancing towards me.

"Lauren, my flatmate." I paused as I read it:

So, if you're not interested in him bring him upstairs so the rest of us can see!

"I would invite you up, but I think you might be in some bodily harm from my flatmates!"

He frowned and looked up at the flat. The girls had the TV on again. He snorted quietly, his eyebrows raising, and then turned to me. "Think I might follow your advice."

"So, will you be going on the night out on Saturday?" I asked, trying not to sound too interested.

"No. Clubbing is not really my scene," he replied.

"Oh well, I'll see you next week then."

"Should do." He smiled.

"Thanks for the company." I turned and walked across to the door.

When I got upstairs Lauren stuck her head out of the living room, an expectant look on her face. When she saw I was alone she sighed and came out of the living room altogether.

"So? Where is he?"

"He decided to stay away from your predatory ways," I joked.

She sighed again, looking disappointed.

"So, what's the story with him then? Are you friends? More than friends? What is it?" she kept on asking.

I went into the living room, to find Natasha and Eilidh there as well. Sitting down on one of the chairs, I thought about Lauren's question.

"I don't know. I'd like us to be more than friends, certainly, but I don't know if he is that interested. He doesn't seem to be."

"He has walked you home, twice. And saved you from that asshole at your kicking thingy," Natasha pointed out, looking for the positives.

"But then he hasn't made any other moves, has he?" Lauren asked.

"No," I conceded, "but apparently that is enough for some people to think he likes me." I told them about Sarah's behaviour at the bar. They couldn't believe it.

"Fuckin' hell min, that's well out o'order! The stupid quine deserves the ass kicking you could gie her!" We all looked at Eilidh and then laughed. Her accent did tend to get stronger when she was annoyed.

"Fit? Well, it's true!" She laughed herself.

"Though very tempting, I don't think I should. I'm probably not that interesting to him. I mean he's a postgrad, looks about twenty-five. Why would he be interested in an eighteen-year-old? When I mentioned the club on Saturday he made it clear he wasn't interested."

"You asked him out?" Lauren shouted. "Way to go, girl!"

"No I didn't. The club are having a social night out. Going to Molokos, then free passes for Club Visage."

"Nice!" Lauren mused. "Club Visage is always queued for ages."

"You can come if you want. We got two passes each," I offered.

"Cool, thanks!"

"So will this Sarah lassie be there as well on Saturday?" Eilidh asked.

"I could almost guarantee it," I responded.

Eilidh grinned. "Think we could be having a flat night out on Saturday! Show this bitch you dinnae mess with us!"

Laughing, we made plans for the weekend. I was going to see if I could get Cathy to give me her spare pass and we would try to sneak in whoever ended up without one. I was starting to feel better about things.

"You could always pull someone else at the club. Sure this Sarah would make sure that Fraser found out. It might just be the push he's needing to make his move," Lauren reasoned.

"I don't think that by pulling someone else I'm going to get the message across that I actually like Fraser," I explained.

"Dunno, like. Sometimes the jealousy thing can work!" Lauren tried to convince me.

"We'll just have to wait and see. I intend to enjoy the night out with or without guys! I'm looking forward to it. I've not been at Visage before and I haven't had a big night out since freshers' week."

"You're far too sensible," Lauren commented.

Chapter Five

Cathy, Ali and I had sorted the free tickets out during our physics lecture the next morning. Whilst Dr Harper was trying to enthuse us on Van der Waals' equation and laws of thermodynamics, we had a whispered conversation on our row. Kev had managed to wangle Ali's spare ticket once he found out it was for Club Visage – apparently this place was *the* place to go. Cathy didn't mind giving her spare ticket to one of my flatmates. We were all convinced that we could sneak in one spare person: with the numbers that were going in they surely wouldn't count. Rachel was busy telling Kev about the layout of the place and where to stand for the best views of the dance floor.

Figures she's been there before.

She wasn't going to be joining us though: she already had plans for this Saturday. We didn't have to worry about inviting Matthew as we hadn't really seen much of him since the first week. He had made other friends and they sat down at the front now. You almost expected to see home-made badges with 'Dungeons and Dragons Club' pinned to their jumpers when they turned round.

Hey, as long as they're happy.

I was just glad he had found people that he felt comfortable with, as Kev clearly hadn't been the company that he was used to.

Cathy arrived early on Saturday, wanting help with choosing clothes and make-up for the evening. This had made Lauren intensely happy as there was nothing that she loved more than dressing up for a night out. Once she had finished with her makeover Cathy came into my room and we adjusted her top so that she felt more comfortable: Lauren and Cathy's styles were just not similar. We were all done up and sitting in the living room having our first drinks, when Ali and Kev arrived.

"Hey, hey!" Kev shouted as he came down the hallway. "Are you guys ready for me?"

Natasha looked at me with her eyebrows raised.

"He's not too bad. He'll probably flirt with everyone for the first hour or two but he'll settle down after that, promise," I assured her.

After a few drinks and pictures for our cameras with us all dressed up, we ordered some taxis and headed into town. We arrived at the bar a half-hour after the meeting time, so everyone was already there. It was great walking in and seeing so many people you knew. They all called out hellos and we moved round, talking to everyone. Our group took up about half the bar. Even the coach turned up for an hour and left with a slightly staggered step as he tried to phone his wife to say he'd was already on his way home.

Sarah looked pleased when she saw me, and headed over, with a grin on her face.

"Hi Steph. So glad you came."

"Hi, Sarah. You're looking nice," I said, trying to be polite. I didn't want to end up with a bitch fight. As I said Sarah's name, Eilidh looked up from the table I was standing next to, nudging Lauren. The two of them made their way round to me.

"So, what friends have you got with you tonight?" Sarah asked. I knew fine she was only interested in one person.

"A few of my flatmates, and Cathy and Ali, of course. This is Lauren and Eilidh here, actually." I gestured to them as they handed me a drink.

"No one else? Fraser not with you?"

Before I could answer Eilidh jumped in.

"Didn't he mention something about the company of certain people got on his nerves when he walked you home, Steph?" she asked me, all innocence.

Sarah's eyes went wide at Eilidh's words. In the pause that followed, Lauren, who had been studying Sarah's dress, spoke up.

"That's the dress that is a rip-off of the one SJP wore to the awards last year," she seemed to muse to herself. "Didn't Marks and Sparks get into some kind of lawsuit for copying the design, though they claimed it was different because of the cheap buttons," she said, pointing to the buttons on the front of Sarah's dress, "instead of the bow detail?"

"This dress is from Oasis, actually." Sarah almost bit off each word. Her face was scarlet. "See you later, Steph." She whirled around and stormed off.

We almost collapsed in laughter. Cathy and Ali drummed on the table and I got a high-five off Kerry.

"Score! That'll put her back in her box for a while!" Kerry grinned.

The rest of the time in the pub went by quick. We were all in good cheer as we headed out for the club.

We walked past the queue outside the club, where people threw envious looks at us whilst rubbing their arms to stay warm. We trooped up to the door and stood in a group. As the bouncers tried to count heads we deliberately milled around and sent Lauren to the front to dazzle the guy at the door. Once the door opened we handed the guy our tickets in two and threes, claiming that so'n'so had ours and this ticket was for that person over there – pointing across the crowd. The bouncers got that fed up they just opened both doors and we all piled in, including about six people from the front of the queue.

Laughing with our success at sneaking folk in, we practically ran past the front desks, where people stood paying. People dropped jackets and bags at the next desk, and we headed upstairs to the music that was already vibrating through the floor.

Noise washed over me as we entered the main room. It was dance music – not really my thing. I could feel the bass beat in my ribs. We had to lean in close to hear each other speak. The group started to split up. Some found tables at the side, others went straight to the dance floor, and the rest went to the bar.

Standing at the bar with Lauren and Kerry, I looked around. I hadn't been in here before and I was trying to decide if I wanted to come back. The dance floor was heaving. Around the sides of it people could look down from the floor upstairs. There was a net across to stop objects being thrown but anyone upstairs could clearly watch everyone downstairs. The girls were dressed up in skimpy outfits, in the style Sarah's friends had been wearing.

Hmm, bit of a cattle market.

As Kerry got an order in I watched as one guy seemed to move around everyone at the bar, speaking to them for a few minutes. Sometimes he moved straight on, other times he talked for a while then shook hands with people. It wasn't until he did this to the person next to me that I realised he was selling drugs. I shook my head as he looked at me hopefully, and he moved onto the next person. This place was definitely not my scene.

Kerry handed me a drink and I turned to see where Lauren was. She was chatting to some guy, leaning in to speak to him. I rolled my eyes at Kerry and she laughed. The friends of the guy Lauren was talking to smiled at us and moved across.

Great.

I leaned across to Kerry. "Why do they always think that because your friend is talking to one of them, that you will automatically be interested in them?" I asked.

She just laughed.

One of them started talking to Kerry. I couldn't hear what was being said as the music was too loud. Another guy, who looked in need of a wash, leaned towards me. I could smell the beer on his breath before he was even close, and his pupils were dilated and unfocussed. I tried to hold my breath.

"You've got beautiful eyes," he slurred, moving his head back to try and focus on my expression.

My eyebrows rose.

"Thanks," I said. I turned my head away, hoping that if I didn't make eye contact he wouldn't be encouraged. I tried to look for Cathy on the dance floor but I couldn't see her.

A sweaty hand went round my chin, turning my head back. I slapped the hand down and the guy frowned at me.

"No need to be like that. I'm being nice to you. Givin' you a compliment!" He got loud.

"Sorry, but I'm not interested. I'm trying to find my friend," I explained.

Please let him get the hint and bugger off!

He turned and talked to his friends, gesturing in my direction. His voice got louder but I still couldn't make out what was being said. Turning away, again I spoke to Kerry. "You happy to move away from here? I dinnae like these guys," I explained in her ear.

"Sure. I'm with you on that one," she replied

I looked at Lauren, who smiled and waved. She was happy where she was. Kerry and I headed round the dance floor, trying to get out of sight of the greasy guys. We were busy talking, when someone grabbed my bum. I whirled round, my hand knocking theirs away with more than a little force. My patience was getting a little thin and with a drink in me I was beginning to get angry.

Greasy Guy looked down at me.

"So what's wrong with me then? Why you running away?" he almost shouted.

He was lifting his hand again, reaching out to me. I moved out of his reach.

"There's nothing wrong with you," I replied, still trying to be diplomatic. "I'm just not interested. I'm not looking for anything tonight."

"So just because you're not looking, you're gonna give up a chance to get with me?" he asked, incredulous that this might be the case.

This guy is unbelievable!

Being polite wasn't getting me anywhere.

"Go away. I don't want to know." I couldn't get any more direct than that.

He scowled and drunkenly staggered off.

I turned back to Kerry and we moved again round the dance floor so we were now on the opposite side from the door. The music changed. This song had a bit more of a tune to it instead of all beats. Beginning to relax, we started chatting again, laughing at the guy who wouldn't take a hint.

I had only a moment's warning.

Kerry's eyes focussed beyond me and went wide. She started to open her mouth. I spun on the spot. My arms came up across my body, knocking the drink that was being thrown at me to the side, the contents spilling everywhere. The greasy guy continued on in my direction, following where he had thrown the drink. I set my feet, bracing myself, then pulled my arms back and slammed them into his chest.

"*FUCK OFF!*"

I screamed it, both out loud and in my head. He fell on his arse and skidded on the now wet floor where the drink had spilled. Everyone next to us turned, watching his progress as he continued to skid a good five metres away from me.

"Wow, Steph!" Kerry exclaimed.

He slipped to his feet. His face red, he was raging. He started to move back towards me but was stopped when two bouncers moved into the gap between us. With everyone staring at Greasy Guy and him being obviously angry, each bouncer hooked an arm under one of his and started dragging him towards the door.

"Oh my god, Steph!" Kerry continued. "You OK?"

"Yeh. Just a bit of a fright." My arms were shaking, adrenaline pumping through me.

"Come on. I think I can see some of our guys at a table over there." She pulled me through the crowd towards some tables. Cathy, Ali and Kev were there, along with some others from the club. Kev was chatting to some girl I'd never seen before.

"You'll never guess what just happened!" Kerry went into full details, filling everyone in.

I tuned out and looked round the room. We were sitting right at the side, with the dance floor between me and the door. Adrenaline was still pumping through me. I started to feel as though everyone was staring at me. It was too loud. My ribs hurt, the music pounding through them. I started to breathe too quickly. I needed to get out of here. I stood up.

"You OK, Steph? You're not looking too great," Cathy asked.

"Yeh, I'm fine. Just tired. I'm going home," I managed between breaths.

"You want us to come with you?"

"No. It's fine. I'll see ya on Monday."

I dived into the crowd on the dance floor. Didn't want them to see me like this. I knew what was happening now. I was having a panic attack. I hadn't had one in years – not since before I started martial arts.

Need to get out.

I tried to head towards the exit, my breathing becoming more exaggerated. People were knocking into me, shoving me.

Have to get out. Have to breathe. Not enough air.

It felt as though someone was tightening a belt around my ribs. I couldn't get enough air in. I was being knocked by dancers. I couldn't figure which way the door was.

I'm lost! I need to get OUT!

Gulping air, I continued to fight my way through the crowd. People were really staring at me now. My throat was tightening.

Fucking Hell! Someone get me OUT OF HERE!

The lights above me were spinning, making it even more disorientating. White, red, green, blue. A strobe light started, making everyone move in a jerky motion. All I could see were the bodies around me, pressing me in, with no way through.

Breathe! Give me AIR! GET ME OUT OF HERE!

I burst free of the dance floor, almost falling to the floor as the last dancers gave way. I ran through the doors leading to the stairs, and clutched the banister to stop me falling. My head was still in a panic.

Get out. Get out. Get out! Get OUT! Need air!

Thankful that I hadn't brought a bag or jacket and had fitted everything that I needed into my jean pockets, I dived passed the desks, with the bored clerks giving me funny looks.

Bursting through the entry doors to the club, I tried to take a deep breath of cold air and almost choked as I got a lungful of smoke from the huddled crowd smoking next to the door.

Coughing, I started walking, giving the bouncers a nervous smile as they watched me. People were still making their way towards the entrance. Everyone was in groups, laughing, talking, drunk.

The panic attack seemed to have removed all traces of alcohol from my system. I was fully aware of everything around me bathed in the orange glow of the streetlamps. All the people talking, slurring, their conversations too loud. The black cabs speeding past, their wheels spraying up water. The smell of grease from the kebab and chip shops, with their harsh strip lights lighting up the pavement in front of the steamed-up windows. I even spotted a cat slinking away behind some boxes up an alley. I registered the fact that it was cold but I didn't really feel it. The adrenaline was keeping me warm. My fingers and toes were tingling.

I kept walking, heading home, taking the time to calm down. Now that I was out of the club my sense of direction was back to normal. I was heading out of the city centre towards the west end, where our flat was. After walking a couple of blocks I was almost calm again. Goose bumps had started on my arms.

I was watching a group of guys at the corner up ahead, when they turned and started walking towards me.

"Well, look who's 'ere!" a voice shouted in a slur.

I looked up.

Fucking hell! No way!

It was Mr Greasy from the club. Except this time he had four friends with him and there were no bouncers here: we were too far away from the clubs.

Oh shit. Shit, shit, SHIT!

My adrenaline rush for the evening was gone. I was washed out.

His friends spread out on the pavement behind him, meaning I couldn't go around past him. He smiled at me. It was an evil grin. He opened his mouth to start speaking, but I heard someone else instead.

"Stephanie, I've been looking for you!" a deep voice called from behind me.

I recognised the voice. Relaxing, I risked a quick glance behind me. It was Fraser jogging towards me, with Chris following behind him. Moving up beside me, Fraser slipped his arm around my waist and pulled me close.

"I didn't see you at the club," he said, looking down at me, his eyes scanning my face.

He looked up then to face Mr Greasy, whose grin was sliding off his face. It was quickly replaced with annoyance now that the odds weren't so much in his favour. Fraser and Chris were both bigger than any of his cronies, and they had an air of calm confidence around them instead of drunken bravado.

"Can I help you?" Fraser asked him. There was a definite edge to the question. Nobody would have answered yes to it. Chris moved up to my other side.

Looking at the two guys either side of me, Mr Greasy glared back at me.

"Suppose not." He spat in front of him, then moved off the pavement and around us, his friends following suit.

I sighed, my legs almost folding underneath me. This was too much for one night. Fraser tightened his grip at my waist, taking some of my weight.

"You OK?" he asked.

"Fine," I managed. After my adrenaline rush and the fright, I was beginning to feel tearful and I *really* didn't want to cry in front of these guys.

We started walking again, slowly.

"What happened?" Chris asked after a while.

I explained what happened in the club. I was surprisingly talkative. Possibly my drunkenness was returning – that and being tired. I was aware I should shut up, but I kept on talking about how crap that club had been, and that I was never going back there even if it was '*the* place to be'.

"So how come you were out here?" I asked, looking up at Fraser. I was leaning into his side now, definitely using him to stay upright.

"Heard you were in trouble. Thought you could use some help," he smiled.

"Don't be stupid. You couldn't have heard me yelling at that guy!" I laughed, still a bit drunk.

"Think everyone in Glasgow who could hear you, did hear you." He laughed.

I frowned, not really understanding him.

Putting it from my mind, I closed my eyes, trusting to Fraser and Chris to keep me going right. It was weird. I'd never felt so safe. Me, the one who always had to be aware of everything around her and watching everything that was happening, was quite happy walking along with my eyes closed, being guided by the man beside me. With these two guys walking either side of me I knew nothing would touch me.

A while later I heard Fraser's voice. "Stephanie. Your key?"

I fumbled at my pocket, and then held out my key. I heard a door open and I opened my eyes.

"Oh, I'm home," I managed.

What a stupid thing to say. No shit, Sherlock!

I stepped away from Fraser, feeling suddenly cold without him there.

I could still feel where his arm had been around my waist. Turning to face them from my doorway, I started to feel really embarrassed about what had happened earlier.

"Well, it seems I've to say thanks once again. Why is it I'm always saying thanks to you?" I joked.

"No problem." Fraser smiled. "Try to stay away from the idiots next time you're out."

I laughed. "Will make it my top priority!"

They turned and started walking up the street. I closed the door and headed upstairs, feeling very alone. Stumbling into my room, I kicked off my shoes and fell into bed. Thinking of Fraser's arm around my waist and hearing him saying my name, I fell asleep.

Chapter Six

Over the next few days we were all talking about the night out. Everyone had enjoyed the pub but there was a split in opinion on the club. Some people loved it; some people hated it. A few stories came out. Both Lauren and Kev had got lucky that night; there was my story, which got exaggerated to throwing the guy across the dance floor; and apparently even Cathy had ended up kissing someone.

We were still talking about it all in physics on Monday.

"So, Steph, where did you get to on Saturday?" Kev asked, as we listened to Mr Stuffy droning on about some mechanics thing. Think he may have something to do with my lack of enthusiasm for the topic. The textbook had provided most of my tuition so far.

"Well, after that jerk tried to hit on me literally, I wasn't really in the mood for dancing, so I headed home," I explained.

"Oh, that's not good. You should have stayed and put that guy out your mind. Had a good time." Cathy seemed determined to see positives.

"Oh yeh? Just like you, I hear!" I joked. "Think I would have struggled with that. It was a good night up till that point though."

Cathy blushed, but she smiled at me anyway.

"I think a good night was had by just about everyone, actually." Kev stretched his arms out in front of him, and then put them behind his head. There was a smug smile on his face.

Rachel, Cathy and I pulled faces, shaking our heads.

I hadn't told them about my rescue by Fraser and Chris. For some reason it seemed quite a private thing, and I still couldn't explain to myself how they had been there, never mind trying to explain it to anyone else.

In our maths tutorial I watched Chris walk in, and I saw him in a slightly different light after the weekend. Where Fraser had a definite presence and was clearly someone capable of looking after himself, Chris hadn't seemed to have these qualities. Now that I had seen him step up to defend me, however, I could see it. It was more subtle than with Fraser but still there: an air of confidence, a sure way of holding himself. I was surprised that I hadn't spotted it before. I normally picked these things up.

Chris went over the set work for today. After we started on other problems he made his way over to our table as usual, to sort out the tons of questions that I normally had.

"So, recovered from your evening of trauma?" he asked me, with a small grin on his face.

Cathy and Ali turned to stare at me. I could almost feel their eyes pushing at me.

They don't know! Don't say anything! Please don't say anything.

I shouted it in my head. I could feel a blush start on my face.

There was no way I was getting out of this now; they would pounce on me as soon as Chris moved away.

Chris stopped grinning and looked from me to Cathy and Ali.

"I mean, when I bumped into you this morning in the park, what you described didn't sound like a great night to me," he said carefully, watching me.

"Yeh." I managed a shaky laugh. "All behind me now. So, I was stuck with questions two, three…"

He pulled up a chair and started to go through the work with me. I could still feel Cathy's intense scrutiny but at least Ali was concentrating more on the maths now.

At lunch I was deep in thought, letting the rest of the table talk away around me. We were a big group today. The way our different lectures worked we were all able to meet up with friends to form a group of about twelve, so it went unnoticed that I didn't join in the conversation.

I was trying to figure something out, and it wasn't a maths problem. I was thinking over all the times that I had met Chris and Fraser. Something in the tutorial this morning was nagging me, and it sparked a link with other situations. I just couldn't put my finger on it.

"You're quiet, Steph," Cathy's voice interrupted.

I almost jumped. Looking round, I saw most people had headed off. It was just Cathy, Ali and Kev left.

"Yeh. Just thinking. Few things on my mind."

"Would one of them be Chris?" she asked with a smile. By her expression I wasn't totally off the hook. She had some questions yet.

"No. Just some stuff at home. I need to phone my sister. Actually I might just head off and do that now. I'll catch you guys later." I picked my stuff up and left.

Walking home, I headed into the park and sat down on one of the wooden benches halfway up the hill to think. I watched the ducks in the pond, just following their random pattern as they paddled about. I was cold but it was nice to see the blue sky and the weak sunshine. Made a change from grey clouds. Pulling my feet up, I rested my chin on my knees, staring off across the trees.

What is it? What is it that's bugging me? Something about tutorial... Chris... talking about the night out.

I didn't want to.

He knew I didn't want to talk about it!

That's probably because it was written across my face.

Hmm. What else?

How did they know where to find me? Right at the best possible moment they turned up. And Fraser said he'd *heard* me.

He always seemed to know what to say to me, answering my worries.

This line wasn't getting me anywhere. The only answer at the end of this was that Fraser and Chris were psychic. My logical brain couldn't accept that. Where were the boundaries, the limits with that? It didn't answer anything; just asked more questions.

But what was it, then? What was it that was bothering me? Where were the connections? Surely, as a scientist I should be able to work through this and join the dots; come to some sort of conclusion.

Frustrated, I sat there, trying to clear my thoughts for what must have been over an hour. Finally, when I couldn't sit in the cold any longer, I got up and went home.

In the flat I followed the smell of something delicious to the kitchen, to find Natasha eating at the table. I dumped my stuff on a chair and grabbed some microwavable sweet 'n' sour chicken and rice from the freezer. After shoving it in the microwave and punching the buttons, I slumped in the chair, waiting for my tea to go ping.

"Bad day?" Natasha eyed me sideways.

"Not really. Just got something on my mind that I can't figure out."

"Wanna talk?" she asked.

"Don't know if it will help. Sometimes I think the best way is to try and forget about it, then the answer will just suddenly pop into your head. But I can't seem to get this out my mind."

The microwave pinged.

Trying not to burn my fingers, I tipped my food onto a plate and sat back at the table.

"So what's been happening with your course, then?" I asked, in a bid to distract myself.

"Well, French is going OK. I've spent the last two summers working in France to try and get ahead of the game, so it's fine. Gaelic, on the other hand, is way more difficult. I didn't think it would be this hard to pick up."

She continued to talk about her course and I felt really bad as my thoughts drifted away.

Finished with my meal, I started doing the dishes, when Eilidh came in.

"Hey, girlies, what's up?"

"Nothing for me. But I think Steph's got something plaguing her," Natasha joked.

"Not literally, I hope!" she laughed, looking at me with a raised eyebrow.

"No. Just got stuff on my mind."

"Hmm, that does sound like guy trouble." She paused. "You know what that calls for?"

We shook our heads.

"Cheesecake!" Delving into her shelf on the freezer, she pulled out a family-sized cherry cheesecake.

"You are such a stereotype!" I laughed.

"What? You gotta have an emergency sugar supply! Are you saying that you don't want a spoon then?" she asked slyly.

"Now I never said that!" I quickly corrected, grabbing the spoon off her.

We ended up eating the whole thing and when Lauren came in we started on some drinks and chocolate. Our impromptu girly night in worked to distract me, and I fell into bed later reasoning that I couldn't figure anything out till I had more information. I'd just have to try and ask a few questions, and hope I didn't end up like Sarah.

The rest of the week was fairly uneventful. I spent a lot of time thinking about Fraser and Chris. I tried to work out what I could ask Fraser, if I should ask him anything. How had he found me that night? Most of the time I ended up distracted, not trying to figure out my questions but imagining him with his arms around me again, except this time I wasn't drunk and about to fall down.

I had just started to get changed for training when the door went. I looked round to see Cathy coming in.

"Hey, you're not late!" I laughed.

"Yeh. Made an effort tonight," she joked.

"So, you never did tell me about this guy at the club," I said, fishing for information.

Cathy filled me in as we got changed and went into the hall. The usual crowd were warming up. Ali and Kerry joined us, chatting away.

"Think Sarah is trying to ignore your existence now," Kerry informed me. "She hasn't mentioned your name or Fraser's since the weekend. Hopefully she'll get over it all and go back to her relatively normal self."

"Hope so," I added.

We did warm up and then split up for pad work. I partnered up with Kerry again and we worked through different combinations. After that we started to learn the basic katas, or patterns, as some of them called it. It was a good workout. I needed to concentrate as I tried to remember and combine all the different moves. It helped to take my mind off everything I'd been wondering about.

I was keeping an eye out for Fraser whenever I remembered, but he was late. As time went on the thought occurred that maybe he wasn't coming. This annoyed me as I had figured I could stay behind at the end of training and ask a few questions, under the pretence of thanking him, of course, and finally get things sorted. Well, if he wasn't coming then

I would just have to quiz Chris instead. He always turned up later with the others anyway.

Training finished. The four of us worked on the bags for a while but I couldn't focus as it was clear that Fraser was not coming. Neither was Chris or anyone else. I finally gave up thinking they were coming. Annoyed, I went and got changed with Cathy and Kerry.

"So, you guys coming to the pub again?" Kerry asked, pulling her jacket on.

"Yeh. That would be good," Cathy replied.

"Think I might pass this week. Don't wanna push my luck too far with Sarah!" I laughed.

"You shouldn't let her decide where you go," said Kerry, frowning.

"Nah, seriously, I just want to get home. Got a few things to sort."

I walked down to the pub with them but left them at the door. Turning away, I headed for the park.

I thought of what Fraser would say to me about walking on my own. It was hardly late though: much earlier than I usually walked through here. Leaving the pavement, I walked into the dusk, the orange glow behind me. I looked round, checking the other paths as usual. All seemed quiet: just a faint rustle of trees. I headed along over the bridge, checking to see if any ducks were out, but they were all hidden away for the night. I started to think again about Fraser and Chris but it just annoyed me.

I should just forget about it.

I was imagining things about them. Coincidences do happen. An overactive imagination was all that was wrong here. Starting to feel better, I looked around again. I was almost out of the park. The orange glow of streetlights were up ahead.

A stone scuffed along the path behind me.

I had only just turned my head, when there was someone already right in front of me. I tried to bring my hands up to push him away. He grabbed my shoulders, his fingers digging in, one hand pulling my hair, tilting my head. Pain exploded at my neck.

What?!

I couldn't think; my thoughts were fuzzy.

"No!" I gasped.

I couldn't move; couldn't see.

I could hear a noise – almost a snarl – but couldn't tell where it was coming from.

A dog?

My thoughts drifted away. I didn't want to pass out. The guy holding me suddenly moved away, as though thrown off. He hadn't in fact let me go, and I fell to the ground, hitting my head as he went flying over me.

I lay there, still unable to move. It was as though my whole body had gone numb. My thoughts were sluggish. Lights flashed in front of my eyes. My neck and head hurt. I tried to think of what was happening. Scuffles and snarls were coming from behind me but I couldn't think what it was.

The noise stopped.

I still lay there. Breathing was taking a lot of effort. I could feel each breath: in, out, in, out, my ribs moving up, the air rushing down my throat.

I knew I should stand up, but I couldn't think why. I couldn't move my legs, anyway.

Someone leaned over me, placing their hand on my shoulder.

Who's that?

"Stephanie?"

That's me.

"It's Fraser. Can you stand?"

"Mmm," I managed.

At least my lips can move!

"Guess not, then."

An arm went underneath me. I sailed through the air and was upright. Fraser's arm was underneath my arms. My bag was in his other hand.

Hey, I can see again!

Why couldn't I see before now?

Why had I been lying down in the park?

The streetlights ahead spun as I tried to focus. I put an arm out to stop the spinning. Fraser caught my hand and tightened his grip around me.

"I think you need to get home." He frowned at me.

Home would be good.

I lifted a leg to start walking, and almost fell on my face. Fraser caught me, and the world spun again as he lifted me up. I closed my eyes to stop the spinning. When I opened them I was curled up against Fraser's chest.

This is better.

I tried to look beyond my shoulder at where we were going. All I could tell was we were going uphill. My flat was downhill.

Where are we going?

I tried to speak. It resulted in another pathetic moan.

"I'm taking you back to my place. You need someone to watch you after hitting your head like that," Fraser explained.

That makes sense, I think.

I closed my eyes again. Fraser's rhythmic step was lulling me to sleep. I was vaguely aware of a door opening, bright lights, warm air, voices; then a comfy bed, and I was gone.

Chapter Seven

I woke.

It was dark.

Lying still, I looked ahead. I didn't have the energy to move. My limbs felt like lead weights. There was a big sash window in front of me, with long, heavy dark curtains framing it. The sky was a dark grey outside. I could see only clouds.

I was lying on my side. As I looked down at my arm curled under my head I realised I was fully clothed and was grateful for that, for some reason. A blanket covered me to my shoulders, the weight of it keeping me warm.

Where am I?

I couldn't remember arriving at this place. How had I ended up in this bed?

Surely I haven't had a one night stand?

My face started to go red. Had I? No. I wouldn't be dressed if I had.

Phew!

Someone cleared their throat behind me. I turned my head slowly.

Why did that take so much effort? Why does it hurt?

I frowned, looking across the room. There was a man sitting in a chair next to a desk on the other side of the room. The chair was turned away from the desk and facing the bed. I knew this person, but I couldn't name them for some reason.

That should worry me.

It didn't, though. I knew I trusted this person, even though he had an air of danger. A tightness around his eyes, he was on edge. I knew that much.

"How are you feeling?" His voice was deep, smooth. It relaxed me more.

Compared to what?

I knew something had happened to me but I didn't know what. If I'd been hit by a bus, then I was feeling great. If I had a paper cut then I was feeling shit.

I tried to open my mouth to speak but I only managed a mumble. The guy stood up and walked across. He sat at the bottom of the bed.

Fraser! That's your name.

He smiled.

"Still pretty tired?"

I nodded. My head was feeling woozy. I was struggling to keep my eyes open.

"Well, it *is* the middle of the night. Go back to sleep. You should feel better in the morning." He stood up, still looking down at me, frowning. With a brief smile he turned and walked out the room, closing the door softly behind him.

I could hear a murmur of voices outside my room.

I fell back to sleep.

My sleep wasn't restful. I dreamed. Dreamed of darkness, people grabbing me, voices snarling. I could hear voices, a debate.

Will she live?

What do we do with her?

Is she wakening up?

I knew people were coming and going in the flat, though I didn't hear any doors. I knew that Fraser came into the room regularly to check on me. Sometimes he just looked at me; other times he pulled the blanket up where I had thrown it off. Once he leaned in close and I could feel fingers pressing at my neck where it was aching. I slept almost in a stupor. I was aware of things but didn't have the energy to move. I ached everywhere, but in particular in my head and neck.

Maybe I've got the flu.

Finally I slipped into a deeper sleep.

I woke up. It was light outside. The curtains had been pulled over but some sunlight slipped through the thin gap between them, highlighting little motes of dust. I sat up. Still feeling a bit dreamy, I stood up. I wobbled and put my arm out to steady myself against the wall.

Standing there for a minute, I decided to try for the door. As I walked across the room the door opened before I was half way there.

Fraser looked at me with surprise. I stopped where I was, watching him.

"Feeling better?" he asked, watching me.

"Much," I managed, my voice cracking. My throat felt incredibly dry.

"Why don't you come and sit through here. I'll get you some water." He held open the door and I walked past carefully. The next room was a large living room, though there was no window to the outside. It was the central room in the flat, with what I presumed were bedrooms and the kitchen behind the doors leading off it. All of the other doors were shut.

Fraser guided me to the largest of two sofas, and I sat down. He then handed me a glass of water, which I drank half of before taking another breath. He sat on the other end of the sofa and stared off into space.

I felt stoned. I'd only ever had one joint before, when I was in high school, and this is exactly how I'd felt. My thoughts were so slow. It was as though they were struggling through mud to get to the surface. My muscles moved slowly, taking a great effort to do simple things. My head fell back onto the couch and I looked at Fraser.

What is he thinking?

He turned to look at me, his eyes considering.

"What happened?" I asked.

He paused.

"You fainted. In the park, after training. You hit your head pretty hard when you fell." He watched me.

"Had you eaten before you went training? I know what you freshers are like with your diets when you get to uni. Living off kebabs and toast. Never a veg in sight." He gave a half-hearted laugh.

I continued to watch him. Something wasn't right, but I had no idea what.

"So how did I end up here?"

"I was just behind you on the path, walking home. I saw you fall," he explained.

But that's not true: you weren't where I'd wanted you to be.

I couldn't make sense of that. I couldn't work out my own thoughts. Turning, I looked round the rest of the room. There were doors leading off everywhere. I remembered he said he stayed here with four other guys. I pulled my knees up, suddenly feeling uneasy.

"Are you cold? I'll go get that blanket." Fraser was out of his seat before I could answer.

The blanket was draped over me and I grabbed the edges, pulling it under my chin, watching as Fraser sat back down again. He picked up a remote and switched on a TV on top of a table against a wall. It was comedy reruns, the volume down low. The flat was quiet, as though it was waiting on something, listening.

"Who's in there?" I nodded towards one of the doors.

Fraser looked at me. "That's Chris's room."

"Oh."

I kept looking round. The walls were a deep cream. The woodwork was all stained dark. There were pictures up on the wall, though not your standard student Bruce Lee posters but proper pictures in dark frames. It was a nice place. Most of the private student flats I'd been in had cracks in the paintwork, damp spots on the ceiling, and cables running everywhere. This place didn't have that. It seemed looked after – a proper home, not just temporary accommodation.

"How long you lived here?"

"Quite a while," Fraser replied, smiling.

I stopped turning my head as my neck was getting sore. I watched the TV for a while and soon dosed off again on the couch.

I was aware that there were more people in the room. Though no one was talking, I could just feel their presence. The TV volume was still down low. I opened my eyes. Fraser was still at the end of the couch, but Chris and some other guy were on the other couch. I looked at them without moving.

Wonder who this guy is?

They both turned.

"Hey, Steph. You're not having much luck recently, are you?" Chris smiled.

"Now there's an understatement," the other guy whispered. I wasn't sure if I was supposed to hear.

I managed a laugh. I was feeling a lot better. I stretched my arms and legs out in front of me, wondering how long I'd slept for.

"Yep, I do seem to be having a run of bad luck recently. But then I've had some good luck too. It could be a lot worse."

"That's true." Chris laughed. "This is Ross." He gestured to the dark-haired guy next to him, who had his feet up on the low table in front of him. He seemed younger than Chris and Fraser, and only a year or two older than me. He had dark eyes, and being built broader than the other two, with bulky shoulders and arms, he seemed shorter, but that could just be the way he was sitting.

"Hi," we both said at the same time. I smiled as I tried to untangle my legs from the blanket.

"Sorry for crashing out here, guys. I owe you one big time. I'd better get back to my own flat and give you some peace."

"Nah, don't go yet. You might as well stay and meet the other two as well," Ross said. He seemed genuine, which surprised me. I didn't think they would appreciate some chick crashing out on their couch. I got the impression that wasn't the normal sort of thing for this flat. Very different from the usual first-years that I knew. Kev sprang to mind.

As I thought of meeting the other guys I looked towards one of the other doors in the flat. For some reason I thought one of them were in there. Why would I think that?

There has been zero noise from there. No reason to think someone is in the room.

Chris followed my stare to the door, and then looked back to Fraser.

"So, Chris, you seen the latest?" Ross asked.

They started chatting away. I settled back into the couch. Fraser turned to me. "If you're not feeling well enough to go back yet, you can easily stay here another night," he offered.

"Thanks, but I should get back. You guys have done enough already. Besides, you'll want your bed back," I laughed.

"I sleep just as well on the couch." He smiled.

As we were talking a guy came out of the room that I had been looking at earlier. I frowned. Surely I hadn't known.

"Hey, Craig, this is Steph," Chris called over.

"Ah, so she wakes." Craig gave me a grin as he bounced into a single chair opposite Chris and Ross. He looked different to the other guys. He was taller than me but nowhere near as tall as the others. He looked light on his feet and had a wiry build. He would be fast at sparring. I kept assessing these guys in martial arts terms. I wasn't forgetting that they all trained with Fraser and I remembered some of the impossible moves he was practising the first time I saw him.

"Yeh, I could sleep for Scotland if I wanted to," I replied, laughing.

"Well, hell, if you can't sleep when you're not well, when can you?" he joked. He seemed good fun: not quite as serious as the others. They were chatting away and I sat listening in to their banter as they joked back and forth. Fraser went to the kitchen and brought back another glass of water for me. When he came back in he interrupted the conversation.

"Jonathon is walking up the street. I'll bet you a two-minute head start in our jog tonight that I can predict when he'll open the door closer than you guys can." He had a smile on his face.

Craig and Ross looked glum.

"You're on!" Chris agreed.

"So where was he when you saw him?" Ross asked.

"Just passing the lamppost to the right of our main door."

"OK, so he's got thirty seconds to get in the door, go up..." Ross tailed off, frowning, concentrating on his calculations.

"You playing, Steph?" Chris turned to me.

"I can't run anyway so a two-minute head start wouldn't help me! Besides, I don't even know what floor we're on!" I laughed.

"Oh, come on," Craig joined in. "Fraser always wins these bets. It gets annoying."

"Right. Think I'm sorted." Ross had his wrist up so he could see his watch.

They fell silent, listening. To what, I had no idea. I started to imagine this guy I had not even met, walking up some flights of stairs, across landings, then up more steps.

"Now!" Ross shouted. We all looked at the main door.

Nothing.

I was still seeing him on some steps, moving up.

"Now!" Craig pointed to the door, as though by magic he would walk through.

I still saw him on the stairs. He was getting to the top of them now.

"Now," Fraser said.

No, he was only onto the landing. Walking towards the door. It was as though I could feel him through the door. He hesitated.

"Now," I whispered.

There was silence as everyone turned to me. Then there was the sound of a key in a lock.

"Hah! You were beaten!" Craig shouted with a wide grin, pointing at Fraser.

Ross and Chris were still watching me.

"Ah, but it doesn't count as Steph won't be running with us, remember? So I still got the closest out of all of us," Fraser reasoned.

"Damn," Ross swore quietly.

Into this argument walked their other flatmate.

"So, who won tonight?" he asked, an eyebrow raised in question. He didn't look too interested in the answer, though, as he turned to hang up his jacket next to the door.

His eyes did a double-take when he saw me sitting on the couch, but he didn't say anything.

"Steph, actually, but Fraser is arguing that he won," Craig replied. "I think he's just scared that he won't get his two-minute head start and we'll all leave him behind."

"Any time you want to try and beat this old man, feel free, kid," Fraser challenged.

"Ah, think I might pass on that, actually." Craig smiled sheepishly.

Jonathon walked into one of the other bedrooms and returned after a minute. Fraser moved towards me on the couch, leaving his seat for Jonathon. I found this odd, but kinda liked it at the same time.

I'd better go. It must be getting late.

Jonathon's head turned towards me, but he focused on Fraser instead.

"Ah, so, Fraser. You're planning a run tonight?" It seemed like an impromptu question.

"Yeh, maybe. Later on."

I stood up. "Well, thanks for putting me up, guys, but I'd better be off." I went back to Fraser's room and grabbed my bag and coat. When I came back out, both Fraser and Chris had their coats in hand. I looked at them, puzzled.

"Well, can't have you passing out again on your own, can we?" Chris joked.

I flushed. One of the guys groaned.

"Come on then." Fraser held the door open for me, frowning at one of his flatmates.

"See ya later, guys." I glanced round at them. They were all watching me.

There were three flights of stairs before we reached the ground floor. All the doors on each floor had polished name plaques on them. They didn't look like flats.

"Are these offices?" I asked.

"Yeh. This building is the office of a solicitors' firm. We've got the top floor to ourselves though. The only tenants," Chris replied.

"How'd that come about?" I asked.

"A bizarre set of circumstances," Fraser answered.

We went out into the chilly afternoon. Their place was right in the middle of Park Circus. There was a bit of green in the middle of the circle, with a few trees and benches. Most of it was overgrown. I checked my watch. It was almost five. My flatmates would definitely be wondering where I was, staying out all night. We walked along their street, and then into the park. It was still light enough to see across the grass, and with the trees starting to lose their leaves, you could see the street on the other side. Chris moved up to my other side and we followed the path downhill.

They walked me all the way to my building and came upstairs with me as well. I unlocked the door and stepped through to our flat. When the door opened I could hear movement in our living room.

"Steph? Is that you?" Lauren called.

"Yeh," I replied.

"Where the hell," – she opened the door – "have… you… been?" She tailed off as Fraser and Chris came in through the door, behind me.

"Hi," she managed, staring at them both, wide-eyed.

There wasn't much room in our hallway. I hadn't expected them to come in: they never had before. I headed to the living room, pinching Lauren's arm on the way past to wake her up.

"Stephanie was staying with us." Fraser walked down the hallway, following me.

"Oh, right," was Lauren's vague reply. She turned round and followed me into the living room, in front of Fraser. She gave me a look as she sat down next to Natasha, who had lifted her head from the book on her lap to see what was going on. Fraser and Chris came into the living room. It immediately felt smaller with their height and presence in this tiny student flat.

"Lauren, Natasha, this is Fraser and Chris. Fraser I met at the martial arts club, and Chris is my maths tutor," I explained, watching their faces.

Lauren seemed in shock. Even Natasha had a slightly vacant look on her face. She shook her head and turned to me.

"So, where have you been for the last two days? You could've sent a text," she asked, a bit annoyed.

"Two days?" I didn't understand.

"Uh, yeh. It's Saturday afternoon, Steph. We haven't seen you since Thursday," Lauren joined in.

I looked at Fraser, confused. He was watching me.

How long was I sleeping?

"Steph fainted after training on the way home. We didn't know if you were in the flat so we thought we'd take her back to ours to keep an eye on her," Chris explained.

"You fainted?" Lauren asked, looking at me.

"Apparently so. I can't really remember. Fraser said I hit my head as I fell."

"Why didn't you take her to the hospital?" Lauren's voice started out firm but as she turned to look at them it lost some of its force.

Fraser spoke. "She seemed fine afterwards. Just needed to rest." His tone put an end to that discussion. "So, as long as you keep an eye on her for the next few days, she should be fine." He turned to me, saying, "Try and eat something…" – he paused – "…healthy."

I frowned at them again. I wasn't a doll to be cradled.

I looked back at my flatmates. They were both staring at Chris and Fraser.

Hmm, looks like I'm not the only one who appreciates their appearance.

"Well, I think we'd better leave you to it then," said Fraser, breaking into the silence.

"I'll walk you out," I offered, standing up.

At the door to the flat they stopped.

"Look after yourself, and I'll see you soon." Fraser smiled.

"Thanks." When I returned to the living room both Lauren and Natasha just looked at me.

"Well?" Lauren asked. "Two days with the guy you like? Spill!" she demanded.

"I literally slept. I thought it'd only been one day. I thought this was Friday night."

"There is no way you're giving me that bullshit! Two nights and two days – you've got to have at least something to say," she continued.

I looked to Natasha for help but she seemed just as eager to hear details as well.

What had happened?

"I can certainly understand your interest in him. They are both very… appealing," Natasha commented.

"Appealing? Drop-dead gorgeous, more like! Why didn't you introduce me before? Obviously I would have not gone near Fraser, as you like him, but that Chris…!" Lauren's voice almost drooled.

I had to laugh then. I'd got used to their looks, though every time I saw Fraser my breath still caught. I just didn't think of the rest of them like that but I suppose they were all good looking in their own ways.

Lauren then proceeded to give us a full description of how much she would like to get her hands on him. Natasha laughed as she got up and started cooking. Judging by the portions, she was cooking for all of us. When I asked hopefully, she reminded me that Fraser had said to make sure I ate healthily, to which I stuck out my tongue at her.

"Hey," Natasha responded, "don't think I'm not going to do anything he says!" We all laughed at that.

As we sat eating tea, I could feel something tugging at me. I checked I hadn't caught my sleeve on anything but I realised it wasn't something *on* me. It felt like someone was trying to distract me. I wanted to point, but to what? The feeling got stronger and it felt closer as well. I suddenly thought of Eilidh and I checked my watch.

"When you expecting Eilidh back?" I asked.

"Should be soon, but she didn't give a time," Natasha replied.

Just then, we heard the door going.

"Well, speak of the devil!" Lauren called through to Eilidh.

"Fit ye sayin' about me now, then?" Eilidh shouted as she walked down the hallway and into the kitchen.

"Hey, you've returned!" She smiled at me.

"Yep. Spent the last two days locked up with her stud muffin and won't say two peeps!" Lauren sounded frustrated.

"No way!" Eilidh looked at me. "Serious?"

"I fainted…" – this was getting embarrassing – "…so Fraser took me back to his to keep an eye on me."

"Good girl! I should have thought of pulling that one."

"Yeh, but apparently she's claiming that she did faint, and there was nothing going on for the two days she was there!" Lauren continued.

"Hey, guys, I am right here!"

"Nah, nae chance. She's covering! We'll just have to get her drunk and make her spill."

"Helloooo?" I said.

Natasha was laughing.

They turned to me then. "You're not getting away with it!" Eilidh grinned.

The rest of the evening was spent trying to answer their questions, and trying not to get drunk. Eventually they gave up and decided to make up their own stories instead. Eilidh was particularly annoyed at having missed meeting both Fraser and Chris so Lauren provided full descriptions, but I was still to bring them back here at the first available opportunity.

In the morning I tidied up our kitchen and did some housework, washing etc. Once all that was done I decided it was time to catch up on coursework, seeing as I had missed two days when I would have done some work. I read up on the next chapters for the physics topics we were doing, and then completed my tutorial questions for physics. Then I finished the report for my physics lab, plotting the graph out on my basic laptop, working out the relationship, and analysing the errors. That took me up until mid-afternoon. I had a break before I could go mad, and phoned home to see how Mum and Ailsa were getting on. Afterwards I made a start on the maths work due for Monday.

Although I had got a lot accomplished during the day, I had really struggled to stay focussed. I constantly felt as though someone was just at the corner of my vision, trying to distract me. I kept looking round from my work to just stare at a blank wall, or my bed, or the door. I didn't understand it. Sometimes the distraction felt stronger, as though something was right next to me; other times it was faint. The girls were coming and going from the flat, and I knew who was in and who wasn't. I probably just recognised the sound of their steps in the hallway and knew which door was opening and closing, but I couldn't explain when I knew one of them was about to come through the main door, as my room was the furthest from the stairwell, meaning that I definitely couldn't hear them there. This puzzle just played on my mind, distracting me further, and I threw my pen down on the table and left my room to find a proper distraction.

Eilidh was in the living room, watching TV.

"Hey, you're just in time for the early-evening weekend film!" she called out with mock enthusiasm.

"Great," I replied. "What we got this week?"

"*Ghostbusters*. You want some crisps?" She held out a bag of tortillas towards me.

"Cheers." I grabbed a handful and sat down facing the TV.

"You been working all afternoon?"

"Yep. One day gone but at least that's me sorted for the week. Howz your courses going?" I asked.

"Yeh, they're going." She shrugged. "Got a 5000-word essay due this Friday, so I'll probably have to spend a few nights at the library." She didn't seem too stressed by it.

"So you got most of it done already then?" I guessed.

"God, no! Haven't started. Been talking to a few people about theirs and had a look over the questions and stuff, so I've got a fair idea of what to do." She ate another handful of crisps.

"I couldn't do that. If I've got deadlines I'm such a stresshead about them. Can't leave things till the last minute," I admitted.

"Hey, it's going to get done some time, so what's the point of stressing about it?" Eilidh reasoned.

"Hmm." I couldn't really agree.

We watched the film for a bit, laughing at Slimer. I felt that strange tugging at my attention again. One of our flatmates was at the door. I concentrated. Lauren. Couldn't say why I thought it was her – I just did. *This is weird.*

A key turned the lock. Eilidh leant back in her chair to see into the hallway.

"Hey, Lauren. Fit like?"

"Hey," Lauren called back. "Fit like yerself?" The words sounded awkward in her mouth. Eilidh laughed at the Glasgow accent trying to pronounce the Aberdonian phrase. I wasn't really paying attention as I was still frustrated by how I'd known that Lauren was coming in.

"So, what you guys been up to today?" Lauren asked, dumping some shopping bags onto an empty seat.

"Steph's been a swot and I've been a lazy shit," was Eilidh's reply.

"That's pretty concise." Lauren nodded. She looked across to me. I was still staring at the TV, wrestling with my puzzle.

"Some good memories got you distracted there, Steph?" she asked with a sly grin.

"What? Oh… no. Just thinking about some coursework." Seemed she was still convinced that something had gone on when I'd stayed at Fraser's.

It was a pretty quiet evening. We watched some TV and Lauren was filling us in about a date that she had on Friday night. It was quite a big deal for her, though she was trying to play it down.

After all our chatting I headed to bed early, still pretty tired though I had no excuse after sleeping for about thirty hours straight. I climbed into bed and fell fast asleep.

A tune was playing. One I recognised. My phone.

My eyes shot open and I grabbed my phone, answering it without looking to see who it was.

"Hello?" My voice was a bit groggy.

"Steph?" It was Cathy. Her voice was shaky.

"Hey, Cathy, you all right?"

"I'm really sorry to phone you so late, Steph. I just couldn't think of anyone else who would be able to help." She sounded panicked. I sat up in bed and switched on my lamp. It was eleven thirty.

"It's no problem. What's up?" I asked, getting worried.

"I'm lost…" – she gave a shaky laugh – "…again. I've got no idea where I am, Steph, and I'm on my own and it's getting late and there are these guys walking round and I'm convinced they are following me!" Her voice was rising in panic.

I could just picture it. Cathy lost, her whole body language shouting 'Victim!' for anyone who was looking, and some shadowy figures following her.

"OK. Stay calm. Where was the last place that you recognised?" As she proceeded to describe how she'd stayed late at the library to work on her lab report, I was getting dressed. I didn't really think about it. Cathy was in trouble and she needed my help. Finding her in person was the quickest way. I juggled the phone between my hands, still listening.

She told me that she had left the library and turned left, thinking to find this short cut people in her halls had been talking about.

Only Cathy would try and find a short cut at night!

I grabbed my wallet and keys and headed out the door, taking the stairs two at a time. The cold air snuck in all the gaps in my jacket when I walked outside, still on the phone.

I could still picture her walking alone. I couldn't hang up: I had to keep her talking. Talking on the phone deterred would-be attackers and hopefully she would calm down, feeling reassured at speaking to someone.

I made her describe with as much detail as possible the route she had taken when she left the library. I didn't go that way regularly as my halls were in the opposite direction, but I knew it roughly. When she had told me as much as she could without working her way back to a panic, I then switched topics. Her lab this week was one I had done last week, so I quizzed her on it, knowing that it would easily distract her.

Where is she?

The whole time, I was walking quickly, almost running, towards where she had described. I was past the library now, still picturing Cathy walking down a street, though she had slowed down now and she was hovering at a corner.

"Cathy, take the next right," I instructed.

"OK. Have you figured out where I am? Have you got one of those street map thingies in your room?" she asked.

"I've got a fair idea where you are. Work in progress." I swapped the topic back again. "So did your plots work out to give you a line? Mine were all over the shot. Then we realised we'd been reading the scale wrong for the first half of the experiment. Had to go back and do half of it again before it would work."

I was totally focussed on Cathy and I was starting to get that feeling I'd been getting all day: a pulling towards a certain direction. I followed it without thinking.

I took loads of turns, in completely unfamiliar territory now, but I still knew that I could point the way out to my own halls and I had the feeling I could point to where Cathy was as well. I turned a corner and could see someone up ahead – someone small.

"Cathy, what colour of jacket you got on?"

"Red. Why?" she answered, puzzled.

"Turn around."

She turned. I waved.

"Oh, Steph!" She ran towards me. "I didn't think you would come out. Thought you could just tell me which way to go!" She smiled with relief, giving me a hug.

"Thought this might be easier, rather than trying to explain directions to you!" I joked. "You all right?"

"Yeh, way better now. Feel really stupid." She looked away.

"It's easy done, especially at night. Promise me you'll never try and find a short cut at night again? In fact, promise me you'll just never try to find a short cut ever?"

She laughed. "Promise, definitely."

"Are those guys still about – the ones you thought were following you?" I asked, looking round at the street corners and alleys.

"I haven't seen them for a while. They were probably just walking home." Cathy gave a shaky smile.

"Oh well, suppose that should be where you're going." I linked my arm through hers and started walking. In the time we'd been standing talking I'd managed to picture where we were in relation to places I knew. I walked confidently, taking the next left.

"So you know how to get back to the main road?" Cathy asked hopefully.

"Yep," I answered. "Have you back in your flat in about fifteen minutes."

"That's mental. Do you have maps imprinted to the inside of your head or something? I just don't know how you do it," Cathy sighed.

"Neither do I, really. I've just always known where I am. Look at a map a couple of times and I know it," I explained.

We chatted as we walked, twisting through a residential area. The rain started again, a soft drizzle making the streetlights reflect from the road. It was quiet here. There was no noise from cars as we were a bit away from the main road.

I stopped. I had that weird feeling again. Somehow I knew there were three guys walking down the next street.

Cathy turned and looked at me.

I couldn't explain it, but I knew they were there, and I knew that there was something different about them. The tugging felt different to what I'd been feeling all day. My arms started to tingle with goose bumps. I made a quick decision to not turn down the next street but to loop around the block instead.

I smiled at Cathy, who was now frowning at me, and moved to her other side so I could react if these guys were closer than I thought.

"So, what did you think of that guy Rachel was talking to the other day?" I asked Cathy, to get her talking again.

We walked towards the corner. The guys would be able to see us straightaway as we would cross their line of sight. We walked beyond the building, left the pavement, and stepped onto the street. I looked down the street out of the corner of my eyes, desperately trying to not turn my head. There they were – three large figures moving towards us on the pavement. They were like shadows, no noise. The glow from the streetlights seemed to stop just before it reached them. If I hadn't already known they were there I never would have seen them.

I tried to square my shoulders, look more confident than I felt. Cathy hadn't noticed the guys. We reached the other pavement and stepped onto it.

"Steph?" A voice asked out of the darkness. Cathy jumped.

Shit!

I didn't like this. How did they know me? Should I answer?

I turned my head and shoulders, shifting my feet to get my balance. I lifted my arm slightly to make sure Cathy didn't go beyond me: she wouldn't have a hope.

"Stephanie." It wasn't a question this time, but a different voice to the first, and it sounded exasperated. It was familiar but it didn't belong here for some reason.

The three guys stepped out of the shadows and into the streetlight. I was surprised and confused. It was Fraser, Chris and Ross.

Why are you here?

Why did I get the feeling they were dangerous? Were they the guys who had been following Cathy? Surely not. I couldn't figure it out: it was too confusing.

I held my stance.

"Oh, hi, Chris!" Cathy called over my shoulder.

I didn't lower my arm in front of her. I was still starring at Fraser, trying to puzzle this out. My instincts were telling me to back away slowly, but this was Fraser. He had helped me home loads of times, and saved me from those assholes outside the club. Yet he still felt dangerous right now.

"Hi, Cathy," Chris replied. Ross was busy looking around, not paying attention to us. Fraser held my gaze.

"Bit late for an evening stroll," Chris ventured.

"I was at the library. Got lost on the way home. Steph came and got me. We're just heading back to my place now." Cathy seemed to have picked up on the air of tension. She looked at me.

"We going, Steph?"

"Yeh," I replied.

Cathy turned. I was struggling to break my gaze from Fraser. I couldn't sort out my thoughts. Part of me was still attracted to him as normal and trusted him, but another part was warning me he was dangerous right now. His eyes were locked onto mine and seemed to bury into me, trying to read my thoughts. He blinked, breaking our eye contact. His hands opened and turned, palms towards me – just a small gesture, but enough to show that he meant no harm.

"We'll walk with you. There are some weirdos out at this hour," he announced. Turning away from me, he looked to the other two and then started to cross the road.

The air of tension melted. I turned back to Cathy and we started walking. I even linked arms with her again, my wariness completely gone. It was Fraser; he wouldn't hurt me. The three guys walked along behind us – our escort, our own bodyguards.

"Yeh, speaking of weirdos, before Steph came to get me there were a group of four guys hanging around. I was beginning to get a bit spooked," Cathy said.

"Four, you say? Sounds like lucky timing," Fraser replied. His voice was bland but when I glanced back at him he was frowning.

We walked along. Chris and Ross were talking quietly – so quietly that I struggled to hear anything they said. Cathy chatted away to me but my full attention wasn't on what she was saying. We reached the main road and continued on. It was busier now, with a mixture of people coming from Byers Road. Most of them had left the pubs and were making their unsteady way home.

We left the main street, heading into a more residential area again for Cathy's halls. I started to slow down, feeling something ahead.

This is getting really annoying.

The distraction had started again. There were people around the next corner, and much like I had felt when it was Fraser, Chris and Ross, I knew these guys were different: dangerous somehow.

"You OK, Steph?" Cathy asked, sounding worried.

I hadn't realised that I'd stopped. I was staring at a building, but I was staring through the building. Somehow I knew I was staring right at the two guys who were round the corner. The rest of our group had carried on a couple of steps, except Fraser, who I could feel standing right behind me. If I leant back a fraction I would be leaning against him.

How do I know they're there?

I looked up at Fraser. His eyes seemed amused at something, and a smile started on his lips. I frowned. He put his arm around my waist, moving to the side the unknown guys were on, and started walking forwards.

What is he not telling me?

Cathy looked at me, a bit surprised. I forgot: this would be the first time anyone else would have seen Fraser walk with me. She looked lost for words.

We walked round the corner. Up ahead were two guys walking towards us. They weren't cloaked in shadows the way Fraser had been, and you could hear them talking. As they approached, Chris called out to them.

"Jonathon. Craig. Thought we'd lost you guys!"

They looked up at us, but didn't seem very surprised at Cathy or I being there. Chris made the introductions to Cathy and she glanced at me, obviously wondering why I wasn't being introduced. I looked away, other things on my mind.

Eventually we reached Cathy's halls, in a much bigger group than had started out. I went upstairs with her, leaving the guys downstairs.

"Thanks again, Steph, for coming and getting me. I probably would have ended up being there until lunchtime tomorrow!" She paused. "You wanting to come in or…?" She looked towards the stairs.

"I'll just head back. Get the feeling that Fraser is going to insist on walking me home again." I rolled my eyes.

"Again?" Cathy's eyebrows went up.

Shit! Forgot I hadn't told her about him walking me home!

"Ha," I laughed. "Long story. Tell you about it later."

"You definitely will be! See you tomorrow." She went inside her flat, and I trotted back downstairs.

I opened the door to step back outside, and shivered at the cold air, pulling the collar on my jacket up. The rain was still drizzling down in a fine mist. Fraser looked at me and stepped away from the rest of the guys chatting in a group. I walked towards him, stopping just a step away.

"That was fortunate timing tonight?" I waited.

"More than you realise. Thought I said to take it easy and look after yourself for the next few days?" he replied.

"I am. Not exactly running a marathon right now."

"True, but I don't class walking around in the middle of the night, in the rain, on your own, as looking after yourself," he continued.

I opened my mouth to retort, but then realised he had managed to evade my question and turn it on me. I closed my mouth and frowned at him.

He smiled.

"Well, I'm going home now. Don't suppose you're heading that way too?" I asked innocently.

"As a matter of fact, we are." He seemed pleased with himself.

"Good. You'll have plenty of time to tell me what you were doing out so late as well, then!"

He frowned at me. I just smiled back. Laughing, he shook his head and put his arm around my shoulder. We started walking down the path towards the main road, the rest of the guys following behind us, still chatting.

I hadn't expected him to put his arm around me. It felt good, like I could hide under here. As we walked I leant into him, feeling his body heat through his jacket. My head rested against his chest. My thoughts drifted away.

We were almost back at my flat when I realised that I hadn't asked him why he'd been out.

Stupid girl, being distracted.

I sidestepped, and Fraser's arm fell away from me. I suddenly felt cold without it. He looked down at me. His concerned eyes seemed a deeper blue than normal, making me catch my breath.

Unfair!

He looked puzzled.

"So, you were saying why you were out so late," I prompted.

"Was I?" He smiled, looking ahead again.

Fine.

It was none of my business anyway. It was just that if he was going to ask what I was doing, then I can at least ask the same question of him. We were on my street now.

"We were looking for some people too, but didn't find them." He wasn't smiling now.

"Oh." I didn't really know what to say to that.

He followed me through the main door and upstairs, the rest of the guys staying downstairs. I turned around at the landing to my flat to find him right behind me again. I looked up into his eyes. They were considering, looking at me as though trying to puzzle something out. My gaze dropped under his scrutiny, but stopped at his mouth. I imagined kissing him. I would only have to lift my hand slightly to touch him – he was so close – but his mouth was out of reach for me. He was too tall. I couldn't make the move. In all honesty I didn't know if I should.

Out of my reach? Out of my league, more like.

I flushed, embarrassed at my daydreams.

"So, thanks for the escort. I'll see ya at training, I suppose." I managed to speak, even if it was a bit breathless.

"That you will." His voice was almost as quiet as mine. He lifted his hand and I held my breath. He paused, seemingly changing his mind, and his hand went to my shoulder and lifted away a small leaf that must have fallen on me when we went through the park.

I managed not to sigh. He smiled at me; then his expression closed again, and he turned for the stairs.

"See you later," he called.

I went into the flat and fell onto my bed, thoroughly confused. It was a long time before I managed to get back to sleep.

Chapter Eight

I was eating my Cheerios, still thinking last night through when Natasha came in.

"You're up early," I commented. I was the only one in the flat with regular lectures in the morning so I normally didn't see the girls until the afternoon.

"Yeh. Got a project to work on. Said I'd meet up with the rest of my group at ten," she explained as she rummaged in her cupboard.

"Do you know who went out last night? Thought I heard the door going at the back of one," she asked, looking up.

"That was me, getting in. A pal from my course, Cathy, phoned. Had to go and meet her as she got lost walking home." I laughed.

"Well you're definitely the person to call for that. Where was she?"

"Past the library, by some flats. Never been up that way before."

"How'd you find her then?" Natasha frowned at me.

I paused.

I don't know.

"Well, got her to describe where she'd gone after leaving the library, and just followed that."

Much use her description had been, though.

"Oh, right." She carried on putting some bread in the toaster.

I dumped my bowl in the sink to wash later, and went to my room to pick up my stuff. The rain still hadn't stopped so I grabbed a slightly more waterproof jacket with a hood for today. Checking my bag had paper and my tutorial work in it, I headed out.

I met Cathy in the physics building before our lecture, and we walked to the room together.

"So, you get home all right?" she asked slyly.

"Yes, of course." I pulled a face at her. "There is certainly nobody stupid enough to hassle those five guys."

"I did notice that they're all quite tall. Except one of them – what was his name?"

"Craig," I supplied.

"Yeh," she considered. "So how do you know all of them?" She was watching me. I realised I'd walked into that one.

"OK, I'll spill! But over lunch; not in physics, where everyone will be listening in to escape from the joys of Mr Stuffy."

She laughed then. "Deal!"

We sat down next to Rachel and Ali, waiting on the lecture to start. Cathy was looking round.

"Wonder where Kev is?" she mused.

"Probably waking up in a stranger's bed, wondering why his hands and legs are tied up," Ali joked.

We laughed.

"It's not like him to be late," Rachel remarked.

Now that I was thinking about Kev and wondering where he was, I started to get the tugging feeling again.

Crap! Thought that had gone.

We got our paper and pens out and started writing as Mr Stuffy droned on about centre of masses and momentum. I took a deep breath and let it out slowly, trying to get rid of this distraction so I could concentrate.

It wouldn't go away. I wanted to point to my right. I thought about it, imagining a street plan. In that direction there was a path that reached the physics building from the main building. Kev was walking along it.

How do I know this? Am I just imagining it? Is the pressure of uni getting too much and I'm cracking up?

I frowned, desperately trying to listen to Mr Stuffy. It didn't help that he was so boring. I imagined Kev walking in the main entrance and walking round the building to the back stairs, taking them up. He went up two floors so he would avoid the front entrance to the lecture theatre.

He's closer now.

It was as though someone was staring at my back. It prickled – the feeling you get when you watch a scary movie and you think there is someone behind you, waiting to jump out.

I heard the door creak at the back of the lecture theatre. I looked up and saw Kev sneaking in and taking a seat in the back row.

Damn it! Is it coincidence?

The rest of the lecture was lost on me. I couldn't concentrate.

At the end we stood up waiting on people moving so we could get out. Cathy was looking round.

"Looks like Kev didn't make it," she commented.

"He's up the back. Saw him sneaking in just after the start," I said. They all looked up to the back. Guess they must have seen him as Cathy gave a wave.

"Maths next, then lunch." Cathy gave me a look. "Will we see you at lunch, Rachel?" she asked.

"Might do. I'm meeting up with some other people beforehand, so might be later on."

The three of us trooped over to maths. Ali was moaning that it was Prof. Drosson again and that his poor hand couldn't keep up with the notes. He was looking hopefully at Cathy when he was talking, and she fell for it.

"You can copy anything you miss from my notes, Ali. But I want them back. You can't just keep them as then I won't have any notes!" she warned.

I laughed. Ali looked at me, winking.

During maths Ali sat texting on his phone, not even bothering to try and take notes, whilst Cathy and I scribbled away. Afterwards Cathy handed her notes to Ali and he smiled.

"Thanks, Cathy. I'll get them back to you quicker than you think!"

We walked into the union. Ali said he would meet us upstairs and to save him a seat. We were just sitting our trays down at a table when Ali reached us. He smiled triumphantly and handed Cathy her notes back. She looked confused.

"The wonders of photocopiers, eh?" Ali grinned.

"That's cheating!" Cathy yelled.

"What? You said I could copy your notes!" He played innocent.

"Yeh, but not just so you could be lazy! You're supposed to put some effort into it." She sat down frowning, and folded her notes back into her bag.

He laughed and went to pick some lunch.

"So…" Cathy settled into her seat and started opening her sandwich.

"So," I replied.

She looked at me. "Don't make me drag this out of you! I know you've got gossip. Or are you really not wanting to tell me?" She sounded disappointed.

"No, it's not that. It's just there really isn't much to say. There is nothing going on." I wish my voice hadn't been quite so regretful.

"But you want there to be?"

"Who wouldn't!" I confessed, laughing.

Cathy grinned. "Start at the beginning."

So I told her of how after the first night at the kick boxing Fraser had seen me in the park and insisted on walking me home. Then after Sarah had been a bitch at the bar he caught up with me and walked me home again. I even told her about the night where I'd been outnumbered by the assholes from the club and both Fraser and Chris had been there to rescue me.

Ali joined us again. He looked about to interrupt when Cathy glared at him and, I think, kicked him under the table, as he grunted. He didn't say anything, but sat munching his lunch and listening in.

I went on to tell her how I had fainted in the park. They both looked concerned at that bit but I rushed on, saying that Fraser had been just behind me and had taken me back to his flat to keep on eye on me.

I didn't say how I had slept for two days – that bit still confused me as well. And I didn't tell them how since I woke up I could tell where people were; had my own inbuilt radar. That might just push their belief in my story too far.

What is going on with me?

"So those guys that were with them last night are their flatmates?" Cathy asked.

I nodded.

"So you weren't in lectures on Friday 'cause you were shacked up with Fraser?" Ali asked.

"I wasn't shacked up! Nothing happened. I just spent the night there."

He looked at me in disbelief.

"He slept on the couch!" I insisted.

We were quiet for a bit, just finishing off our lunch. Cathy looked as though she was thinking things over. Ali was looking round the canteen, his mind already off the subject.

"Can you imagine Sarah's face when she hears about this?" Cathy laughed.

"She's not going to! Seriously, it's all just a bit embarrassing. He acts like my personal escort but he doesn't seem interested in anything else. Any other guy going to all that bother would have at least tried to kiss me by now, but there's been no moves by him."

My thoughts suddenly went to last night, at my door just before he left. He had been looking at me much like I knew I had been looking at him. I flushed.

"Now you can't take a beamer after saying that and expect us to believe you," Ali pointed out.

"It's embarrassing. Sure I would like there to be something, but he obviously doesn't think of me that way."

And why would he? He's way out of my league.

I'd never been that popular with guys. I hadn't been in the cool group at school who had new boyfriends each week. I think the guys had been a bit intimidated by me. I wasn't a girly girl into all things pink and fluffy, wearing short skirts and make-up. I was good at the stereotypical bloke's subjects and could probably have beaten all of them up with my hands tied behind my back. Yeh, most of the guys had wanted me as a mate, and that was it. Not that any of them had really caught my eye – they'd been immature boys. Fraser, on the other hand, was something different.

We finished up our lunch and went to the first maths tutorial for the week. Chris was as helpful as ever but I was a bit preoccupied. My full attention wasn't on the work so I just listened in as Ali asked questions, not bothering to phrase my own. Chris looked over at me a couple of times but didn't say anything, for which I was grateful.

Afterwards Ali went away to meet up with some other friend whilst Cathy and I headed to the library to go over her lab report. We sat at the computers on the physics floor, away from the librarians and their frowns. As we sorted her graph and equations she asked a few more questions about Fraser, but there wasn't really much to add to what I'd already said. It was a bit of a relief to finally talk about him to someone. My flatmates' advice was generally along one line and that wasn't really me. Cathy could at least empathise with my hesitance.

Once her report was done, Cathy left to go back to her flat. I stayed behind to check my e-mails and look a few things up, my mind drifting whilst I browsed the net. Cathy's questions had just added to the questions of my own. What was between Fraser and me? Was he just an acquaintance? A friend? Potential lover? Why did he seem so mysterious? Why did he always end up meeting me? Why had I slept for two days in his flat? I knew what some people would think of it – that he'd spiked my drink or something – but I knew that wasn't the case. Why did I trust him so completely, yet why had he seemed dangerous when we'd met the other night?

These thoughts were whirling round in my head and my arguments were just going in circles. It wasn't until the wind sent a chill up my back that I realised that I'd packed up, left the library and was walking into the park, taking the path uphill. I didn't want to stop. I knew that if I did I would never get the answers I wanted.

Leaving the park, I walked along Park Circus, thinking about Fraser. As I did I got the now familiar tugging feeling, but it wasn't in the direction of his flat. This did make me stop.

He's not in.

This just asked another question: how did I know that? It had started since I'd stayed with them. This made me determined to not waste the resolve I'd managed to muster. I wasn't going home. I crossed to the little bit of green in the middle of the circle, past the railings and the overgrown bushes, and sat down on a dilapidated bench to think my questions over. If I could work out an answer I would leave without looking stupid in front of Fraser. If I couldn't work out answers, then I'd ask him when he arrived, and I would know when he arrived.

I sat there, trying to figure out how to phrase my questions. I watched some birds dodge in and out of the trees, a rare break in the rain allowing some sunshine through to play off their colours. I let my mind drift, thinking that some answers might come if I distracted myself, then I'd give up and go back to tackling the questions from different angles. The rain started again, but it was so soft it didn't really bother me. I just pulled up my hood and brought my feet up so that my legs weren't on the bench. I sat thinking, my thoughts wandering.

"Stephanie?" Fraser called.

Shit! Didn't hear him walk up!

I jumped where I sat, my foot slipping off the wet bench. I turned to look at him, thrown off guard. He was on the path, walking towards me, just visible round some bushes.

"Are you OK?" he asked, sounding concerned.

"Fine," I managed.

He walked up to the bench, paused, and then sat down at the other end. I noticed the distance. I looked away from him then, not wanting to get distracted. I hadn't realised how dark it had got. The sun was gone, with shadows replacing it – definitely evening time.

I opened my mouth to speak but couldn't get anything out, so shut it again before he noticed my hesitation. I pointed my toe and scraped it along the ground, trying to work out a way to phrase my questions without sounding ridiculous. All I could see were his long legs reaching far out from the bench, whilst mine barely reached the ground.

"So, are you fully recovered from the weekend? Chris was saying you were quiet today." He turned his head towards me slightly. His voice sounded as though he was searching for something to say.

Here was my chance.

"Yes and no."

His head came up, his eyes trying to find mine. I kept my head slightly turned.

"Was it just chance that you were right behind me when I fainted? I don't remember anyone being on the path." I took a breath and continued, "And if you were there to start with, why didn't you catch me up? And why is it that whenever I'm out at night I always seem to bump into you anyway?" My voice got more confident as I went on, and by the end I was looking him right in the eyes and almost demanding an answer.

"Why did you say you *heard* me when that guy was being an ass?" I asked, quieter.

He just looked back at me. I couldn't figure out what he was thinking. His expression was almost fierce. His eyes were still focussed on mine. I couldn't meet his gaze for long. I looked away into the shadows.

Looks as though he'll never speak to me again. This is stupid. What am I doing? I've made a decent friend and now I'm accusing him of something when he's done you a favour.

Well, if I'm asking everything…

"Why do I know that Ross is standing at the gate over there?" I asked quietly, still not meeting his gaze. I lifted my hand, pointing to where I knew Ross stood waiting. I dropped it back down to the bench and leant back, lifting my face to the sky and letting the drops of rain fall on my face. If Fraser walked away now I didn't want to watch him go.

I sat like that, waiting to hear footsteps fade away, but I didn't hear them. I kept my head where it was but looked across to where he had been sitting. He was still there, and still looking at me, but his face wasn't angry now.

"So… I'm crazy, right?" I asked.

"No, not crazy." He gave a small smile.

"Don't know if many people would agree with you." I tilted my head forward again.

I was relieved that he hadn't run away from me, but I still didn't have any answers.

"So… anything?" I asked.

"I don't think you're crazy; far from it. I think your mind is better at retaining information and analysing it than I gave you credit for." He smiled apologetically.

I didn't know whether to be insulted or pleased. It was definitely a backhanded compliment.

I just looked at him. He shifted where he sat, and looked forward.

"Are you sure you want answers? You might not like them." He turned and leant towards me. This time his face did look angry. "Maybe you should just be happy with what you've got and get on with things." His voice was harsh.

I leant back from him on the bench. I didn't understand the shift.

What is he trying to do? Scare me? Hah, now he doesn't want me around when he has already saved me several times.

"Think I've got a right to know. It does involve me." My stubborn streak emerged.

"Are you sure? You can think on it." His voice was serious, giving me a choice. I knew if I left here I was never going to know.

"I'm sure."

He stood up then, all traces of anger gone. It had been a front. He held out his hand towards me,

"Come on then. We should go inside before you freeze."

Chapter Nine

Inside his flat Fraser motioned me to the couch, and then disappeared to his room. I took off my now soaking jacket and sat down in the same seat as I'd sat in before. Ross stopped just inside the door, watching where Fraser had gone. He looked to me and frowned, then went to another room, closing the door behind him.

I sat rubbing my cold arms, looking at the door Ross had just walked through, wondering what his problem was. Fraser came back out with the blanket that had covered me the other day. As he walked around the couch he draped it over my shoulders.

"I'm not that cold," I lied, pulling it around my front.

"Yes you are," he replied, his eyes amused.

I frowned at him as he sat down.

"So these answers I'm waiting on then?" I prompted.

He hesitated now. He was sitting across from me, not on the same sofa. Although I was disappointed that he wasn't closer, it did mean that we had better eye contact.

Pros and cons.

"What are your views on the supernatural?" he asked, sitting back on the couch.

I raised my eyebrows, looking at him.

"You serious?" I asked.

He nodded once, waiting on my response.

"Well, that depends on what you're classing as supernatural. I know of quite a few natural phenomenons that lots of people claim are due to the supernatural forces, but are actually explained by science." I stopped, looking across at him to see if that was what he was after. He didn't move so I carried on.

"If you're talking about ghosts, then I'm not sure. The logical side of me says that there's nothing after we die, our body stops working and all brain function ends. I would like to think that there is something afterwards but I don't know about souls or consciousness – it's probably just romantic wishing. Hulk, Superman, etc – just pure fiction."

That was probably the longest speech I had ever made in front of Fraser, and it was on a subject I was not comfortable talking about. I looked at him, slightly nervous as to the response I would get from my ramblings.

"Hmm, that covers quite a few things. What about psychics?" he asked.

"Psychics?"

"Psychics or telepaths. Do you believe in them? Most people know a few stories about twins or siblings or something."

Where is this going?

"I don't know. Think people who do readings and things like that are usually just good readers of body language, making educated guesses. I've never seen any first-hand evidence of anything supernatural. But, who knows? Just because I haven't seen something doesn't mean that it doesn't exist."

"No family stories about psychics?"

"What is this about? I thought I was supposed to be getting the answers here!" I frowned at him, pulling the blanket tighter around me.

"Yes, you are right. I just wanted to get some background." He looked at me.

"What would your response be if I said that I was telepathic?" he asked, watching me.

"Not sure. Suppose I would want to test that. You know, 'think of a number' stuff."

We just stared at each other. My mind started to turn this over. He was being serious.

"So what would the limits be then? Like, could you pick a number out of someone's head only if they were concentrating, or do you know every thought they have? Do you have to be near them, touching them?"

He started to smile. "You definitely have a scientific mind."

"Well…" I shrugged, looking away.

I thought about it some more.

So, can you hear this?

I didn't look at Fraser, careful not to give him any clues. I just focussed on the words, trying to frame them clearly in my mind.

"You don't have to shout, you know," he replied, almost wincing.

I looked at him in shock. I felt goose bumps emerge all over my arms.

What the fuck?

This time he did wince. I pulled the blanket closer around me, trying to get some warmth back into my body. I stared at him, my thoughts whirling.

"So…" I tailed off. I looked away, staring at a painting on the wall.

*So if you **can** hear me, let's do a test. I'll think of some words and you repeat them out loud. First one, nine.*

"Nine," he said quietly.

Piano.

"Piano."

Holy shit!

"Stephanie, you don't expect me to repeat everything, do you?" he asked.

"Suppose not." I swallowed.

I sat still, thinking, looking away from him again.

"So you have been able to hear everything that I've thought around you?" I asked.

"Most of it, yes." He looked apologetic. "I'm not able to catch it all – only what you form as proper thoughts, not your general musings."

I suddenly started thinking about what I'd thought of Fraser in the past weeks. I felt my face starting to flush, so I quickly tried to change my train of thought.

"So does it not get a bit confusing, hearing people's thoughts all the time?"

He paused, watching me again.

"I'm not able to hear everyone's thoughts the way I hear yours. Normally I have to focus to hear a person's thoughts – deliberately pry – and so I rarely do it. But you project your thoughts; they are not hidden. I hear them without searching for them."

I stared at him, trying to take this in.

"So, I'm not like everyone else?" There was something I should have guessed.

"Never met anyone like you," he replied, smiling. "There do exist real psychics and better telepaths than me. I've met a couple of them. They have always known about their skills and are able to hear others as well as project their own thoughts, so that is not what you are," he explained, frowning over the puzzle.

"Right." My voice sounded vague.

I curled back on the sofa, resting my head and tucking the blanket under my chin. I sat staring at the paintings and thinking things through. This explained quite a bit. When I had first seen Fraser, he had turned to look at me without me making a noise. The first time at training, when I was annoyed at the hulk wannabe, he had come over; and he knew where to find me when he was walking in the park. It didn't explain, though, how I knew where to find people.

Fraser was sitting still on the other couch, just watching me. He had leant back after our first bit of the conversation. He must have relaxed, no longer thinking I was going to freak and run out of the building screaming.

"So when I'd been at the club and that creep was trying to make his move…" I tailed off: he knew the story.

"I never heard anything like it." He shook his head. "Now that was loud. Chris heard it all crystal clear, and even Craig heard some of it."

He looked across at me as I suddenly went still, my eyes widening further.

"All of you…?"

"Ah, sorry. Yes. Though I'm the most proficient. I suppose there is more to explain yet." He looked at me hesitantly.

"More?" I asked. "Well go on then. Think you've proved your case for the psychic part. What else you gonna shock me with?"

"I apologise: this part isn't as benign." His face was closed again, emotion gone. His eyes seemed grey, with hardly any blue in them. I started to get worried.

"When you spent a few days here it wasn't because you fainted in the park." He avoided eye contact. I could feel my back prickling. "Someone attacked you in the park." He paused. "I say some*one* – should really say some*thing*." He shook his head, still avoiding my gaze, which was fixed to his face. "I didn't get there until he already had a hold on you. I threw him off, hoping that I hadn't been too late, and chased him away. I couldn't leave you lying in the park though, so I stayed with you."

I had vague memories and emotions floating back to me: feeling scared, hearing growls, and being carried.

"I brought you back here to keep an eye on you. Most people don't survive that." He looked up at me then.

"Survive what?" My voice was almost a whisper.

"Being bitten by a vampire," he said quietly.

I looked at him, and then laughed too loud. "You're having me on!"

His face was still. "I'm not."

There was silence. I couldn't think, frozen.

"Most vampires kill when they feed. We," – he gestured round the flat – "do not. We only take what we need to survive. When I first felt the presence of new vampires in the area we started patrolling to find them. When I heard your thoughts in the park that night I ran to you, realising it was a likely place for them to hang out. I ran to find you but I was too slow." He still wouldn't look at me. "I thought he had killed you."

"You're all…" I *did* whisper this time.

"Sheer luck got me there just in time. I didn't know if he had bitten you yet or if he was just about to. As it turned out he had bitten you but had not taken any blood yet." He looked up at me then, his face a mixture of fear and anger. "That is what not many people survive."

"So what are you saying? I'm a vampire?" My voice was incredulous.

"No. That is an easier process. You would have to lose some blood and take in some blood of the vampire. That is not what happened to you." He sighed, and then continued, "When someone is bitten, part of what is the vampire goes into the victim. This usually leaves the victim as the vampire feeds, but that vampire never got the chance to feed on you. He left part of what is a vampire behind. This normally acts like a poison to people and they die. It is almost unheard of for this type of case to happen, as if a vampire has got to the stage of biting there is not much that will stop him drinking." He smiled ruefully.

"But I didn't die."

"No, and I think it's got something to do with the fact that you can project your thoughts as well. You slept solid for twenty-four hours and the next day you slept again, if not quite so soundly."

I remembered waking up in his room and seeing him sitting in the chair watching me.

"But after that you were fine. Almost back to normal. The one difference we all noticed immediately was that your projection was even stronger. Before, only myself and Chris could hear you. Craig heard you once in the unique circumstance when you were both drunk and very angry, but never normally. That next evening we could all hear you. Craig, Jonathon, and Ross haven't developed telepathically yet, so they shouldn't have been able to hear you." He frowned, looking down at his clasped hands, his elbows leaning on his knees.

I struggled to get this straight in my head.

"So you guys are vampires. I'm sitting in a flat with two vampires, but you don't kill people? Some other vampire bit me – you don't know who – he left vampire spit back in my blood, and now you can all hear my thoughts. There's also the fact that I can tell wherever anyone is. Great!" My eyes were wide and my voice was getting higher but I couldn't do anything about it. My ribs were starting to feel tight.

Fraser looked up at me, his eyes narrowing. Each breath was coming faster, my throat closing.

Not now!

"What's wrong, Stephanie?" Fraser asked, sitting up straight.

God, I hated having a panic attack in front of people. They were bad enough on their own, without having someone I knew witnessing my total meltdown.

My limbs felt shaky. I couldn't take a full breath. I felt too hot, and tried to push the blanket off me. I looked around the room. The dark paintings seemed to be moving in towards me. My thoughts became more panicked.

Not here!

"Stephanie! What is wrong?" Fraser's voice was more insistent now.

I locked my eyes on his, to avoid the walls leaning in.

"Nothing is wrong. That's the problem."

That made more sense before it came out my mouth.

"Claustrophobic," I managed. That condition was more acceptable. He frowned.

"Do you need to see more space?" he asked.

I nodded, not trusting my voice.

"Come on then." He stood up. I struggled to unwrap myself from the blanket and get my shaky legs onto the ground. His hands circled my forearms, helping me up, and he guided me towards his room.

Once in there he lifted up the huge sash window, and a burst of cold air swirled into the room, cooling my too-hot skin. I leant against the windowsill, with the top half of my body out of the window, and sucked the cold air into my lungs, feeling as though it was my first proper breath in ten minutes.

I could see the dark clouds above, and could see over the trees across to the other buildings and down the street. Feeling the drizzle dampening my cheeks and forehead, I dropped my face from the sky. I could see the cars parked on the street, their colours skewed by the orange streetlights, the lamps reflecting off the uneven paving stones and puddles. As my gaze lowered, my breathing calmed, the cold air calming me down.

A hand came round my side, stopping at my stomach and then pulled me back from over the edge of the window.

"Don't want you falling out." His voice was quiet.

I stepped back. Fraser was right behind me. I hesitated, then leant against his body as my legs were still a bit shaky. His arm stayed around me, making catching my breath a bit more difficult than it should have been, but not because he was holding too tight. For some reason I wasn't concerned that I was currently leaning against a vampire. I really couldn't digest that fact right now.

"You OK now?"

"Yeh, better."

"I'm sorry. I just unloaded all that information on you. It wasn't fair of me," he apologised.

"Well, how else were you going to do it? Send me a new text every day?" I joked.

He laughed. "I suppose not. Could have found a better way, though."

We stood in front of the open window for a few minutes longer. I was enjoying feeling his body next to mine, his arm around me. The back of my head lay on his chest. I could feel his breath on my hair.

I shivered as a gust of air came in. As Fraser moved around me and closed the window, I sat down on his bed. He brought the big office chair from the desk over to the bed and sat in it, stopping a bit away, giving me some space.

"It still doesn't explain how I can suddenly tell where people are now though," I mentioned.

"When someone changes from human to vampire…" He looked up at me hesitantly as he said this, checking I wasn't about to start hyper-ventilating again. "…they retain their personality, their likes and dislikes, and any talents which they had before. Being a vampire enhances things. Physically we are stronger, harder, faster than any human. Mentally we can process information quicker – some have photographic memory etc. Your own unique talent depends on if you had any particular skill to start with and how good you were with it. Not everyone has one. For you, being able to locate where people are must have developed from a skill you already had." He looked at me.

I looked out the window, considering this.

A skill I already had?

I'd never been able to find people before. I'd always been aware of my surroundings but that was through self-defence, not any hyperawareness of my own. I'd worked at it. Frowning, I continued to think.

When I knew where people were I felt a tugging in a general direc-tion. I had to think of them and focus on where I thought they were. It helped when I thought of a map.

My sense of direction!

"Stephanie?" Fraser asked.

I turned to him, smiling. "It's my sense of direction!"

"That much I picked up." He smiled.

"Oh, right." I laughed. "I've always had a good sense of direction. Spin me around in a strange place and I would find my way out. There might be a few wrong turns but I'd get there eventually. And if I had been there even once before, I would definitely find my way out – no wrong turns. I've never been lost, ever.

"But now it's not just knowing where to go: I know where other people are as well. I found Cathy the other night. There was no way her directions were any good – she was too panicked. I knew when Kev was about to arrive at the lecture. I know which of my flatmates are home before I go in. I knew that you weren't in when I arrived today. It's like seeing pins on a map. Each pin is a person. I've got my own tracking device for anyone."

I smiled, relieved at having figured it out, relieved that I wasn't going mad.

"That certainly is a useful talent." He looked thoughtful. "So, how far have you tested it?" he asked.

"Tested it?" I choked. "I haven't."

He looked surprised. "Thought you would have worked out all the limits by now!" He gave a laugh.

"I thought I was going nuts!" My voice was exasperated. "I thought I was under too much stress; wasn't coping with uni. I've been swapping between trying to figure it out and forgetting about it altogether, not testing it."

"Ah, sorry. It's just when someone changes to a vampire, after the initial shock and adjusting period they normally start to experiment to see what they can do; see if they enhanced a talent. I was forgetting this isn't a normal case."

I sat quietly, picking at a loose thread on his duvet, thinking things through.

"So, what is it that you can do then?" I asked.

"I've got a talent for languages. Before I was changed I already knew three fluently, and was in the process of learning three others. Now all I have to do is speak to someone who knows the language and I can converse with them. I don't need to hear all the new words. I know them immediately. It took me a while to get control of it as I didn't realise what I was doing to start with. People would be astounded as I just started talking to a native of some far-off place. I didn't even know where they were from but I could talk to them." He laughed at some memory.

"Now that is impressive," I said, with admiration in my voice.

"Not really. Most people can learn new languages and for vampires it is even easier, taking into consideration they have all the time in the world to learn, and the increased memory and quick uptake of information." He shrugged. "So, you see, not that much of a skill."

"Natasha would be so jealous. She's struggling with Gaelic. Completely new language for her," I explained.

He smiled. "My native tongue. You can offer my help to her if you wish."

"Thanks." I looked at him, a dozen questions springing to mind about his life. I didn't want to be rude though; didn't know if he would be willing to share. I tried to keep the questions from forming properly in my head. There were some I didn't want to know the answers to.

"So… what about the other guys? What are their talents?" I diverged.

"Like I said earlier, not everyone has a particular talent. Chris hasn't found his yet but I'm beginning to suspect it is linked to teaching – something to do with explaining things, making people understand."

I nodded.

Makes sense; he's the only one who can explain any of the maths work to me.
Fraser smiled.

"Craig was proficient with weapons in his previous life. Since then, I haven't found a weapon he couldn't use straightaway. Hand it to him, and he knows how to use it. Has all the technique, everything."

"Jonathon and Ross are the youngest of our group. So far Jonathon hasn't shown any particular area of expertise. Ross is just really starting to think of what his talent might be. It can be a long process to find it, and some never do. Like I said, it depends if you had one, and how strong it was in the first place."

I sat quietly, trying to take this all in. I looked out the window. It was completely dark now.

Must be night. Wonder what time it is?

"Just the back of nine," Fraser replied.

I smiled, then sat thinking some more.

"Do you want to go home?" Fraser asked.

I considered that. Fraser clearly wasn't going to harm me; that idea was ridiculous. Chris didn't mean any harm either. What about the other guys? I'd been in their company before but only for a short time. They'd thought I was about to die anyway. How would they feel about me now – this girl who was neither one thing nor another?

"Am I OK to stay here a while?" I asked.

"Of course." Fraser's voice was sure. "No harm will come to you here."

"I need to think about things, without having to dodge questions from my flatmates," I explained. "And I might come up with a few questions of my own." I smiled at him.

He smiled back. His eyes seemed a darker blue now. "Thought you might."

We moved to the living room. Ross had come out of his room and was sitting on the couch opposite, again watching me out of the corner of his eye. It was like he was watching a nervous horse, waiting on me bolting. They had the TV on low and were pretending to watch it. I was sitting in the same seat as before, deep in thought.

"Chris is coming back," Fraser announced.

I looked up at him, coming out of my thoughts.

"Now how do you know that? Thought I was the one to know where people are," I joked.

"I can hear him coming in the front door."

"Oh." I paused, thinking. "Does he know I'm here?"

"He'll probably smell your scent on the stairs, but he won't know why you're here."

"Right."

I smiled, a thought coming to my head. I tried to not let it form completely, but kept it vague, not focussing on it.

Fraser frowned towards me. I focused on the TV, ignoring everything else. He turned his torso towards me and started to open his mouth, when we all heard the door to the flat opening.

Chris walked in, looking round. He wasn't surprised to see me. He looked to Fraser but he was still focussed on me and didn't acknowledge him.

"Hi, Steph, wasn't expecting to see you here." His voice was friendly but his expression was a bit confused.

Hey, Chris! Still raining out?

He froze, his arms half out of his coat. His eyes darted from me to Fraser. I tried hard not to laugh at his expression. Ross had turned his back to Chris so he wouldn't see the big grin on his face. Fraser snorted a laugh.

Fraser looked at Chris then, something silent passing between them.

"Oh." Chris reanimated and finished taking his coat off. He walked over and sat at the other end of my couch. He looked at me then.

"You OK?"

"Just trying to get my head round it all," I replied.

He nodded. "A lot to get your head round."

He turned back to Fraser. "How much did you tell her?"

Fraser didn't say anything aloud.

Chris nodded.

I frowned at Fraser. "So you just projected your thoughts the way I do?"

He nodded. "I can speak to the others as they are vampires as well. The older they are, the easier it is. I can say anything to Chris, but if I was talking to Ross I have to focus a lot more and, even then, keep it short and simple."

Ross frowned at this. Seemed he didn't like being at the bottom. I quickly moved on. "So, with you, thoughts can be both incoming and outgoing?"

He laughed. "Yes."

"But with the rest of you guys you can only get incoming?" I asked.

Chris answered, "It depends on our age how much our psychic has developed. First of all we hear more advanced vampires. The more developed we are the clearer we hear them. Then we can start to hear humans. After that we are able to start projecting thoughts. Again, only the more advanced vampires can hear us, and then any vampire can hear us as we get stronger. Eventually we can project thoughts to humans as well. I'm at the stage where I can hear Fraser clearly – as he is older than me – and I'm starting to hear humans, but I only catch about half of what they are thinking and I have to be close to them. If I practise with one person it becomes easier with them. I was starting to hear you more clearly before… the incident… but now I hear you clearer than I hear Fraser." He turned to look at Ross.

"I only hear Fraser faintly. The more information he tries to send, the more confused it ends up. You, I couldn't hear at all before the incident in the park, but now I hear every word crystal clear."

I frowned, thinking this through. Ross turned back to the TV. Fraser and Chris watched my expression.

I looked to Fraser. "You can only speak to them because you are all… vampires?" I stumbled over the word. "You can't talk to ordinary folk?"

"I will be able to eventually, but I'm not quite that old." He smiled.

"And you think that I had some psychic ability before?"

"Definitely." He nodded, serious now.

I was still trying to puzzle this out.

"So I can already send outgoing, which is a more advanced stage?"

Fraser nodded.

"So shouldn't I be able to receive incoming?" I asked.

He blinked. His face went thoughtful, a frown appearing.

"If you were a vampire, then yes, if you could send a thought you would definitely be able to receive one. But you're not a vampire, so I don't know."

"Try it then."

He looked up at me then, slightly concerned.

"I don't know if that will work. I don't know how it would affect you." He sounded unsure.

"You said yourself that at some point you would be able to speak to normal people, I imagine, without hurting them. I'm not normal! I can already project. Try it!"

"It could work, Fraser," Chris commented. "None of the rest of us are anywhere near that stage. Only you could try it."

Fraser was frowning. "Maybe. Not tonight though. Think you have had enough strange things today. How about we talk about the things we already know you can do."

I sighed, slightly disappointed.

Chicken!

He raised one eyebrow at me. Ross laughed.

I had to admit this was going to be kinda cool. Couldn't think of too many practical applications but it could be fun. Then I thought of the downside: they could hear every formed thought, anything I framed properly in my head.

Everything? I asked.

"Everything," he said quietly. Ross looked away again. I suddenly felt uncomfortable. This was too intrusive.

"Are there any limits? Chris said he had to be close to hear other people."

"I have been hearing you since you moved to Glasgow," Fraser replied with a wry grin on his face. "Before the incident in the park it used to be only fully formed thoughts, but now I can hear almost everything. Before the park, distance had an effect for me making you quieter. Now it doesn't. Wherever you have been recently I've been able to hear you. Distance doesn't make you quieter to me."

I gasped. "You hear everything?" I asked in horror. My thoughts whirled. I tried not to focus on a single particularly embarrassing thought, and just let them pass quickly through. I hoped it was too quick for them.

"'Fraid so." He looked away now, avoiding my eyes.

"There is some good news," Ross smiled at me. "Distance does have an effect for me. I have to be quite close. In the same room, actually. Once I'm more than about five metres away you start to get quiet. Ten metres, and you're gone." Ross smiled at me.

That was something at least.

"So, you'll all range in between this?" I gestured between Ross and Fraser.

"Yes," Chris replied. "I can hear you when we're on campus at the same time, so I figure about a half-mile radius."

"Right." My voice was quiet.

That was quite a difference between Ross, Chris and Fraser.

Wonder what the age difference is?

I immediately regretted thinking that.

"Sorry," I said.

Ross just laughed. "Yep. Fraser is officially old. Me, on the other hand, I could still be alive."

My eyes couldn't leave his face. My curiosity was afire. I wanted to ask, but didn't know if it would be incredibly rude. I couldn't imagine them being old. Fraser's eyes certainly held a look of knowledge. Chris, as well, had such a calm exterior you knew they weren't the same as the party-obsessed students I saw every day. But Ross's comment led me to believe they were beyond the normal span of a human lifetime. I just couldn't match that up.

"Ross, you are lucky that Fraser and I are so easygoing. At some point you are going offend a vampire who will gladly teach you a lesson." Chris shook his head as he spoke. He looked across to Fraser, who was frowning at Ross, "Think we should stop being easy on him. He's easily out of adjustment period now. Maybe it is time he should learn some manners."

Fraser glanced at me. I was frozen to the spot, listening to the exchange, wondering what it all meant.

"Hmm," was all he replied.

I tried to think of other things. My thoughts were slow and I realised that I was knackered. It must be late. All my thinking and questions must have taken a while.

What time is it?

"Almost midnight," Fraser replied.

"Wow! Didn't think it was that late." It was as if the confirmation made me even more tired. I yawned.

Do you guys even sleep?

"Rarely," Chris replied. "We've no real need to. It's more like a deep meditation than actual sleep."

Hmm.

"You're welcome to my bed, if you don't want to walk home." Fraser turned to me.

That sounded like a good idea. The thought of walking home in the cold rain didn't appeal.

"Would that be OK?" I asked.

"No problem." He stood up.

I followed his action, stretching my arms out in front of me. I followed him into his room, standing in the middle as he moved the chair back and picked up a book and some papers from his desk. He faced me.

"I'll be in the living room if you need anything. If you want to leave, just say, and I'll walk you home." He paused, watching me.

I was trying to not think of him now that I realised my thoughts were open to him, but it was difficult with him standing so close to me. I could have easily stretched out my arms and touched him.

"You've been incredibly calm about all of this," he commented.

"Ah, I don't think so." I thought about my panic attack earlier, trying not to flush.

He smiled. "I'll be next door."

He turned and left the room. It felt very empty without his presence. I tried not to think about it and climbed under the covers on the bed, wondering why he had a bed at all if he didn't need it. I fell asleep within seconds.

Chapter Ten

I woke but kept my eyes shut. I lay there enjoying the warmth, with the sunlight shining through my eyelids.

That was a weird dream.

I'd dreamt of being at Fraser's flat, talking about psychics, telepaths, projecting thoughts and, of all things, vampires! I smiled.

How daft!

Sunlight on my face.

Hang on. Sunlight doesn't come in my window in the morning.

My eyes popped open. I was in Fraser's flat again.

"Oh." It all came flooding back.

Wasn't a dream.

There was a knock on the door. As I rolled round it opened, and Fraser walked in.

"Morning. How are you?" he asked.

"Umm, OK. Just coming to," I replied groggily.

I stretched and sat up in the bed as Fraser sat down in the chair.

"Judging by the fact I can see daylight outside, I guess I've missed my morning lectures?"

"I'm afraid so. I thought it best to let you sleep. Give you a chance to sort things out." He smiled apologetically. "I'm sure we'll be able to catch you up on anything you missed."

"Really? Know much about thermodynamics, do you?" I joked sarcastically.

"Well, it has been about forty years since I did my degree in Physics but I'm sure I'll remember the basics." He grinned.

My mouth fell open. I tried to recover before I looked even more stupid.

"So, what are you studying here?"

"I'm doing a PhD on the poet William Soutar," he replied.

"Never heard of him."

"He's quite a well known poet from Perth – early twentieth century. He seems to be going through something of a revival right now, so it seemed fairly appropriate to study him for just now."

"So you've got a few degrees then? You study whatever is popular?" I asked.

"We have quite a few degrees between us. It fits in easier with our younger appearance, and is easier socially than a workplace. We spend time doing degrees, masters etc, then sometimes work for a few years, then move on to a new university. We've stayed in Scotland recently, but all of us except Ross have spent time abroad."

"Oh, right."

This was more information than he had ever divulged before. I wondered if I was going to get more information out of him.

So you can still hear me, right?

"Clear as a bell," he replied, smiling.

The rest of the guys in?

"Nope. All away out."

My head was a lot clearer after my sleep. I could think of questions rather than lots of ideas bouncing off the inside of my skull.

"Is there any way I could stop projecting my thoughts?" I asked.

"Normally, yes. With time and plenty of practice vampires are able to shield their thoughts so that others can't read them. This would also stop you projecting every thought. You would have to specifically send a thought out of your shield. But for you I'm not sure. As projecting came naturally it wasn't a skill developed with time," he answered.

"So you gonna tell me how? So you don't have to put up with my comments about everything?"

He smiled, his eyes amused.

"Don't tell me you've been enjoying my assessment of everything?" I asked, horrified.

"I must admit it has been refreshing to see another viewpoint, through a new pair of eyes. A vampire can become detached from his surroundings, bored with things." He wasn't smiling now, but was focussed on something distant. "You must understand we've seen most of it before. Human nature hasn't changed that much over the years. Occasionally something will catch our interest and we re-engage with our surroundings again. It's one of the reasons I stay at universities – there is generally more energy in these places than at the usual office job." He looked up at me.

"But to hear your thoughts on everything has honestly been like a breath of fresh air. Someone so young, experiencing new situations – it's been a reminder of what life is like." He smiled.

I was chewing over the word 'young'. I'd always hated to be considered young. Most people who knew me didn't think of me as young. I found most people my own age petty and difficult to relate to. I'd been lucky that my flatmates were reasonably like me, with liveable differences.

"I meant no offence." Fraser's quiet voice intruded into my thoughts.

"None taken." I smiled briefly. I suppose I was young compared to what-ever age he was. This thought depressed me, but I tried not to focus on it.

"So, a shield? How does that work?"

He smiled.

"It is a mental skill. People view it in different ways. Some see a wall with their thoughts on the inside; others picture emptiness, absolutely nothing, no thoughts in their head. This is a more advanced technique as it requires you to process thoughts quickly and then get rid of them. You've got to find something that works for you. I would get Chris to explain this to you, but he hasn't progressed this far himself." He paused. "You actually did something similar last night, though I don't think you realised it. Before Chris arrived, you thought something but then hid it. How did you do that?"

I tried to remember.

"Well, I knew if I thought about it properly I would project it, and Chris would realise what I was up to. So I tried to forget about it and just immersed myself in the TV programme, trying not to think of anything else. Then I wouldn't project what I was about to do."

Fraser thought about this, his eyebrows lowering.

"It's a good distraction technique, but it isn't actual shielding as I could still read your thoughts. It was just that they were all about the programme we had on."

I watched him. He still looked thoughtful.

"It is like a middle ground. You stopped me seeing the thing you wanted to hide."

It still wasn't enough for me, though. I couldn't do that all the time, and I would have had to think about something before I could then hide it.

"So, what do you see then when you are shielding?"

He looked back to me. "I see a clear film. Picture it moulded to the inside of my skull, like shaped bullet-proof Perspex. I can still see through it and so let thoughts from others enter, but nobody can break through the Perspex to see my thoughts."

"So it's kinda like polarisation? You let things through on one axis – people's thoughts, but if it's on the other axis – people trying to hear your thoughts – it gets stopped?"

"Yes, that's it exactly, though I've never seen it in that way before." He looked surprised.

Hmm. Perspex.

For some reason I just couldn't see that working. The way I had it in my head was seeing as well as hearing other people's thoughts, and you could still see through Perspex. I knew if I had any doubt then it wouldn't work: just like with martial arts, you had to believe it would work. Any hesitation, and it wouldn't work.

So not Perspex. What else? Polarised filters? Nah.

Filters just didn't fit for some reason. I turned and looked out the window again, thinking. I could feel Fraser's eyes on my face. He was following my thought processes as well.

Why not just go with basics? A brick wall?

I started building a wall in my mind. One brick down, some mortar, then another brick on top. I built a circle, with my thoughts on the inside. I looked across at Fraser, my eyebrows raised.

He looked back.

"Well?" I asked.

He frowned.

"You're not projecting anything. Try and hold that and think of some-thing else at the same time," he instructed.

I tried. My wall was around the inside edge of my head, my thoughts on the inside of the wall. I pictured a tree – one that I passed each day going to uni. Once I had it fixed in my head I looked back at Fraser.

"You're still not projecting. That is quite remarkable; you definitely have some telepathic links somewhere." He paused, watching me. "Let's see if you can hold that."

He didn't do anything, didn't say anything.

I started to feel a strange pressure on my brick wall. It was as though I had dived into a pool and the water was pushing on my head, but this was on the inside, on my wall. Suddenly a brick fell, and then more came crashing down. My wall was gone.

I gasped.

"The tree in the park." He didn't even sound smug. I almost wanted him to.

I stared at him.

Crap.

I didn't mind if he heard that.

"Quite the opposite, actually."

"And how do you figure that?" My voice had an edge to it. I looked away from him.

He frowned at me. "You have just managed to stop projecting on your first attempt. You've built an effective shield, and you held me out to start with. You are forgetting, Stephanie, that you are not a vampire. You should not be able to do any of this. There is also the fact that at two hundred and eighty years old there are not many vampires around here that *can* hold me out, and certainly no humans." His own voice had an exasperated edge.

"Oh" was all I could manage. I suddenly felt young, and embarrassed at my mini temper tantrum. I avoided looking at him.

There was silence for a while. I was trying to picture my wall again. If I could stop projecting, that was something at least.

Fraser blew out a breath slowly. "With practice, I am sure that you will be able to hold a shield. You have picked this up remarkably quick. You are already more adept at this than any of the others here." He moved his head, trying to make eye contact with me. I couldn't resist but to look at him.

You are doing well.

I gasped. He hadn't spoken out loud. His voice was so clear, so close, so intimate. Goose bumps appeared all down my arms. I tried to grasp it, stupid though that may sound. I tried to hold onto the sound of his voice in my head.

He blinked and stood up.

"I'll leave you to think. I'll be next door." He left the bedroom.

I sat motionless on the bed, still trying to recover from the sound of his voice in my head. Was that what I sounded like to the rest of the guys? I flushed at the thought. That had been weirdly personal, almost like a full on kiss, his thoughts in mine. I knew that I wanted to feel that again though. I was suddenly glad that most of them couldn't hear me when I wasn't close.

So I knew how to shield. I just had to practise and I would stop projecting to them. I stood up, fixing my clothes and running my hand through my hair. I checked my phone for the time: half eleven.

Definitely missed lectures then.

I'd have to borrow Cathy's notes if Ali didn't already have them. I grabbed my bag and jacket, and headed out to the living room. Fraser was standing in the doorway to another room, a book in his hand.

"Thought I'd better head off," I said.

He looked up. "I'll walk you back." He put the book down on a desk further in the room.

"You don't have to. It's not as though it's the middle of the night or anything. And you know I won't get lost." I laughed.

"I'm heading out anyway. Might as well see you back." He shrugged. Grabbing a coat off a table, he walked to the door.

I followed him down the stairs and outside. I looked towards the little bit of green in the middle of the street, and the bench where I had sat the other night.

Well, definitely got my questions answered. How bizarre!

I never would have believed the answers a week ago. There was evidence to back it up, wasn't there? I started thinking back over everything that had been discussed. There was no doubting Fraser's telepathic part, and I certainly had developed the radar system after that fainting spell. The rest? Vampires? Was that something I really wanted to ask for evidence for? What evidence could they give me? Don't think they would appreciate me asking to see their fangs.

"So, vampire myths then." I started, as we entered the park.

Fraser looked over, an amused expression on his face. He'd probably heard my thoughts: I hadn't been thinking of a wall.

"Garlic?"

"No effect."

"Stake in the heart?"

"Does work, or decapitation, but not many humans are capable of doing that."

"Oh." That kind of stopped my thoughts for a moment.

"Daylight?" I asked, looking up at the sky.

"An annoyance for the first few years. We are oversensitive to it in the beginning, but after a while we can stand it. Ross still wears long sleeves and hats most of the time. One of the advantages of the west coast is lots of rain clouds." He smiled.

"So, is it the UV? What would happen?" I asked.

"The UV irritates our skin, and eventually we would literally burn. But, like I said, it is more of an inconvenience than a threat to older vampires. Only for the very young would it actually be a threat, and they would have to be somewhere quite sunny."

"Being invited into someone's house?"

"Pure myth."

"Oh, yeh." I thought about Fraser and Chris coming into my flat before.

"That's about it, isn't it?" I asked.

"Oh, there are quite a few more," he chuckled. Holding up his hand, he started ticking off his fingers. "You can see my reflection. You can see me in a picture and on film. I have a heartbeat, but it is a lot slower than yours. I don't have to breathe but habits are hard to break. I'm not cold – not unless I haven't fed for a while – though I am sensitive to heat in others: I can feel it radiating off them. Our senses are better than humans, with exceptional eyesight, a very good sense of smell and hearing – most of the perks of a hunter. We do also have a natural appeal to most people, but this can be controlled. If it is used, people are attracted to us, trust us, are not afraid. We don't use ours: it is really just to make it easier to…" He drifted off, looking across to me.

"Oh, right." I looked away.

I hadn't really been thinking about that side of it; just been focusing on my stuff. I didn't want to think about it right now, with Fraser right next to me. I didn't think I would be able to keep my wall up.

We carried on walking downhill. The park was busier than normal, with the rare sunshine pulling people outside. It was still cold though, so the young kids were well swaddled up as they threw bread into the pond for the ducks.

We walked towards the exit, still side by side. I was trying really hard to not think of my attraction to Fraser, but sometimes it couldn't help but appear in my thoughts. I tried to focus on my wall. Fraser remained silent beside me.

We walked down the street to my flat. I didn't hang around at the main door, and Fraser followed me in. As we were going up the stairs we met Lauren coming down.

"Hey, Steph." Her eyes widened as she took in who was behind me.

"Hey Lauren. You got lectures?" I asked.

"Group study," she replied vaguely, finally looking back to me. "You must have been out early this morning. Didn't hear you leave." Her eyebrow was raised.

"Yeh. I headed in early. Was meeting my lab partner to go over stuff before we handed in our report."

"Oh." She sounded slightly disappointed.

"Well, I'll catch you later." I started up the stairs again.

She kept watching us until we went round the corner.

"Lab report?" Fraser's amused voice was quiet beside me. Lauren wouldn't have heard it.

More questions than it's worth.

There was a pause.

"See what you mean."

I turned to stare at him. "You didn't!"

"Had to check what those questions were. Didn't want her getting suspicious," he explained.

"Lauren's suspicions are generally more towards other things! Which I could have told you."

"Yes, I see that now."

My face flushed.

I tried to think of a change of topic.

"Thought you said you could control the attraction thing?" I asked, thinking about Lauren's daydreamy voice and staring.

"We do. As I explained earlier, it isn't really necessary. Most people have some initial attraction to us anyway but then they never normally approach unless we make them. They feel intimidated. You are probably one of a handful of people who have approached me of their own will."

I thought about that as we finished climbing the stairs. Sarah's behaviour at the martial arts club showed the fascination and also the reluctance to find things out for herself. Our maths tutorial had loads of girls sighing for Chris but none of them made a move for him. In the pub the guys had all been standing in a group of their own. None of the willing girls had approached.

"So when did I approach you?" I couldn't remember.

"At the end of training. When I'd held the bag," he reminded me.

"Oh yeh."

"The fact that you approached us caught all of our attention. And it finally allowed Chris to realise that it was you he was starting to hear. He'd been thoroughly confused earlier." He laughed. "I'd already realised it was you."

He paused. "You really didn't like that guy, did you?" he asked, a grin on his face.

"No." I blushed, remembering the rampage I'd had at Hulk in my head. Of course I hadn't realised that Fraser could hear those names.

We went into the flat and walked towards the kitchen area. Natasha was in, with a spread of books in front of her on the table. She looked up to see who had arrived, with a frazzled expression.

"Hey, Steph!" she called. Her eyes passed me and then darted back to my face again as Fraser followed me into the kitchen.

"Hey, Natasha."

I grabbed some bread and shoved it into the toaster, not realising how hungry I was until the smell of the kitchen hit me. We both sat in the plastic chairs at the table. I checked one of the book titles.

"Gaelic not going any better then?"

She sighed. "No. Most of the people on the course are native speakers and have formed their own little groups. I can't find anyone else who is struggling. Just need to spend more time on it, I suppose." She flopped back in her chair, throwing her pen on a pad of paper on the table.

My toast popped. I stood up to grab it as Fraser started talking.

"I know the language. If you want some help, I'd be happy to."

"Really?" Natasha's face showed she couldn't believe her luck.

"Really." He smiled.

"Oh, that's great!" She reached for a book. "Could you tell me what this phrase is? I just can't work it out and I'm sure it changes the meaning of the rest of the paragraph."

"I'm just gonna grab a quick shower," I called over my shoulder as I headed into my room, stuffing the toast in my mouth.

I rushed a shower, washing my hair quickly, and flung on some new clothes. Dumping my notes from yesterday, I reached for my phone to send Cathy a text about notes for today. Once that was all sorted and I looked reasonably presentable, I went back to the kitchen, hoping they were getting on fine and it wasn't just awkward.

I needn't have worried. They were both sitting talking and I couldn't understand a word of it. There were too many 'ughs' and 'oichs', so I knew that it wasn't French – my basic high school learning told me that much. Natasha looked relaxed; her panic must have been over. Should've figured Fraser would sort any problem.

Natasha looked up at me, smiling.

"Hey, you want some lunch?" she asked.

"That would be great! I'm starving." I smiled, anticipating Natasha's cooking.

She turned to Fraser. "You want some?"

"Ah, no, sorry. I've actually arranged to meet up with someone for lunch. Wouldn't want to ruin it."

"That's OK." She turned and started raking in her cupboards.

Do you eat normal food?

Fraser glanced to me and shook his head.

I sat down at the table. Natasha pulled some ingredients out and started chopping.

"Thank you so much for going over that stuff, Fraser. You've no idea how much of a help it is." She turned side-on to look at him as she spoke.

"No problem." He smiled. "Actually I'd better be going. Meeting Jonathon later." He stood up, and I moved on my seat, about to follow him.

"No, no. You stay here." He put his hand on my shoulder, covering it completely, his thumb and forefinger resting round my neck. It sent tingles down my arm. He looked down at me. "I'll see you tomorrow some time. If not, then on Thursday at training."

"Yeh." My voice was faint. I cleared my throat. "Thanks. I'll see you later."

He smiled, nodded to Natasha and headed down the hallway. I watched him till he was out the door.

"So…?" Natasha asked as soon as she heard the door shut. She'd stopped chopping and was staring at me.

"I don't know," I shrugged. "Bumped into him on my way home this morning and he decided to walk me back."

"He seemed to be pretty friendly." Her eyes flickered to my shoulder, where his hand had been. It still seemed hot where his hand had touched, though the tingles had changed to goose bumps on my arm.

"Yeh. Think he likes me, but maybe I'm just too young." I couldn't help my voice sounding disappointed.

"You're both adults. He's like, what, twenty six? It's not that much older than you – only about seven years or so."

Try two hundred and sixty years older.

I sighed. I must seem so naive and stupid to him. But I couldn't help wishing.

Thankfully Natasha didn't hassle me too much. I was just glad that it had been Lauren who was leaving: she would have grilled me way longer than Natasha did.

I went out later to meet Cathy for her notes, telling her that I'd slept in this morning. I did my food shop on the way home as I hadn't had the chance at the weekend – my usual trip to Farmfoods. Natasha was having some influence though, as I did go to a normal shop as well for a few fresh ingredients – the odd bit of fruit etc.

The afternoon was spent copying notes and then sitting chatting to the girls in the evening. Lauren, of course, had just a few questions for me, though I think I managed to avoid the worst of them by pretending to have gone out early.

Eventually I pretended that I had to phone home, and disappeared into my room. I didn't phone but did send both Ailsa and my mum a text each. Ailsa replied immediately. My mum probably wouldn't pick hers up until tomorrow. I climbed into bed and lay listening to the rain, and thinking of Fraser, again.

Chapter Eleven

It was still dark outside when my alarm woke me up in the morning. I got showered and dressed and ate a bowl of cereal whilst checking the weather. It was cloudy but not raining. I grabbed a fleece, and then left the flat.

It was cold outside. Couldn't be long till we started getting sleet. I pulled my zip right up and walked quickly, trying to keep myself warm. I cut through the park and up the steps to the main building. I liked this part of the uni. You could see across the trees to the museum, could see the science centre, and the top of the SECC. It was nice and open. On a day like this it also meant it was really windy, so I didn't slow down to appreciate the view, but kept going to the physics building.

I saw Rachel heading into the lecture theatre in front of me. I followed her in a minute later. I already knew where Cathy and Ali were sitting, and headed for them.

One handy advantage found.

I didn't have to stand at the front, looking stupid as I tried to find my friends. I could just go straight to them.

"Hey, guys." I sat down as they said hi.

"You make sense of my notes?" Cathy asked.

"Yeh, thanks for that. I've got them in my bag here for you." I dug around for them and handed the papers back to Cathy.

"Cool," she replied, taking them off me and putting them in her bag.

The lecturer came in at that point and we turned our attention to him as he started to scribble on the overhead. Halfway through the lecture he decided to take an 'interesting aside', as he called it, apparently not hearing the collective groan of the students. I tuned out, and decided to try and locate people. I started with something easy, as I knew Matthew was bound to be at the front of the lecture theatre somewhere. I concentrated on him, eventually feeling a tug towards the front. It was weak though.

Wonder why?

I put it out of my mind and moved on. Seemed that Kev had been late again as I could feel him at the back of the room. The pull was stronger than that with Matthew. I twisted round, just to check, and found him almost immediately. Smiling to myself, I turned back round. I tried to find Fraser. The pull was stronger again. I closed my eyes, trying to place him. He was a few buildings away, inside one that I'd never been in before. I could almost picture him in a room at a computer, but that was probably just imagination. I moved to Chris. The pull was weaker than the one with Fraser, but stronger than with Matthew and Kev. He was in the maths building. Didn't have to think much about that as I knew the building at his position.

Cathy nudged my ribs, and my eyes sprang open. She looked at me, grinning, and started writing again.

Oops!

The lecturer had finished his aside and was writing again on the overhead. Well, looked like I could still do the radar thing.

We finished up and made our way over to maths.

"What's keeping you awake at night, Steph? Slept in yesterday, then falling asleep today!" Cathy joked.

"I didn't fall asleep. I was just resting my eyes!" I laughed.

"Wouldn't blame you if you had. That aside lost everyone apart from the front row," Ali grumbled.

We entered the maths building and climbed the stairs up a couple of floors. We had to hang around the corridor as the previous class hadn't left yet, so everyone was in groups, chatting. I was facing Ali when I saw a familiar figure over his shoulder.

Morning, Chris!

He paused mid-step, his head snapping up. His searching eyes found mine.

Boo!

He laughed, shaking his head, and then carried on walking towards us. I grinned, thinking there probably weren't many people who could say they gave a vampire a fright.

"Steph? What you laughing at?" Ali asked me.

My eyes focused back to him. "Sorry, Ali. I was just laughing at someone over there." I pointed to a group of guys down the other end of the corridor.

He glanced briefly over his shoulder. "Oh, right."

Chris was passing us at this point. "Morning." He gave us a nod, a small smile on his face.

The girls in a group next to us all went quiet as he drew near, watching him as he passed, and then glared at us once he was gone. How dare we get his acknowledgement and they don't!

You've just torn some girls' hearts back here. You're gonna have to say hi to everyone next time.

His shoulders moved in a chuckle as he kept walking.

Maths wasn't too bad. I found this new topic easier than previous stuff. It helped that the lecturer didn't write loads of notes. He even gave us handouts of the key points. Ali definitely approved.

Kev and Rachel joined us at lunch, with some of Rachel's friends. Kev spent most of the time chatting the new girls up, whilst Rachel, Cathy and Ali discussed a new pub that had opened en route to their halls. My attention drifted, not really that interested in their conversation.

Instead, I sat thinking of my wall, trying to hold it in place whilst still thinking about normal things. It was surprisingly difficult to do as once I started to think of other things the wall would fade away, and I'd have to start again. But I persevered.

Eventually people started to drift away, and I decided to head off too. Saying cheerio to the guys left at the table, I jogged down the stairs and outside. I walked along the street, looking up at the trees, which had lost almost all of their leaves now. The leaves that were clinging on were all shades of orange and brown. There were piles of them along the pavement and side of the road. It reminded me of the trees on a walk that was by our house back home. It'd been a while since I was last home. I should probably go back at a weekend and see how they were doing. Check my mum wasn't doing Ailsa's head in.

I walked along the street and past the main building, careful not to slip on the leaves as I started downhill. Eventually I reached the park and stopped for a while on the bridge, watching the water underneath and the ducks paddling round. It always managed to put me at ease and make me forget my worries.

"Penny for your thoughts."

I smiled and turned to see Fraser standing beside me.

"Like you'd need to ask!" I laughed.

He smiled and moved up to stand next to me, leaning on the stone railing.

"But that wouldn't be polite. You've been a lot quieter this morning." He looked down at me.

"Yeh. Been practising. It's more difficult than it seems though." I frowned, trying to bring the wall back to mind.

"I've no doubt that you can do it. You've certainly got natural talent." He looked down at the water flowing underneath us.

We stood, lost in our own thoughts for a while. At least I was. Eventually he turned to face me.

"So, any more questions for me today?" His tone was light.

I thought about it. Stepping back from the stone wall, I turned to start walking further into the park, with Fraser at my side.

"I've got questions. But I think I've covered most of the ones to do with the whole projection thing. As long as I can stop doing that, so you don't have to hear me all the time, that's the main thing."

He walked on for a bit, not looking at me. "So, you have questions about us." He wasn't really asking, his tone correctly identifying the 'us' as himself and his vampire flatmates.

I nodded. "I'm just curious about you. If you don't want to talk about it then that's fine. I'm probably being really nosy anyway."

He sighed, looking into the distance as we walked. He was aiming for the path uphill and I followed his lead. Near the top he walked over to one of the benches so we could look over the park. He sat down and looked across at me before he started talking again.

"I'm happy to answer some of the questions you might have. Just be aware that not all of the answers will be… easy." He paused. "In all honesty I'm surprised that you are still even coming near us, never mind wanting to find out more."

"I've never felt threatened by you, or any of the other guys. You've never giving me any reason for staying away. In fact, you keep on being my rescuer!" I laughed.

"Surely, just what we are is reason enough." He turned his face away from me.

I looked across at his profile. "But you said that you don't kill people; you only do what you must to survive."

"And that is true. But it wasn't always the case." He looked at me.

"Everyone changes. None of us are the same people we once were." It was my turn to look away now.

We watched a couple walk towards us on the path. Passing us by, they were busy chatting animatedly.

"So, what do you want to know?"

"When were you born?" I asked.

"Surely your maths isn't that bad?"

I just smiled.

"1730."

Wow.

"How old were you when you… changed?"

"I was twenty five."

"So…" My history was very sketchy. "Wouldn't you have been around when there were Jacobites?"

He chuckled. "They weren't a separate breed. Yes, I would have been, but my father sent me away to family in France to avoid the trouble. I was only a teenager but he didn't want me to get drawn in by it all. He had already lost his brother during the first uprising. He wasn't about to lose his son, though by the time I returned, in 1765, I wasn't really his son any more."

"So it happened in France?"

"Yes."

We sat quietly for a while. I didn't know what questions to ask, which ones he would answer.

"What about the other guys? How long have you known them?"

"I've known Chris for about a hundred years now. We met in London, got on well, so we travelled together for a while. Eventually we met Craig about eighty years ago. Jonathon, we met almost thirty years ago. Ross, we took in about twenty years ago. We found him not long after he had been changed. He had been left without guidance. It was only a matter of time before he was discovered and exposed."

The numbers were going round and round in my head. They were all *way* older than me. Even Ross was twice my age, at least. I could only imagine what it must be like to live with someone for over a hundred years.

"You must know each other incredibly well."

He smiled, looking at me. "Chris and I know each other well. Craig too."

"You don't think you know Jonathon and Ross well, even though you've lived with them for over twenty years?" My voice was disbelieving.

He hesitated, frowning.

"There is a difference between knowing someone well and living with them. We all have a past, with stories and secrets that we don't tell everyone we meet. Would you say that your flatmates know you well?"

I opened my mouth to confirm, thought about it, and then changed my mind. "I suppose not."

"I'm not denying that you get on with them and that you are happy living with them, but it doesn't mean that they know everything about you."

I could see his point. I liked living with the girls and we got on well for all our different personalities, but none of them knew anything about my panic attacks, and they didn't know about my family. They didn't know everything about Fraser. Yet these things were a huge part of my life.

"So. You said that Ross was going to be discovered. Do people really believe in vampires?"

He just looked at me with one eyebrow raised. "Don't you?"

"I mean, other than when they are faced with one. Do people actually come to their own conclusion that there must be vampires out there?"

"There are some groups who make it their business to hunt us. Generally they only find young vampires who are foolish enough to expose themselves. Most established vampires leave them to it, as it makes it less likely that we will be found if they are busy with young ones. Even if things became public the groups are generally quite fanatical, appearing like cults in the press, and so are rarely believed."

"Right." My voice felt a bit weak after his calm tone. So calm, yet he was talking about the fact that there were groups hunting him.

"There is nothing for you to be alarmed about, Stephanie. There are no such groups in Glasgow, and we do not make foolish mistakes."

I gave a half-smile, and looked away. The sky was still a blanket grey. In the distance there was the dull haze of rain. A wind was starting, pushing the clouds along in a hurry. There weren't many people in the park today, most just walking through and not stopping: it was too cold. I pushed my hands further into my pockets and leant back on the bench, bringing my feet up to the edge of the seat. Fraser may have been able to sit right back and have his feet reach the ground, but I couldn't.

"So how am I doing with my wall?" I asked. I'd been trying to keep it in place during our conversation.

"Not bad. It's slipped a couple of times but your thoughts are definitely not as loud as they were."

"Cool."

I shivered; couldn't help it. We'd been sitting still for too long.

"I should've realised it was too cold to be sitting out here. Come on. Let's get you inside." Fraser stood up and I followed.

At a branch in the path he looked to me. I deliberated for a while, then nodded downhill with a sigh. I had too much work to do.

Got tutorial work to get done.

He smiled and we headed down the path back to my flat.

"Will you be training tomorrow night?" I asked.

"That is the plan."

We carried on towards the other side of the park.

"If you are still curious as to what we can do, you could stay behind after training and join in with us, if you'd like."

"Yeh. That would be good." My answer was a bit too quick. "Might just watch though. I have the feeling I'm not going to be able to keep up, anyway!"

He smiled at me. "You never know."

I laughed.

He stepped in beside me. I thought he was going to put his arm around me but he stopped just centimetres away. Our arms brushed against each other as we kept walking. My thoughts were a bit more scrambled, with him so close. I tried to keep the wall in place.

"My turn for a question this time, if you'll answer."

"I'll try." I half laughed. Surely if he wanted an answer, he could have plucked it out of my thoughts.

"Who is Ailsa?"

Suddenly it was easy to visualise my wall.

"She's my sister," I answered.

He nodded.

"You are close?"

"Very close."

He nodded again as we carried along the street. I was trying to think how he knew the name, but then realised he must have heard it from me at some point. This struck me as odd. For all Fraser must have heard many of my thoughts in the time I'd lived in Glasgow, he had never mentioned them. He had given me some measure of privacy, for which I was very grateful.

Against my shield I felt a light pressure, as though someone was stroking their finger across my cheek. I looked at Fraser sharply.

"Was that you?"

He hesitated. "Yes. I'm sorry. I wasn't trying to pry. I just wanted to test a theory."

"Could've asked."

"It wouldn't have been a valid test then, as you know. You would have been expecting it."

"Hmm." I frowned at him, but couldn't do it for long. "So what was your theory then?"

"I've often heard you mention the name Ailsa but as soon as she comes to mind your thoughts go quiet; your shield stops you projecting. Is she by any chance a younger sister?"

"What makes you think that?" I was scowling now, wondering why he was so interested in Ailsa. We were almost back at my flat and I had been hoping he would come in again, but this conversation had me on edge.

"Your protectiveness. Even now you are avoiding my questions."

I stared at him. It took me a second to realise that I'd stopped walking and was standing facing him. I gave myself a mental shake and started walking again. There would be no point in a face-off with Fraser, not that I wanted one anyway.

Why does he have to be asking me these questions?

"She's older than me, by three years."

"Hmm." He walked beside me again, not acknowledging the fact that I had been getting ready to fight, though he clearly must have recognised it. Ever since the accident I was overprotective of Ailsa. If she needed anything, I did it. I knew this but didn't really admit it to anyone else. Didn't have to.

Lost in my own thoughts, I unlocked the main door. Fraser followed me in and up the stairs. In the flat I dumped my bags in my room, whilst Fraser took a seat in the living room. I grabbed a juice from the kitchen and then sat down opposite him on the padded chairs.

"None of the girls are in," I said. I couldn't sense any of them nearby. He smiled and nodded.

What do I say?

I couldn't think of a conversation. Our previous topic didn't make me want to talk and I couldn't move my thoughts on from it.

"So what did your test show then?" I asked.

"That you can block very well if you have the motivation. That was the same strength that I used the first time you shielded. The first time, it got through, but this time it didn't even come close to getting through."

"Oh, right." I suppose that was something to be grateful for. I looked out the window, not really wanting eye contact just now. I stared out at the street. The trees across the way were swaying in the wind that was picking up.

"Stephanie."

I couldn't help but look round at him. It was the way he said my name; nobody says it like that. His blue eyes locked with mine. They pulled at me, made me want to close the space between us.

"I'm sorry. I didn't realise this would upset you."

I had to clear my throat before I could speak. "It's not your fault."

He opened his mouth again to speak so I jumped in, keen to move on.

"Think Natasha will try to pick your brains again about her course-work next time she sees you. She's been talking about trying to change her second language to something else like Spanish or Italian. She's probably doing fine but she seems to be a bit of a perfectionist."

Fraser hesitated, obviously thinking about whether to go with this new topic or not.

"I'd be happy to help her any time I'm here."

We sat in quiet for a bit. I started to relax again, the tension from before leaving me.

"So when you guys are training, is it one style of martial arts that you do, or a mixture?" This was a safe enough topic.

"A mixture. I've obviously tried a few different ones over the years, and trained under different masters. We've developed our own style really, combining moves with our natural strengths."

I nodded. It made sense. I used techniques that worked for me and forgot about the ones that didn't, using my flexibility to my advantage.

"Craig obviously has a talent for it. Chris enjoys it; has got used to my... obsession for it. Jonathon humours me and Ross doesn't yet realise its advantages. They train just as something to do."

"I see."

"What about you? Why do you like it so much?" he asked.

I paused before answering. Without him realising it, he was back to the topic I had been trying to get away from.

"Distraction. I needed somewhere to vent frustration, anger. I needed something I could escape into."

"That sounds very familiar." He gave a half-smile. Funnily enough, I believed him. I didn't think anyone would really understand my reasons, but I believed that Fraser did. He didn't ask any more, maybe recognising the emotions behind those feelings.

It felt odd having him sitting in our living room. He seemed out of place. It was such stereotypical student surroundings, with the shabby furnishings, dirty dishes piled up in the kitchen, the traffic cone still sitting against the wall; whilst Fraser was definitely not your typical student.

I turned to look out the window again.

What is he doing here?

I hoped my wall was still strong. It wasn't that I didn't want him here, but at times he seemed so much… more than anything I was.

How can someone sit with elegance? Yet he managed it. He seemed relaxed yet ready to move instantly. Confident, perfectly at ease with who he was. His clothes fit him well. They didn't look very flashy but you knew they cost more than my jeans and T-shirt. His perfect good looks and body. The feeling that you could ask him any question and he would be able to answer it correctly. I felt very inadequate sitting opposite him.

"What are you thinking?" he asked.

I laughed. "Bet you haven't had to ask someone *that* for a while."

He smiled. "Admittedly, no."

"I'm not thinking about much."

"I should probably tell you now, that it's not very easy to lie to a vampire. All these extra senses, you see." He waved his hand at himself. "I can hear your heartbeat increase, see your pupils change, and hear the change in your voice tone as well. So you can't say you weren't thinking something." He smiled at me.

Thankfully he hadn't mentioned the fact that you sweat more when you lie. That would have made me feel even worse next to him. I decided to avoid.

"Eilidh's coming in the stairwell. She'll be glad to finally meet you."

He laughed, shaking his head. "I get the feeling you are practised at avoiding things. Not many people can resist answering a vampire's questions. Yet again, something different about you."

I flushed. If I hadn't been looking straight at him I would have missed his quick glance at my cheeks when they heated. He didn't move or say anything, though. I looked away, picking up my glass for a drink.

Eilidh's key turned in the main door and we listened as she rustled through the doorway with what sounded a like a load of shopping bags. When she entered the living room she stopped where she was and stared at Fraser. She stood there for what must have been about three seconds before I realised she couldn't break away without some help.

"Hey, Eilidh. Been shopping?"

She literally jumped at my voice, her head jerking towards me.

She didn't even realise I was here!

"Steph! Hey, um, yeh, been shopping." She lifted an arm, showing me the bags. I tried not to smile at her dumbstruck expression.

"Right, eh, I'll get these away then." She moved through to the kitchen, dumping her bags on the table to unpack them.

I let my wall down deliberately,

That so isn't fair what you can do to people!

Fraser just smiled across at me.

But not on you?

I drew in a sharp breath, my muscles melting. He was projecting to me again, and again it sounded so intimate, so close, like a caress in my head. There was a blur in front of my eyes. When it resolved, Fraser was standing, leaning down right in front of me. In his hand was my glass, the juice sloshing from where he had caught it. It hadn't even reached my lap yet. My eyes widened even more, realising the speed that he must have moved at.

"Sorry. I shouldn't have done that here." His voice was quiet. Eilidh wouldn't have heard it in the kitchen.

"It's fine." My voice was weak. I cleared my throat, trying to get back to normal. "I've thought of another question for you, actually." I managed a quick grin.

He smiled back, glanced towards the kitchen, then sat down next to me, out of Eilidh's line of sight in the kitchen.

"Shoot."

I rushed it out, not knowing how long Eilidh would stay in the kitchen for.

"When I project, do I sound like you do to me?" He didn't say anything. "I mean, you sound very… close. I don't just hear you." I didn't bother explaining further. Surely he knew what I meant, with all his boosted senses.

He looked away from me before he answered. "No, it does not have the same effect on us. I'm trying to figure it out. I think it has something to do with the fact that you are generally broadcasting rather than sending a specific thought to one person. But even when a vampire sends a specific thought to someone, it shouldn't have this effect. I've heard of it, but never seen it."

"Right." I frowned, confused about how that made me feel. It was a relief to know that I wasn't being that personal with guys I barely knew, but it was a bit worrying that Fraser didn't know why it had this effect. I just figured he would have all the answers.

He leant back in the seat, his arm going around the back of my chair but not touching me. It still seemed very far away after what I'd felt when he projected to me, even if his leg was resting against mine.

Eilidh came back through from the kitchen. She hesitated when she saw us sitting so close together but then switched on the TV and sat down across from us, where Fraser had been sitting.

"So, fit you guys up to then?" She asked.

"Nothing much. Just gossiping about training," I replied.

She nodded, then looked over to the TV and started flicking through channels.

"I should probably be going. Let you get on with your work."

Eilidh's head turned back to us at the sound of Fraser's voice. He moved forward, his hand touching my shoulders as he stood up.

I tried to give myself a mental shake. I *so* needed to stop noticing every time he touched me. I was making more of it than he was, and I would only end up upsetting myself.

He picked up his coat and headed up the hallway, with me following behind. He paused just outside our door again, looking back at me.

"So, I'll see you tomorrow night." I tried to sound casual, and wondered if he could detect the forced tone. My stomach always clenched when it came to saying bye to him.

I can be such a ditzy girl sometimes. Get a grip!

I really hoped my wall was back up again. I looked down, trying to find something to hold my attention – anything other than his face.

"Yeh, we'll be there, and hopefully you'll show us how it's done afterwards."

I laughed at that, looking back up at him. "I'll think about it."

He smiled.

"I'm sorry I upset you earlier. I didn't mean to." His eyes were fixed on me, watching my face carefully.

"It's fine."

How much can he read me? What does he know?

He lifted his eyebrows, clearly not believing me. So he really was a human lie detector. Great! I smiled again, trying to show that I was fine.

"I'll see you tomorrow then." I moved back, putting more distance between us.

"See you tomorrow." He turned and jogged down the steps.

I closed the door and leant against it, taking a minute to catch my breath. Even though I could hear the TV in the living room, and Eilidh was in there watching it, the place felt empty. I flicked the light on in the hall as I walked towards the living room. There wasn't much daylight coming in the tiny window.

I sat down opposite Eilidh as she looked away from the teatime chat show.

"I'm guessing that's Fraser?" she asked.

"Yeh. I didn't actually introduce you, did I?"

"Nope, but I'll forgive you. If he was sitting that close to me I think I might forget about formalities as well!"

I gave a laugh. "Yeh, he still has that effect on me."

"So, have you made a move on him yet?"

"No. I don't know whether I should or not. I mean, he is just so…"

"Gorgeous?" Eilidh provided. "Perfect? Fit? Pin-up good?"

I laughed. "Yeh! All of that! What chance have I got? I think we could become good friends, and maybe that is all I should be aiming for."

"You're crazy! You seriously gonna give up a chance on that? What have you got to lose?" Eilidh tried to convince me.

But I had a lot to lose. He was one of a few people who knew what I could do. Even now I knew exactly where he was, walking up the hill in the park towards his flat. He was moving quicker than your average person walking.

Wonder if he's jogging or running? Maybe just walking fast?

I shook my head and put Fraser out of my mind as much as I could. I chatted with Eilidh for a while, though she seemed a bit quieter than usual. Maybe she was annoyed that I didn't introduce her after all.

I left her to watch the TV, and went to my room to work on maths questions for tomorrow. I sat at my desk with my sheets and textbook in front of me, calculator on hand, and stared away into space. Well not quite anywhere: I was staring at Fraser again, just from a distance. My maths problems lay forgotten on my desk as I daydreamed, wondering what training would bring tomorrow night. What would it be like? Would he walk me home again afterwards? It got dark outside as I sat dreaming.

Chapter Twelve

"But how the hell can that line turn into that one?" Ali gestured at the paper on the desk in front of us as he muttered under his breath.

My eyes met Cathy's as we shared a look across Ali's frowning head. She gave a sigh, and then patiently started explaining it for about the fourth time. By some miracle I got this section, and that seemed to just annoy Ali even more. I'd been his comrade before – someone else who thought it made as much sense as Egyptian hieroglyphs.

I looked over to the front, where Chris was shuffling some papers.

Your expertise is needed across here. Think Ali might shred the work with his teeth, then run out the room howling if he doesn't get a break soon.

He looked up. His eyes crinkled at the corners, trying not to smile for no apparent reason. Even had I not been able to see Chris walk towards our table, I would have been able to track his movement by the turning of heads and sighing from the class as he walked past.

"Anything I can help you guys with?" His voice interrupted Cathy's explanation.

Ali looked up from his work, sighed, and then gave in. "Yeh. This doesn't make any sense to me."

I went back to my own work as Chris set about sorting Ali's maths problems.

We met Kev and a few others when we came out of maths, and joined them for lunch in the union. They were all chatting away but I couldn't quite get into the conversation. Nights out, shopping trips, TV programmes – I just wasn't that interested. I was too busy thinking about training tonight and how long I had to wait till then.

"Looking forward to training tonight, Steph?" Cathy asked, with a grin on her face.

"Yep. You coming back again?" I asked her.

"Yeh. Think I might be converted to your ways!" She laughed.

I smiled. We sat chatting for a while but I didn't stay too long. I dawdled on my way back to the flat but didn't meet Fraser in the park. It was daft. I knew he wasn't nearby but couldn't help walking slowly, as though he might just appear beside me.

The afternoon was spent doing a bit of cleaning and then I phoned home. For all Ailsa and Mum didn't say anything directly, the atmosphere on the phone seemed strained. They must have argued. I just wish they would tell me what it was but they obviously thought they could fool me. Maybe it was time for that visit home. I didn't have any plans for the weekend yet, and I could easily catch a train back. Buy a return ticket. That way Mum wouldn't have to drive me back to Glasgow. I didn't discuss my plans with them on the phone, so they couldn't object and say that there was no need for me to visit.

At training that evening I was surprised when Cathy and I walked into the hall to see Craig chatting to our coach. He gave me a friendly nod and a grin, and then carried on his conversation.

"Isn't that one of Fraser's flatmates that I met the other week?" Cathy asked as we waited on Ali joining us.

"Yeh. It's Craig." My voice was a bit vague as I tried to figure out why he was about to join in with our class. Fraser had invited me to join in with them afterwards but I didn't think one of them would join our training session.

We did our usual warm-up session and then were instructed to partner up for pad work. I looked around for Kerry but didn't get a chance to call over to her as Craig appeared at my side.

"I'm booking you for this part." He tossed me some pads.

"Oh, really?"

"Yep. In fact, I'm booking you for the rest of the evening!" He grinned at me. His smile was infectious.

"Any particular reason for this?" I asked, whilst pulling the targets onto my hands.

"Yep. Wanna see what you can do. Especially after last week. Fraser said you had a bit of a talent for this before. Need to check and see if it has progressed any."

I froze. I hadn't even considered that.

"You mean people can have more than one particular talent?"

"Oh, yeh." He held up his hands ready to punch. "You ready?"

I finished strapping the Velcro and held up the targets, letting Craig start on the routine we were to practise.

My thoughts tumbled. I just assumed that knowing where people were was going to be it. I hadn't thought that there could be more.

Shit! What happens if I am better? Will I notice? Will other people notice? Should I even be trying it in front of others?

"Wakey, wakey, Steph. Time to swap." I looked up. Craig was looking at me expectantly. I pulled off the targets and tossed them. He caught them both with one hand, and started to pull them on.

I took a step closer to him. "Should I be even trying this out for the first time here?" I looked around at all the other people in the hall.

"Yeh. It'll be fine." His voice didn't have any concern in it, but I couldn't help frowning.

"But what if – "

"Just punch," his voice interrupted me. He held up the targets.

I still hesitated.

He did the old coach trick of hitting me round the head with the pad because I didn't have my hands up. I lifted my arm to block it, and he smiled.

"That's the idea! Now hit the pad!"

I laughed and started the routine. Couldn't say I noticed any difference. Relieved, I relaxed a bit more and just got on with it. Craig was good to work with, giving encouragement and advice as we went along. I remembered that this was his area of expertise – fighting – and wondered if that was why he was here rather than anyone else.

By the end of the class I was knackered. All the encouragement and constant pushing had got the most out of me. I stood trying to catch my breath as Cathy and Ali came over to join us.

"That was a hard class. Don't know how you could keep that pace up, Steph," Ali's voice was a bit wheezy, his arms on his hips.

"Remember, she's done this stuff before," Craig cut in.

"That's true." Cathy said, her cheeks red from the effort she'd put in.

I noticed that Craig was nowhere near out of breath and had retained normal composure throughout the session. I hope no one looked too closely at him. As we stood chatting I felt, rather than saw, the rest of Craig's flatmates enter the hall. Craig excused himself and made his way over to them.

"So you coming to the pub again?" Ali asked.

"Actually I might catch you up later." My eyes followed Fraser as he walked the length of the hall. Ali snorted, and Cathy stuck an elbow in his ribs.

"Ow. No need for that!" He rubbed his side.

"We'll catch you later," Cathy said, smiling, "or maybe just see you tomorrow." She winked, and then pulled Ali along after her as she left the hall.

I started to do some stretches before my muscles tightened up. I tried not to watch Fraser too openly. Sarah couldn't help but follow his movement round the room. She switched between watching him and shooting glares at me. The room got quieter and she eventually left, but clearly wasn't happy with me staying. She didn't say anything to me though.

Fraser walked towards me but stopped when there were still a few steps between us.

"Are you happy to stay and train then?" he asked.

I moved closer to him. "Yep. What was Craig's assessment then?"

He smiled. I'd hit it right on.

"He says you're good. You haven't got any extra strength but your speed is quick. We can test it properly now that the rest have gone."

"So I'm good, am I?" I felt slightly disappointed with that assessment.

"Trust me, that is quite a compliment, coming from Craig."

"Huh."

We walked over to the rest. Chris and Jonathon had picked up some kick shields, and Ross and Craig were currently doing turning kicks on them. It took a second to register the power that they were doing it with, as both Chris and Jonathon hardly moved when the kick landed. There was certainly no way I was holding the bags unless they wanted to scrape me off the wall.

Fraser and I joined in, taking turns to kick after Ross and Craig. My kicks seemed so pathetic after watching them, even when I was trying my hardest. I eventually gave up trying to compete, and just had to accept the bruised ego. They were vampires after all. That brought a smile to my face.

There's a sentence you wouldn't say very often!

After a few rotations Fraser called a stop. "Think everyone has cleared out of this floor now. We can start sparring. You and I'll watch to begin with." He nodded at me.

The guys didn't bother putting on mitts or any guards. Jonathon partnered Ross, and Chris was with Craig, which was odd to look at – the tallest guy with the smallest. Fraser moved beside me and they started.

It was so fast: constant attack and defence, no gaps, no thinking time, no consideration, just a constant flow of movement. Then they would break apart and just circle for a while, then another flurry of movement. My mouth hung open. I turned to Fraser. "You expect me to do that?" My voice was incredulous.

"Well, maybe not quite so quick." He smiled back at me.

"You're crazy. There is no way I can keep up with you guys."

They had stopped now and swapped partners. Craig was now with Ross.

"This should be good. Ross always tries to get one over Craig. Hasn't managed yet but still thinks he can." Fraser's voice held some amusement as his focus turned back to the guys.

I watched as Ross concentrated on finding Craig's weaknesses. I couldn't see any. I could barely follow their movement once they got into it. The testers, the fake attacks – I could follow as they were slower; but the real attacks – I struggled to see. I just heard the resulting whack.

"Think you're ready for a shot yet?" Fraser asked.

"Do you seriously think there is any point?" I replied.

"Let's see what you are capable of. At the very least you can learn a few new moves." He smiled at me and started walking over to the guys, who had stopped, but the only one out of breath was Ross, which made me frown.

I thought they didn't need to breathe?

"Craig, do you want to start?" Fraser asked, though it didn't really sound like a question.

Craig took a few steps away from Ross and faced me. Giving me a nod, he brought his hands up to start. I settled into fighting stance, bouncing on my toes a couple of times to keep my feet light. Craig circled around me, keeping eye contact, and I turned, staying square on to him. He started off easy, a backhand strike to my head. I blocked and countered with a punch. He kept on moving, picking up speed. The attacks became quicker, moving in with a variety of techniques, punching and kicking. I kept blocking but was struggling to counter as he recovered from strikes so quickly. I hadn't even tried to attack him yet.

Eventually Fraser called time. I was panting, trying to get my breath back quickly. It seemed all the more embarrassing as Craig wasn't even out of breath.

Surely that's an advantage, if they can't be winded?

"Jonathon?" Fraser looked across at him, then turned and smiled at me. It looked as though he was trying to be reassuring. Couldn't say it worked. At least with Craig we had kind of chatted before; he was always friendly. Jonathon was a bit of an unknown.

Craig moved over to the other guys, who were standing at the side of the room watching as Jonathon walked towards me. He was taller than Craig, meaning he was going to have a bigger range. I'd have to move more to get out of striking distance.

We started circling, the same as the first round. Jonathon didn't ease me in though and was soon striking faster than Craig. I gave up trying to retaliate and just concentrated on blocking and moving. A few hits got through, making contact. I'd had worse but they were still enough to catch my breath.

Suppose he's got no concept of what would be sore.

Another strike sped towards my head. I just saw a blur of movement and managed to dodge it, leaning my head to the side, but I'd leant too much. I winced as his sweep made contact with my ankle and I felt the sudden loss of balance. The room tilted as I started to fall, one hand going out to try and ease my landing.

Except I never reached the floor. A hand wrapped around my forearm and another went under my back, stopping my downward motion. Air whirred and I was suddenly upright again, with Fraser's hand on my shoulder keeping me steady.

Wonder how fast he can actually move?

He had covered the gap between us incredibly quickly to catch me. I hadn't even had time to catch my balance and he had moved across the width of the room.

"You did well against that." He gave me a nod.

Even I heard Jonathon's snort. Fraser's eyes flickered across to him, his expression considering.

"Give you a chance to catch your breath." He gave my shoulder a slight squeeze and then walked back to the other guys, with Jonathon following.

They started sparring again. Whoever was unpartnered watched the rest and called time. Then they swapped and started again. When Craig was spare he came over to talk.

"So, with your talent you can tell where people are?" he asked.

"Yep."

"Is it like knowing their general location, or would you be able to narrow it down so you knew their exact position?"

I frowned. "I'm not sure what you mean. If I was to close my eyes I would still be able to point out where specific people are in this room."

"So, I'm standing next you just now. If I leant towards you, would you know that?"

"I don't know." I frowned, not following his train of thought.

He stood watching the other guys for a minute.

"I was thinking: if you were able to narrow into a smaller range, you might be able to follow where people are striking."

I must have still looked confused.

"Right now we move too fast; you can't follow our moves with your eyes. That's how Jonathon managed to make contact. But if you were to rely on your talent you would know where the attacker was and what his body was doing. So you could follow the position of their arm or leg and know where they are attacking. That way you would have time to move and counter. Rather than relying on your eyes, use your talent."

I stared at Craig, amazed.

"I would have never thought of that. Don't even know if I could do it. Suppose it makes sense but I haven't focused on people that are close in detail; only thought about their general position in relation to me."

He grinned. "That's my skill though: how to use weapons in a fight. Hope you're not offended by me thinking of you as a weapon."

"Hey, if it gives me a chance of levelling the field, I don't care!" I laughed.

We turned back to watch the guys sparring. This time though I focussed beyond them and tried to follow their movements but not with my eyes. I couldn't do it, but kept trying. If I thought it was possible, then it would be.

The guys swapped around partners again and I kept trying to follow their movements without looking at them. I stared at the mirrors beyond them or sometimes looked away completely.

It started to work, eventually. There were a few different rotations before I started to see figures in my head. It was just a pull in a certain direction. When I focussed on the cause of that pull I would see a blob, which resolved into the rough shape of a person. Then that blob would move and change shape as either arms or legs moved out from it.

This is cool! If I can use it properly.

"Stephanie?"

I focussed back in the room again. Fraser was next to me. The rest were still sparring.

"Are you OK?"

"Yeh." I smiled. "Craig just gave me a pointer. Think it could help but I'll need to practise."

He smiled back. "Craig's advice is always good when it comes to sparring."

Eventually they stopped rotating round. Ross and Jonathon left the hall and Fraser, Chris and Craig stayed to practise kata. It was nice to get some room to practise the katas from my old style of karate rather than the new ones I'd learnt. I worked through a few different forms, and then finally sat down on the floor to do stretches and watch the three guys doing their katas.

It wasn't too bad a view, sitting and watching them. I knew quite a few girls who would have paid money to see these guys working out.

The moves were impressive – playing to their strengths – but not quite as intimidating as watching them spar.

After a while they stopped, and Chris and Craig headed for the door, calling over that they would see me some time soon. Fraser stood next to me, waiting on them leaving.

"So how was that then?" he asked.

"Wasn't too bad. Certainly won't be picking a fight with any of you any time soon!" I laughed.

"Are you wanting to meet up with Cathy and Ali at the pub?" He started walking towards the doors.

"I might pass. They won't be there for that much longer anyway." I glanced at the clock on the wall. "Think I'll just head back to the flat. Got a few things to do."

"I'll meet you downstairs then, and see you home."

We split up going into the changing rooms. I got changed in record time but when I jumped the last couple of steps down to the entrance Fraser was already standing waiting.

Guess I shouldn't be surprised.

He smiled when he saw me, and moved over to the door, holding it open for me. His hand lightly touched my back as I walked through, sending tingles radiating out from it. We took the normal route through the park, and I gave my usual glance around at the paths next to us.

Don't know why I'm bothering: not as though anyone is going to sneak up on Fraser.

"So how come Ross and Jonathon left after the sparring?" I asked.

"They don't see the benefits of kata. Practice for fighting – they can see the advantages of, but kata is just a bit too boring for them." He smiled.

"Huh." I'd always enjoyed both parts. The kata provided a good chill-out and focus for your mind. I'd never rated people highly if they dismissed kata.

"What was Craig's assessment of me then?"

Fraser smiled down at me and then looked ahead again. "He thinks you're good. Better than most humans. I think your reflexes have been enhanced slightly, but your strength seems to have stayed the same."

I nodded, considering this. It wasn't too big a change. We continued walking close together on the path, our arms brushing against each other. Each time we touched I could feel tingles through my jacket, as though the whole side of my body next to his was being warmed by him. It made it particularly difficult to keep my wall in place but I tried my best.

He left me at the outside door to my flat and I tried not to linger with him. It was difficult, like ripping a wax strip off: you know it's gonna hurt and you don't want to do it but you'll look really stupid if it stays. I turned resolutely and opened up the door, heading for a restless night as I thought about the sparring.

Chapter Thirteen

I woke Friday morning two minutes before my alarm went off. I hit the button so it wouldn't beep at me, and then stretched out my legs and arms, feeling a dull ache. My muscles weren't sore yet but they would be tomorrow.

I went through my usual morning routine of watching the weather outside whilst I sat and ate my cereal. It was pouring down and I was struggling to remember where my umbrella was, in the hope that I wouldn't look like a drowned rat when I arrived at uni. Thankfully I found it under the bed and so still looked fairly human when I walked in the doors for my lecture. I walked over to Cathy as I tried to shake out my umbrella without soaking my jeans.

"Hey, Cathy." I plopped down in the seat next to her.

"Hey." She looked up from reading some notes. "You have fun last night?"

I caught her cheeky grin before she put on an innocent face again.

"I stayed and did a bit of training with Fraser and some of his group. Then he walked me home again. So you can get rid of that grin, Missus!" I warned her.

"So things haven't changed yet?"

I sighed. "No, not yet." I turned to the front of the room and watched people coming in. "Maybe we'll just stay friends."

"You never know if it will work unless you try. He certainly seems to like you, and you apparently get more conversation out of him than anyone else. You should have heard Sarah in the changing rooms last night. She was not in a good mood!"

I couldn't help but smile at that. Unfortunately I knew that Fraser talked to me more because of the ability I had; it wasn't really a sign that he liked me in that way. I daydreamed, thinking about him.

"Here comes Ali." Cathy's voice interrupted my thoughts. I looked up to see him squeezing past people at the end of our row, trying to reach us. He fell into the seat beside me.

"My legs are killing me. Took me for ages to get down the stairs this morning." He rubbed the back of his thighs, as if to emphasise his pain.

"Hate to tell you, buddy, but it is normally the day after the day after, that it really kicks in. You'd better do some stretches today if you expect to walk at all tomorrow," I advised. He just groaned in response.

We sat through the lecture without speaking to each other, not because there was a huge volume of notes to copy, but I think we all appreciated the style of this lecturer: he made it seem obvious. It was nice to understand something the first time it was explained.

The rain had stopped when we walked over for our maths lecture, but the clouds threatened that the break wouldn't be for long. Sure enough, after our usual dull maths, it was raining again. Thankfully it wasn't far to the union for lunch. We grabbed some food and drinks and sat down near Kev, Rachel and a few of their friends.

"Cool. So I'll meet you at six; then we'll head to the pub. Hopefully get in before the queues start." Kev sounded excited.

Rachel looked over to us. "You guys want to come out on Saturday?"

"Where you heading?" Ali asked.

"We're going to Legend. They've got DJ Storm doing a set. Last time he was in Glasgow he completely sold out the Arches. We're going early to try and beat the crowds."

"Sounds impressive, but dance music isn't for me. Whole load of beats and no tune." Ali shook his head.

"That's the new place on Byers Road, right?" Cathy asked. Rachel nodded as she bit into her wrap. "Think I might join you then. See what it's like. You going to come, Steph?"

"Not this time. I'm going back home for the weekend. See how everyone's getting on."

"Can you not do it some other weekend? This is not a night to miss," Kev wheedled.

"No, 'fraid not. Anyway, I'm kinda like Ali. Dance music isn't really my thing. I'd probably just be bored."

"No chance. This place is supposed to be really good, and I definitely know the DJ will be," Kev continued.

"Well, maybe some other time."

"Don't know what you're missing."

I just smiled at him. The rest of the time was spent discussing their plans for the weekend, and debating music.

After lunch I walked Cathy and Ali back towards their flats. I wanted to check out a music shop on their route home. It was pouring rain again and Cathy and I huddled under my umbrella as we walked up Byers Road. Ali refused to get an umbrella and just got soaked instead.

At the top of the street I left Cathy making a beeline for the nearest shop selling umbrellas as Ali squelched after her. I made my way into the music shop, pausing for a minute at the door under the heater, trying to thaw out a bit. I had a quick glance over the DVDs, looking at the new titles out, and then made my way over to the CDs. It was nice to spend some time just flicking through music, trying to find some of the groups I'd heard of recently and older groups that were just new to me. My fingers tapped along with the music playing in the shop as I walked along the rows. I picked out a few albums that I thought I might like, and was currently weighing up how much I could spend and which ones would be the best.

I felt a familiar tugging at my mind, and looked up to see who had come into the shop who I knew. I couldn't see anyone I knew. Frowning, I looked back at the display in front of me. I concentrated on what I was feeling.

I can't put a name to them. I know where they are, but I don't know who.

I looked towards the door but couldn't see it clearly as there was a group of guys in the way. Whoever it was had moved away from the door and was walking along one side of the room, next to the DVDs.

Why can I sense them if I don't know them? Sure, if I concentrated I could pinpoint everyone in this room, but only people that I know catch my attention.

I tried to think about what I was feeling. It was a strong pull, meaning that I must know them or…

A vampire?

When I was first able to do this I could tell where Fraser and his flatmates were straightaway, even though I didn't really know them. That night when I went to get Cathy, I'd known they were around the corner and I knew they were different to anyone else, it wasn't the same pull as my other friends.

This is the same! Shit!

My head went up involuntarily, my eyes scanning the room. There were several people standing looking at the DVDs beyond the group of guys. I couldn't pinpoint which one was the vampire yet.

What does this mean? Does Fraser know there are other vampires here? He's only ever mentioned them when he was explaining it all to me. Is this the one that bit me in the park?

My heart started to beat faster. I put the CDs down and started making my way towards the door. I could feel a pair of eyes on me but I couldn't look round, couldn't meet them. Time for backup. I let my wall down.

Fraser?

I walked out the shop and started down Byers Road. I didn't bother with the umbrella: it would only get in the way.

Stephanie? Everything OK?

For once, his voice didn't make me melt on the spot.

Not sure. I can sense a vampire in the same shop as me, and it's not one of you guys.

Where are you?

At the top of Byers Road.

Leave. Make your way towards the uni. Chris is closest, but we are both on our way.

I didn't know whether to feel reassured or more panicked by that. They were coming to help, but why did they need to? I could still feel a presence behind me, following. I couldn't help but look round. The street was busy and I couldn't really see past the people behind me. If I concentrated I would be able to pinpoint the person, but my mind just couldn't focus. I wanted to see them, wanted to know who I was dealing with.

I left the main street, turning onto one parallel to it. It wasn't as busy, so I might be able to get a look at whoever it was. I almost ran for a few steps, trying to get ahead, and then stopped, moving over to look in the window of a jewellery shop. I angled myself so I could see the corner that I'd just come around.

Seconds seemed to drag. I tried to get my breathing under control, and have a glance around to see who else was in this street.

Think I've made a wrong move.

In my eagerness to see who I was dealing with, I'd gone onto a quieter street with less witnesses, and cobbles making my footing much less reliable. I wouldn't be able to run without breaking an ankle.

Crap!

Just as my mistake sank in, a guy turned the corner, his eyes scanning the street. I managed to break my gaze away before he met my stare. I faced the necklaces in the shop window, moving my head to face different ones. All the while I tried to watch him out the corner of my eye.

He looked at me, stuffed his hands in his jacket pockets, and then sauntered down the street. A smug smile sat on his face. I had played right into his hands coming onto a quieter street.

Time to move.

I turned away from the window and started walking towards the uni again. My back was prickling, and I knew he was behind me. I could feel him start to pick up speed, closing the space between us. I couldn't run though: as soon as I did that he would know he was rumbled, and just move in quicker before I got away. I continued walking, back straight, not looking round.

My thoughts spun. What do I do if he reaches me? Where were Fraser and Chris? What does he want? Should I run? I tried to keep my breathing steady, but I could feel each breath getting shallower.

The gap between us was suddenly getting smaller. He was running towards me.

Shit! What do I do?

A hand closed around my upper arm.

"There you are! You won't believe how long I've been looking for you." His voice held amusement but it wasn't making me smile. He turned me around roughly and pushed me back towards one side of the street, his grip on my arm bruising. He leant over me, his face not far from mine. His lank hair was pulled back into a ponytail. His stubble had grown beyond trendy and was now adding to the whole unwashed look. To passers-by we might look like a couple about to kiss. The thought made me shudder.

He smiled at that. "Remember me, do you? Didn't think you would. So where is your interfering friend this time?" He stared at me.

I didn't answer. Didn't know what to say. Didn't know if I could say anything. I had a suspicion my voice might just not work right now. His grip on my arm tightened again at my lack of response, and my fingers started to tingle due to the lack of blood.

"It's very rude to interrupt someone at their meal. Made me curious as to why he would do that. Can't see anything particularly interesting about you."

He slowly ran his gaze over me and I suddenly felt in need of a hot shower. I moved my free arm across my body. He just sneered. "Never mind. He'll get the message soon enough. Nobody stops me doing what I want."

He pushed his face towards mine and I turned my head to the side, desperately trying to avoid him. My heart rate doubled. I could feel it pounding. His face went to my hair and moved down to my neck, and I could hear him breathing in. I tried to bring up my arms to push him away but even with adrenaline only one of them would work. I might as well have been a puppy trying to fight off a lion. He just laughed.

"Don't worry. You've got a few more hours yet. I like to take my time, and here isn't really the place. The audience might object to what I have in mind for you."

He straightened up, pulling me away from the wall. I looked down the street, wondering how the hell I was going to get away from this guy. A familiar figure entered the bottom of the street at a jog. My eyes met Chris's and his speed increased. I struggled against the grip this sleaze had on my arm but it was difficult now that it was completely numb. At least he couldn't do too much without drawing attention to us.

Chris reached us just as Sleazeball leant towards me with a fist clenched and half raised. I saw his nostrils flare and his eyes narrow before he straightened up and turned to Chris.

"My argument isn't with you. Stay out of it," he snarled.

Chris just stared back at him, not showing any emotion.

"No. It's with me," Fraser said quietly.

I almost laughed as Sleazeball jumped and spun a one-eighty to face him, but the sudden movement and release of my arm sent me staggering into Chris instead. He had arrived so quietly, and it must have been quick as I barely knew he was close before he was there. Chris checked I was upright, and then moved me behind him.

"You!" Sleazeball's voice was loaded with venom. His hands clenched into fists. "Should've known you wouldn't come alone."

"Why are you here?" Fraser asked. His voice was calm but I thought I could detect some strain in it. His posture betrayed nothing to the casual glance but it was incredibly still. He was ready to move.

"Because I want to be. Nobody stops me doing what I want. I'll go where I want and take what I want." His gaze drifted back to me.

Fraser's eyes narrowed at that. "Wrong. We stay here, and have done so without any trouble for a long time. You are either part of our group or you are not in central Glasgow. And you are certainly not part of our group. It's time for you to leave." Fraser's voice was like ice. I'd never heard it like that. It put a chill in me and I was his friend, but Sleazeball didn't seem to notice.

"What? I'm supposed to go running because you say? I don't think so. If I want to stay here then that's what I'm going to do, and there ain't nothing you can do about it." He spat onto the street to emphasis his point.

Fraser stepped in close to him, barely a hand's width away from him. He leant down so he was staring the guy in the eyes, his voice low and full of intent. "This is your one chance to leave now, without any repercussions. If you do not follow this advice it will turn out badly for you, not us." He then took a step to the side and looked beyond him – a clear dismissal if ever there was one. I couldn't take my eyes from Fraser's face.

"You don't scare me. I've beaten way more guys than you. I'll be seeing you around." With a last glance at me, he stalked off. Fraser still didn't acknowledge him.

I watched him go, my attention finally coming back to the street around us and not just the couple of metres surrounding me. As I felt the distance between us increase, I also felt lots of different tuggings at my attention. Craig and Ross were coming from the direction of the uni, but more worryingly there were two other pulls from beyond the sleazeball.

"Fraser, there are more of them." My voice was weak, my throat still not recovered from being so dry.

His eyes met mine. "Where?"

"Beyond him, round the corner to the left at the end of the street. They are keeping out of view."

He came and stood beside me then, and we watched the sleazeball walk down the street and out of sight. He joined the other two and walked with them, I told Fraser.

"So he's got his own group." Fraser looked thoughtful. He looked back at me but didn't say anything. Ross and Craig joined us at that point, and Fraser quickly filled them in on what had happened and then sent them to follow the group to try and find where they were going.

I was aware of the rain again, running down the inside of my collar. My arm was a riot of pins and needles from the returning blood supply. Just below my shoulder was agony where Sleazeball had grabbed me. My arms were shaking, their strength leaving with the adrenaline. It was enough to have tears stinging my eyes.

"We'd better get you home." Fraser was looking at me, but my focus was beyond him.

"I'll walk back with you as well," Chris offered to Fraser, who was still watching me. I could only see Chris out of the corner of my eye. Both of their voices seemed to be fading out. I couldn't hear them properly.

"I think we'd better get a taxi. I don't think Stephanie can walk that far right now."

Everything was fading now, not just sound. It felt as though things were spinning. Last thing I noticed was Chris's voice:

"Shit."

I could hear a low rumble. Over that I could hear blowing air, but I was warm. I knew I was lying down but nothing else. My eyes opened, to see Fraser sitting across from me. I could only look at him. It took me a few moments to come to. I blinked and looked around. We were in a black cab.

I was sprawled across the back seats and Fraser was sitting in one of the fold-down seats opposite me, his elbows on his knees, leaning towards me.

"I didn't know if you would want to go to your place or mine so I thought we'd wait and see," he explained.

I looked out the cab window and saw we were still near Byers Road, parked at the side of the street. In the front the cab driver looked up from reading his paper.

"I passed out, didn't I?" I cringed.

"Yes." Fraser was trying not to smile.

I moaned and put a hand over my face. "Nightmare."

"No. I would say that's what you went through before you passed out." He lifted my hand off my face. This time his eyes weren't smiling.

"Hmm, suppose I should go back to mine." I felt as though I could sleep for a week. I tried to sit up, and got about halfway before everything started to swim again. Fraser moved over as my arm went out to try and steady myself. Sitting next to me, he pulled me towards him, so I slouched against him in a half upright position.

"One step at a time." He sounded amused.

He gave the cabby my address, and we set off. I kept my eyes closed to start with. Cab drivers were enough to make you dizzy at the best of times, never mind if you weren't feeling great. By the time we got to my flat though I was well enough to be sitting up and to have my eyes open. I wasn't looking forward to the stairs though.

Pathetic. Can't even face stairs, never mind vampires.

"Hope yur feelin be'er, hen," the cabby called as I hobbled out. Fraser paid him. Don't know what that must have cost him to have the cab sitting idling whilst I was out of it, but he waved me away when I went to get my purse out.

Fraser's arm went around my waist to help me up the stairs. We were at the door to the flat when I remembered there was a lift.

Typical.

"We'll just go to my room." I looked at Fraser, but he didn't say anything. "Lauren's in the living room, and I really can't be bothered with an inquisition. Hopefully she won't realise there are two of us coming in."

I unlocked the door and made my way down the hall to my room.

Fraser made no sound at all behind me. I actually looked over my shoulder to check that he had come in, not believing what my instincts told me.

I peeled off my sodden jacket and hung it up on the back of the door. Fraser dropped his over the only chair in the room. The room seemed even smaller than normal with him in here. I flopped onto the bed, my head finding the pillow and my body curling up instinctively into a ball. Fraser sat halfway down, his hand going to my shoulder.

"Stephanie, I need to know what he said to you, and what happened before I arrived… before it fades."

"Believe me, it isn't going to fade any time soon." My voice was dry as I rolled onto my back and looked up at him.

How can I feel so many things at one time?

Here he was, in my room, sitting on my bed – probably what I'd wanted since I first saw him. He had just saved me from some asshole who wanted to kill me, for which I was incredibly grateful, yet I was still scared, shaky and tired after the adrenaline rush, and frustrated at being so close to and yet so far from Fraser.

I sighed. Pulling myself up to lean against the wall, I told him everything that had happened. It wasn't much. He had arrived pretty quick.

"So what happens now?" I asked.

"We will find him and get rid of him. He shouldn't be too difficult to deal with. He is young, otherwise he would have heard you call me. Probably even younger than Ross. That is not a threat to us." His voice was very matter of fact, no emotion. He was looking out the window as he talked. I watched his profile.

"What about the others that were with him." My voice was quiet.

"I expect they are even younger, if they let him take the lead. With Jason gone I imagine the others will quickly leave."

"How do you know his name?"

"He is young so he didn't have real shields, only the barest idea of one. I was able to get some information from him before he went. Not that he realises it."

"Oh." Right now I could see the scary side of Fraser: the lack of worry, the coolness with which he talked about killing one of his own kind. The really scary bit was I had the feeling this was only the tip of the iceberg.

He must have sensed some of my concern because he looked back down at me again.

"You don't need to worry. Nothing will happen to you, I promise." He smiled at me, but for once it couldn't completely get rid of my unease. The only reason I was here now was because they had come to help. But they couldn't be by my side all the time.

"You normally show a remarkable trust for us; trust me now." His face was serious.

"I do trust you, but I don't see how you can find him. He could be anywhere."

"You don't need to worry about that. Let us deal with it." He moved back on the bed and leant against the wall. "Come here." He held his arm out from his side, and I moved over to lean against him. It was good to finally feel him next to me. I let my head rest on his chest, and my hand on his stomach. My eyes started closing on their own.

"You need to get some sleep."

That was all it took. I fell fast asleep.

When I opened my eyes, I found I was in my bed, with the duvet pulled up over me. My bedside light was on, giving off a soft light. The curtains were pulled over the window. There was no one else in the room. I looked over to my clock. It was after seven. I'd slept all afternoon. I sat up and spotted a note on my desk, and a little jar next to it. I got up and went to read it.

> Stephanie,
> Hope you are feeling better. The balm should help the bruise on your arm heal quicker. If you need me just call, otherwise I will see you tomorrow.
> Fraser

I picked up the jar: Tiger balm.

No miracle cure for me then.

I didn't want to look at my arm yet: it was still aching. I'd put some on before bed. That way I wouldn't stink out the whole flat. I put a fleece on top of my T-shirt, and went to the kitchen to get some food.

All the girls were in. Natasha was sitting in the kitchen eating something that smelled delicious. Lauren and Eilidh were watching TV and chatting. Lauren was all done up for a night out. I grabbed a frozen meal and stuck it in the microwave and attempted conversation, answering any questions that I had to.

I pushed around heated mash as Lauren talked animatedly about her night ahead. She was hoping to meet up with a guy later on, purely by accident of course. Eilidh was going out as well but was meeting her friends later. She tried to convince Natasha and me to join her but I explained my plans for going home tomorrow and the early start that would need. Natasha claimed coursework for her reason to dodge another night out. Eventually Lauren left to meet her friends, and Eilidh went to get ready.

"You seem quiet, Steph. You all right?" Natasha asked. She was doing her dishes now. All the pots were stacked at the side. One thing to be grateful for with ready meals – zero mess to clean up.

"Yeh, just tired. Today's been a bit hectic." I looked back down at my plastic carton with the remains of shepherds pie in it. I hadn't eaten much. For all the smells of Natasha's meal having me drooling, as soon as I put food in my mouth it tasted like ash.

"So, are the courses still a bit of a nightmare?" I asked, to change the conversation. She took the bait and filled me in on the details of her latest assignment from Hell. I tried to appear interested but my mind was still playing over this afternoon. Eventually Natasha tailed off and I guiltily tried to think of what she had just been saying, wondering if I needed to make a response. I didn't have to, thankfully, as the pause had been a bit too long to be natural.

"Well, I'll see you on Sunday or Monday. I'd better go look out some stuff to take with me, and check the train times. Hope your work isn't too bad."

"I'm sure it will be. Catch you later," she called as I walked back to my room. Once there, I leant my head back against the door, relieved to be on my own again and not having to pretend that everything was OK. I got on well with my flatmates but I couldn't tell them everything, and that was becoming more difficult.

I packed a bag with some clothes for the weekend, a few textbooks to read on the train, and some music to swap with Ailsa. I went and brushed my teeth, then came back and got changed for bed, looking at my arm for the first time.

Ouch!

I had a handprint around my arm. It was bright red with some darker bits in places. You could clearly see the shape of the guy's hand. I tried to match it up with my hand but it was bigger than mine. I opened up the tiger balm and started to rub some in. I quickly went through the clothes I'd packed for the weekend, making sure they all had long sleeves. I would definitely need to cover my arms for a while.

I put some music on low, then climbed into bed and pulled the duvet tight around me. For all I felt tired, I knew I wouldn't sleep any time soon. I stared off into space, replaying events and wondering what it all meant, and what impact it would have on the guys, because of me. Would he try to find me again? What would he do if he did find me? Why had he come back for me? Would he leave after Fraser's threat? Would Fraser carry out his threat? Were Ross and Craig annoyed at me for having to tail that group around?

Eventually I fell asleep, but it wasn't restful. My normal nightmares of screeching metal and screaming now had a new factor in them – a leering face inches from mine,

"Nobody stops me taking what I want."

Chapter Fourteen

My alarm beeped at me. My arm escaped the duvet and hit it, making it fall on its side. I groaned. It hadn't been a good night and I just wanted to go back to sleep. I got up with a sigh, grabbing my towel, and went for a shower. Over breakfast I had a look out the window on another dreary day, the rain a fine mist. I cleared up my dishes seeing as I wouldn't be back for a few days, grabbed my bag, jacket, and umbrella, and then trotted down the stairs. I paused at the main door, making sure I had everything, and settled my bag so it wouldn't rub on the walk to the train station. I went out and put up the umbrella, turning my collar up to keep out the rain.

"Stephanie," a familiar voice called.

I turned to see Fraser standing next to the open door of a black saloon car. I walked towards him, frowning, stopping a few steps away from the car.

"I heard about your plans to go home for the weekend and I thought I could give you a lift."

My eyes shot to the car. It was low with a smooth outline. I didn't need to know much about it to realise that it would go fast. I recognised the Audi symbol on the front but that was it.

"Thanks, but you really don't have to do that. The train is just as easy; it's not a hassle," I replied, staying exactly where I was.

A frown appeared on his forehead. He stepped around the door, closing it as he walked over towards me. I tilted the umbrella back so I wouldn't poke his eye out.

"I'm offering you a lift. You'll get there quicker and you don't have to pay." He laughed. "I'm a safe driver: better senses and reflexes, remember?" The frown came back.

Man, this is awkward.

"I'm really not that great with cars," I tried to explain.

"You get car sick?" He still looked puzzled.

"No…" I sighed. "Just really anxious in them. I get stressed." I rushed it out, watching his face for a reaction.

"Well, you have no reason to worry whilst I am driving. I have been doing it for quite a long time." He smiled confidently at me. I couldn't quite return it. He held out his hand towards the shoulder with my bag. As I let it slide down he grasped it and then put it in his boot. I stayed where I was. He walked back up to me, watching my face. Putting his arm around my shoulder, he walked me towards the passenger side of the car. His hand went over mine on the umbrella, and he looked down at me.

"You really have no reason to worry. I will keep you safe."

These words seemed to sink in to me, making my back tingle. He kept his eyes on mine as he lowered his head. My heart started to hammer. His lips touched mine. I gasped. I hadn't been expecting this. He started to pull away, misreading my gasp. My hand flew up to his cheek, pulling him towards me again, and I kissed him back. It started slow, but as time went on it got deeper and my insides started to melt. I could feel heat flushing through me. I completely lost my surroundings, could only think of us.

Too soon he pulled back. Taking the umbrella out of my now limp hand, he spun me around and sat me in the car. I stared out of the windshield, still feeling the pressure of his lips on mine, the feel of his hand on my waist. Then he was sitting beside me, and the car was pulling out of the parking space and heading towards the motorway.

"You might want to put on your seat belt." His deep voice woke me out of my daydream.

I quickly grabbed the seat belt, clicking it into place, and looked around me to get my bearings.

"That was cheating." My voice was lower than normal as well.

He chuckled. "Do you regret it?"

"No." My answer was a bit too quick.

"Good. Neither do I."

I looked across to see him smiling back at me.

"Try and keep your eyes on the road. I don't need any extra reasons to get panicky in the car."

He chuckled but turned back to the road anyway.

"I'm curious. What makes you nervous of cars? Most people enjoy travelling in them."

"I'd really rather not go into it when I'm in one. It won't help." My voice had returned to normal now, but my throat was starting to feel tight. I could feel his glance towards me but I didn't turn; I just kept my eyes front, on the road. We had left Glasgow and were currently circling round the outskirts on the motorway. I'd never travelled to Glasgow by car so I didn't know if this was quick or not. It always felt quick to me. I couldn't take my eyes away from the road and the other cars to check his speed. I guessed he was going quick as we were certainly passing other cars with ease, but the engine was not loud – just a background murmur.

"Will music help?" Fraser asked.

"Possibly." I eyed the lorry we were passing, looking at the size of wheels.

He flicked some dials and I heard the start of a classical piece.

"What do you want to listen to? I've got a few different CDs in. Relaxing Classical, Red Hot Chillis, Linkin Park, Jose Gonsalez, Train."

"Anything. Not bothered." I couldn't help my short answers: my throat just wouldn't let me speak a whole sentence.

His eyes flickered to me again but he didn't say anything, just pressed a few more buttons. The music changed, still playing quietly though, enough to drown out the sound of the engine though that wasn't hard. We were now out of Glasgow and its suburbs. The road was quiet as it was still early. I had been planning to get an early train to arrive in Perth at half nine, and then get a bus back home. Buses weren't as bad as cars: they were slower and everyone gave them room. You just didn't feel as exposed in them.

I concentrated on my breathing. Slow breaths in, out. I started to feel a bit calmer. The quiet roads helped, and so did Fraser's smooth driving. There were no sudden lane changes, no sudden breaking. Everything was smooth, controlled. I honestly started to relax.

Soon after, I was able to look round the car and not just stare out the front windscreen. The dash had so many buttons on it that it was lit up like the cockpit of a plane. I was glad Fraser had selected the music as

I wouldn't have had a clue where to start. The seats were half leather, half dark material, and shaped around the sides like rally seats. It was very comfortable.

I was surprised how secure I felt. I just wasn't like this in cars. Normally I managed short journeys OK but eventually I would end up having a panic attack and would have to stop. Either that or take a lot of medication before going in the car, like enough to sedate an elephant. But here I was, able to start thinking about other things, and not just the cars around me.

"So, how come you knew I was going home today?" I asked Fraser, giving him a quick glance before I looked back to the road.

"Ah, I eavesdropped last night," he said apologetically.

"Oh," I managed. "How? I mean, you weren't reading my mind, were you?"

"No. You would be able to tell now if anyone tried to read your mind. I checked with the other girls every now and then. Skimmed Eilidh and Lauren's minds as they left last night."

"Oh, right." I continued to think. My thoughts weren't as coherent as they normally would be. "So, not that I don't appreciate it, but why the offer of a lift?"

He laughed before he answered, maybe realising my slight white lie. "I agreed with you that it would be a good idea for you to be away for the weekend. Give the guys a chance to try and track down Jason. This way I get to keep an eye on you too."

"You don't think he would follow me home, do you?" My throat started to get tight again. I didn't want to lead him to my mum and Ailsa.

"I don't think so, but he could have easily followed you to the train station."

"Right." I looked out the side window, but that just made it seem as though we were going really fast, so I quickly turned back to the front.

"How long were you outside last night?"

He paused again, giving me another look. This time our eyes met and held for a while before he looked back to the road. "After I left you I called Chris to watch over your flat, then went home and got changed, packed a few things, then came back in the car. I wanted to be close by just in case… you needed me."

"Oh, um, thanks." He stayed outside my flat all night?

We were quiet for a while as we cruised along. Stirling Castle passed by. The Wallace monument looked small from the road but I remembered all too well the endless curving staircases from a school trip.

Would Fraser have been around during that time?

My history really wasn't good. I couldn't remember the dates that Wallace would have been around. I frowned, trying to picture what Fraser would have been like back then. What did he do? He certainly couldn't have been a student. I looked back across at him, trying to read some answers from his face but that was impossible. Instead I just ended up admiring his profile, my eyes lingering.

He kissed me!

It sent tingles across my arms thinking about it. Hopefully it hadn't just been a ploy to get me in the car, but I wasn't sure. His face turned to me and I quickly looked out the front. I could feel my face starting to heat but I tried to control it.

"So, what do I say when I arrive with you?" I asked.

"Whatever you want," he replied. I thought I could hear the hint of a smile. "I will stay in Perth. I've got a flat there, but I'll come back to see you, if you don't mind."

"Don't mind at all." That saved one hassle at least. Didn't know how my mum would react to a stranger staying in the house.

That's daft. Seeing as it's Fraser, she would probably be just fine with it!

"Where is it that you stay, exactly?" Fraser asked.

"Take the next turn-off and I'll guide you there." Conversation pretty much stopped as we went along the country roads towards my home town. The scenery around here was gorgeous but my eyes were glued to the road again. I couldn't see very far with all the corners, and Fraser's speed didn't decrease all that much. Eventually we pulled into my street.

"It's the last house on the left."

"Nice house," Fraser commented as he pulled into the driveway.

I saw my sister looking out the window at the sound of a car. My mum opened the front door as I was stretching out the tension from my back, and Fraser was lifting my bag from the boot.

"Steph?" Her voice was unsure.

"Hey, Mum, surprise!" I went over and gave her a hug.

"What are you doing here?" she asked.

"What? Am I not allowed back for a visit every now and then?" I joked.

"Of course. I just wasn't expecting you." She pulled me back into a hug.

Ailsa came out of the house, giving me a smile as she wheeled past to get a better look at Fraser and the car.

"Nice wheels," she commented, smiling at Fraser.

"Could say the same." He held out his hand. "I'm Fraser."

Ailsa grinned back as she shook his hand. "Ailsa. But I have to disagree with you: these things are sadly outdated." She tapped her hands against her own wheels. "So, did you pick Steph up at the train station?"

"No. We drove up from Glasgow this morning. I was going to Perth anyway, so I thought I could drop her off on the way."

"Really?" Ailsa couldn't help the shock in her voice. She looked round to me, her eyebrows raised. She was as surprised as me that I'd managed the trip in a car.

"Do you want to come in and have a cup of tea?" my mum asked.

"Thanks but no. I'll leave you guys to catch up. I'll see you tomorrow some time?" He looked at me.

"Yeh. That would be good. Thanks, Fraser."

He smiled back at me, giving a wave to my mum and Ailsa, then got back in the car and drove off with a soft purr. The engine was just as quiet on the outside.

"Well, you didn't do him any justice on the phone," said Ailsa as she turned to me. I laughed at her, and then grabbed the back of her chair, making her do a wheelie, before pushing her into the house ahead of me.

It was good to chill out and just catch up with them. I'd missed all the little things, like the way they would joke with each other and nag at you. It was nice to be around people who you knew well and you could relax with, and who knew what you meant the first time you said it.

We sat on the couch all afternoon, eating biscuits, drinking cups of tea, and just generally gossiping. We then went into town and got a takeaway and a DVD and munchies for watching the film, and had a good girly night in. My mum went to bed early and that left Ailsa and me to chat into the wee hours of the morning. She wanted to know everything about Fraser, of course, and I told her as much as I could. Then she was keen to hear what uni life was like. She was getting fed up living at home. Think just having two people at home was a bit suffocating.

I slept like a log that night. Nothing disturbed me – no screeching metal and no leering faces.

I woke to darkness. I knew it was morning though because I could hear the birds outside twittering away. The only birds you heard in my part of Glasgow were seagulls, pigeons and the odd crow. I smiled listening to them, stretching out in bed. My door opened and Ailsa stuck her head through.

"You awake?"

"Am now," I grumped back at her with a grin.

She rolled in, then pulled herself onto my bed and lay down next to me.

"It's nice having you back. I've missed you."

"I've missed you too."

"So what's the plan for today then? When is Mr Fraser coming back?" I laughed at the eagerness on her face.

"I don't know. You know, I don't even have his number to give him a call."

Not that it's a problem.

She just frowned at me. "I'm sure he'll turn up. If not, you'll just have to stay here!"

We got up and had a lazy breakfast, still in our dressing gowns. After Mum nagging about the time of day we went and got showered and dressed. We were sitting in the living room chatting, when I got interrupted.

Stephanie? Can you talk?

I almost jumped out of my seat. Thankfully Ailsa was looking at the TV at that point.

Yeh. Might get a bit distracted though.

That's OK. I was wondering if you would mind a visitor.

Not if it's you.

I could almost hear him laughing.

I will be there in ten minutes.

My mood immediately brightened. I continued talking to Ailsa but was trying to feel where Fraser was. It didn't take me long to pinpoint him.

"Hello, Steph? Where is your mind wandering?" Ailsa waved at me.

"Sorry, Ailsa. Just daydreaming there." I pulled my gaze from the window I'd been staring out of, and stopped trying to hear his car. He'd be here any minute.

"So what do you think of the idea?" I'd finally found out why my mum and Ailsa were arguing, Ailsa was wanting to move out and get her own place. I did feel a bit guilty; it was probably because I was gone that she was thinking about it.

"Well, there is no reason you can't, but how are you going to pay rent if you don't have a job?"

"I'll get a job – get shop work or something," she replied, a bit defensive.

"Wouldn't you get bored? I can't really see you behind a till all day."

Thankfully I heard Fraser's car pull into the drive at that point. I think I'd hit a nerve. This was going to need more concentration.

"Here's lover boy," Ailsa teased.

"He's not lover boy." I scowled at her.

"Not yet," she muttered as I left the room.

I met Fraser at the door and led him into the living room, where my mum had joined us when she heard the front door. After the second introduction and niceties were out the road we sat down, and there was a bit of an awkward silence, where both my mum and Ailsa struggled to stop staring at Fraser. Yet again he didn't seem to fit in to our house; he was just a different being. Gorgeous, and smartly dressed without being too formal, he seemed relaxed yet ready to move, and had a certain air around him. I recognised it now as dangerous, but to others it was just mesmerising. I struggled myself, and I had certainly had more practice. My mum coughed. "Fraser, would you like some lunch? I was just about to make it." She stood up to make her move into the kitchen.

"No, thank you. I had some in Perth before I came out." His voice mesmerised us all. It was a second before my mum responded.

"Oh well, too bad." She sounded genuinely disappointed. I just raised my eyebrows at Fraser.

Eaten already, have you?

His eyes crinkled, the corners of his mouth curving up, and he shook his head slightly. No one else noticed.

"Ailsa? Steph? Are you wanting anything?"

"Still full from breakfast, Mum," Ailsa replied for us both. It was only an hour after we'd eaten.

"Oh, that's right, sleepy heads." She went to the kitchen and started banging about.

"I'm going to get a drink. You guys want anything?" Ailsa moved towards the door.

"No thanks," we replied at the same time. Ailsa just laughed and went to help Mum.

It was quiet when she was gone. I couldn't think of anything to say to Fraser that wouldn't sound really odd to Ailsa, who was undoubtedly listening to us in the kitchen.

"Did you have a good day yesterday?" Fraser asked, his eyes on my face.

"Yeh. Just chilled out and had a catch-up. It was good."

Again, nothing else came to mind to move the conversation on.

"Do you want to go out for a walk? See the local sights?" I looked across at him.

"That sounds ideal." He smiled.

I sighed with relief and jumped up, going to grab my shoes and coat. I paused in the kitchen doorway, catching my mum with her mouth full of sandwich.

"We're just going a walk. Probably go down by the river. Won't be too long."

"Mmm-hm!" Was all I got for a reply.

Feeling relieved, I stepped out the front door. The house had suddenly seemed suffocating.

I led Fraser along some footpaths between the houses in our

neighbourhood, and then joined the farm track, eager to leave the house behind. Fraser followed silently, a half-step behind. Once on the walk I slowed down, enjoying the views. You could see all around you here, see the woods edging the fields and spreading onto the hills beyond. It wasn't closed in like the city. The trees at this time of year were a mixture of colours. Some were already bare, with brown or pale silver branches; others clung on to a rainbow of leaves; whilst some were still green. The fields themselves were in a variety of stages: some with cows grazing the weak grass, some with the stubble of crops left over. Others had been cleared, and were waiting to be ploughed next spring.

I took in a deep breath, letting the cool air fill my lungs, and blew it out, along with all my tension. Thankfully it wasn't the time of year for spreading the fields. Those lungfuls, you could do without. I turned round to Fraser to find him watching me with a smile on his face.

"I get the feeling this is a well worn route for you."

"You could say that." I laughed. "This is where I would come when-ever I needed to get out the house, to just escape. There is a nice bit further on: a wee beach down by the river that nobody goes to. You can just sit and watch time flow by."

He reached out and took my hand in his, pulling me closer in the process. That stopped me thinking about my surroundings for a while. My hand felt so small in his. His fingers wrapped right around the back of my hand. I was conscious of the feel of his skin against mine: some parts smooth, other parts rough. His hand wasn't cold, which surprised me.

I suppose that's just another myth.

"What are you thinking?" he asked.

I gave him a quick glance, embarrassed. "You'll just laugh at me."

"Promise I won't." He smiled, trying to make eye contact again.

I sighed. "I was thinking that your hands aren't cold and that it was probably another myth that I had wrong."

His mouth twitched.

"Hey! You promised you wouldn't laugh!" I was laughing myself.

"I'm not laughing!" His face turned smooth again.

Liar!

Now he gave a laugh.

We carried on walking into the woods, away from the fields. You could hear the river further ahead. Fraser asked a few questions about my home town, and I described growing up here. It wasn't anything spectacular; just a typical small town in Scotland – older population, bored teenagers, and lots of tourists due to the picturesque countryside.

Eventually we reached the river and walked alongside it for a while. I pulled my hand out of Fraser's and moved over to the side of the path. Pushing aside some overgrown ferns, I jumped down the bank and landed on a stony beach area. I looked back to see Fraser mimicking my actions, though much more gracefully.

Of course.

He looked round my secret haven, which was completely hidden from view due to the high bank and the overgrown plants on top of it.

"A hidden sanctuary." I smiled and walked towards the giant rock that was stranded here. How it got here I had no idea, as the rest of the beach was covered in small pebbles, but it had worked as my seat for contemplation for many years. I pulled myself up onto it, crossed my legs, and looked back at Fraser. He stood watching the river, and I turned back to look at it myself.

I was always mesmerised by the movement of the water over the stones. It wasn't particularly wide. I could have swam across it but I didn't fancy the middle part. The smooth surface with calm swirls at the top hinted at strong currents in the depths. Further up there was a rocky bit, where the water bubbled over, making white foam. Sometimes swans came along but usually it was just the ducks.

None in sight today though.

I woke up out of my daydream when I heard Fraser move onto the stone behind me. He put a leg either side of mine, letting them hang over the edge of the rock. His hand went around my waist and he pulled me back to lean on his chest.

Surely this is the best thing.

I completely lost track of time. I sat watching the water rushing over rocks, then watched the branches on the trees opposite sway in the breeze, and then got lost in the swirls on the surface of the calm parts. Fraser's arms stayed around me, his warmth heating my back through my jacket, he rested his chin on top of my head at one point, which made me smile.

Eventually I came out of my reverie and sat forward. Fraser let his arms drop from me. I shuffled round so I sat side-on to him, so I could see his face.

"I've got a question for you, about the whole talking to each other thing."

"Ask away."

"Well, you know before when you would speak to me directly it had more of an effect on me than I expected?"

His lips twitched up in a smile, and he nodded for me to go on.

"You've spoken to me twice since then and it hasn't had that effect. Why is that?"

His gaze broke away from mine and his eyes moved over the water before he answered.

"The full answer is something I'll give you in the future. Right now, the explanation is a bit too complicated. It was to do with emotions and since I've realised that, I can control my thoughts better. So when I speak to you directly now, it doesn't have the same effect."

"Right." I knew there was a frown on my face, but I also knew that it was probably the best answer I was going to get.

"Nothing clearer than that?" I asked.

He smiled. "In time" was all I got by way of reply.

I sighed and leant back against him, my head on his shoulder and my face towards his neck. His arm went back around my waist. His other hand rested on my knee.

I could feel my heart beat quicker as I tried to work up the courage to ask about us, and not about the telepathy part. It was stupid; here we were sitting in each other's arms, but I was still nervous to ask.

Scared I'll ruin it. Burst the bubble and make him run.

"So," I started.

"So?" He sounded as though he was smiling, but I couldn't see.

"So was your kiss yesterday just a ploy to get me in the car?" I rushed it out.

He smiled now. I could see it in the silhouette of his face. "Yes and no."

"That doesn't really help me any."

S. C. M. REID

He laughed. "Well, I could see that you were going to cause problems with the car and I did think if I distracted you enough we could head that off. Then I have been wanting to kiss you for a while, and although I thought you would want to, I haven't been able to read your thoughts for a while either, so I couldn't be entirely sure."

"Oh." My voice broke on the one word.

He looked down at me, moving me off his shoulder.

"So, would you say that we were together, then?"

God, my voice is pathetic!

"If you wanted that." His eyes were locked on mine. My skin was tingling, radiating out from his hand on my back. I was suddenly aware of how close we were to each other.

"Yeh." The end of my word was lost as his mouth found mine and all thoughts stopped. I was floating. Lost, his mouth and hands were my anchors. The pressure on my lips, his taste, all made my heart race. Heat flooded through my body. My hand moved up the back of his head, keeping him with me, not letting him pull away. He was obviously thinking the same, as his arm pulled my body closer to him. His other hand went to the back of my neck, almost supporting my head.

Our island of Heaven was interrupted by the ringing of a phone. I have to admit it didn't stop me, but then it didn't stop Fraser either. It kept ringing. Then Fraser made a sound that could only be described as a growl. I could feel it through his chest. He pulled away from me.

"Sorry. It must be Chris if it keeps ringing." He reached into his jeans pocket whilst I tried to catch my breath against his chest.

"Yes?" His voice was deep and not altogether welcoming.

There was a muted voice on the other end. I let them talk, and stared out over the water, my heart rate finally returning to normal. I heard the snap of the phone as Fraser finished talking and returned it to his pocket.

"Chris?" I asked.

"Yes." He seemed distant somehow – not at all what he had been two minutes ago.

"Something wrong?"

He sighed, and looked back down at me as I sat up.

"The guys have been trying to find out where Jason and his friends are hiding out. They haven't come across him yet, though they've found plenty of trails in a few different areas. They seem to be playing hide and seek. Ross even caught sight of one of them, but lost him during the chase."

His eyes narrowed as he spoke, his face hardening. He looked older. It was easier to see the dangerous side of him now.

I've just been kissing a vampire. What am I doing?

There was no denying my feelings for him though. As to whether I was incredibly stupid or brave, I would just have to wait and see.

We left my secret beach behind. I scrambled up the bank, using stones in the earth as footholds. Fraser just jumped up in one sudden movement. I shook my head in wonder as we started out on the walk once more.

We changed between holding hands, sharing brief kisses, and having our arms around each other as we walked along. When the path joined up with the main walk I spotted some familiar figures ahead.

"They really have no concept of subtlety." I shook my head.

"Your mum is worried about you," Fraser replied.

"Worried about me?" I shook my head again, sighing. "What's she worrying about me for? Need to try and sort out these two before I leave, before they never speak to each other again."

We had almost caught them up, though they were walking away from us and hadn't spotted us yet.

"Mum!" She turned at my call. Ailsa leaned around her to see us.

"Fancied a stroll, did you?" I lifted my eyebrows at her. Ailsa at least had the grace to blush.

"A walk sounded a good idea. Get some fresh air, you know," she replied. Her eyes darted between us, taking in the fact that we were still holding hands.

Would you mind pushing Ailsa for a while? There's a bit up ahead that my mum struggles with.

No problem.

"So, Ailsa, you must have lots of stories you can tell me about Stephanie." Fraser sounded enthusiastic.

I shot Ailsa a warning look, to which she just grinned. "Don't get me started!"

They moved ahead, leaving me to walk with my mum. She was quiet to start with and I gave her time to phrase her questions.

"Things are going well at uni? Coursework is OK?" she asked.

"Yeh. Managing all the work OK. It's difficult but I get there with it. Flatmates are doing fine as well."

It's just the vampire trying to kill me to prove a point that's a problem.

"So Fraser is on your course?" She was getting there.

"No. He's studying an English course."

"How did you guys meet?"

"We both go to the same martial arts club."

"Oh, right." She was quiet for a while after that, obviously lining up the next question.

"How old is he?"

Wow, she just came right out with that one.

"He's twenty-five. Mum, you know I'm never going to end up with someone my own age, right? Not that I'm saying this is it. We'll wait and see how it goes. We've only just got together."

"Oh, of course. He just seems a bit… He just reminds me of some people… Well I'm sure you know what you're doing." She smiled at me then.

I smiled back but my mind was whirring.

What isn't she saying?

We could hear Ailsa and Fraser talking up ahead, the occasional laughter floating back to us.

I started talking to Mum about Ailsa and her idea to move out. By the end of the walk I think I had most of it ironed out. Mum could understand her viewpoint now and was willing to give her more independence and encourage her as long as she didn't take it to extremes. Now I just had to work on Ailsa to give up on the idea of moving out, and go for other options to show her independence.

It was as though I'd never left. Well not strictly true; it never normally got to the full-blown argument stage. It made it more awkward for me to sort out without being obvious.

Back at the house we stayed for another hour or so, and then it was time to leave. I said my goodbyes, reminding them it was only a few more weeks till the end of term. Even though it was only late afternoon it was dark by now – definitely into winter. Back in the car there were positives and negatives to it being dark. I couldn't see everything that was out there, which was a negative, but cars all had their headlights on, which made them more difficult to miss – positive.

I sat thinking about the short weekend. The fact that I could think of anything else but the road was, in itself, amazing. It had felt weird being home, like it had changed in the time I'd been away, though I knew it hadn't. I missed my mum and sister, yet it was nice to have some time away as well, which made me feel guilty. I was worried whether they would work out their arguments.

Then there were the developments with Fraser – they were definitely positive. I grinned as I thought about my flatmates' responses to the news.

"You never told me your dad died in a car crash." Fraser's voice broke the silence.

My grin vanished. "Not much to say, really."

He opened his mouth as though to carry this on, so I rushed to interrupt him.

"I'd really rather not talk about this when I'm in a car."

He paused, and then closed his mouth over. I could feel tension building in my body again.

Why did he have to bring that up now? Ailsa must have told him.

I felt angry at my sister, but then why should I be?

Because it's my choice to tell people.

I knew this was daft. I shouldn't be angry, but she shouldn't be telling these things to my friends. That was up to me.

I sat watching the road again for the next hour. The headlights were washing over things, showing flashes of colour in the otherwise monotonous shadows.

Eventually we reached Glasgow. The orange haze over the city was giving everything a weird glow. It seemed to stand out more since we'd been away. Fraser drove smoothly through the streets, and stopped outside my flat.

I suddenly felt awkward. I hadn't been thinking about what to say at this point, and I cursed myself for not spending some of the car journey considering that dilemma.

"I'll get your bag." His voice was quiet as he opened the door and got out of the car. This at least put it off for a while.

I stood up and stretched my back, easing some of the tense muscles. Fishing around for my keys, I made my way to the door. The car beeped behind me as Fraser locked it and followed me into the stairwell.

In the flat Lauren stuck her head out of the living room when she heard the door.

"Hey, Steph!" she called. Her eyes then focussed beyond me as Fraser moved into the hall behind me.

"Hey, Lauren, good weekend?" I pulled a smile onto my face.

"Yeh." Her eyes came back to me then, her face expectant.

I just carried on walking to my room and she finally ducked back to watch the TV again. Fraser followed me into my room and dropped my bag on the bottom of my bed. He turned to look at me.

"I'm sorry I brought up the car crash. I didn't realise it was so difficult for you." His voice was soft, quiet.

"You don't need to apologise. It's just something I don't really talk about."

I moved over to my bag, unzipping it. His hands went over mine, stopping them.

"You should, though. You know that?"

"It's in the past." I tried to make my voice light. He pulled me towards him and hugged me. I blinked back tears.

I'm not going to break down! This isn't the time for it!

Whether he sensed my reluctance or not I don't know, but Fraser let me go. As I moved round the room, unpacking my bag, he sat on the chair and pulled out his phone. Soon he was talking, and from what I could pick up I guessed it was Chris.

"Any news?" I asked when he hung up.

He shook his head, frowning. "They can't seem to track him. He's still playing games." He stared off into space, his face thoughtful.

"So, is it just a case of wait and see?" I asked.

"Unfortunately, yes. I was hoping to have this sorted by the time we were back. I don't like the idea of him hanging around. A new vampire should be easy to deal with, even if he does have a few friends."

He continued staring away, thinking about something. I'd been trying to forget about the weird situation when I was away, but there was no avoiding it now. A vampire wanted me dead. If it came to a straight fight there was no way I could win. My stomach tensed at the thought. I just had to try and avoid him, and continue on as normal. Now I did have an advantage for the avoiding, but not much. It wasn't even as though I'd done anything personally to annoy him. I was just a pawn, just a tool for him to make a point, make a statement that he wasn't going to be told what to do.

I suddenly felt very insignificant, very small. Weak as well. There was nothing I could do. I couldn't fight, couldn't find him. I just had to wait like a duck at a shooting gallery, waiting for the crosshairs to find me.

This'll teach me not to walk through parks at night.

If I'd never gone through the park he wouldn't have found me, and Fraser wouldn't have stopped him – no problems. Now all of them were busy looking for this creep.

"Are the guys pissed off spending their time looking for this guy?" I asked.

Fraser's eyes flicked back to mine. He seemed surprised. "No, not at all. Craig likes this type of thing; it's right up his street. Ross is excited by it. We don't have any real problems round here – none that Chris, Craig and myself haven't been able to deal with – so he's just happy to be in on the action for a change."

He hadn't mentioned Chris or Jonathon. I wondered why. I could feel my stomach sinking slightly at the thought of annoying even more vampires. I really didn't need to be doing that.

"Right." I didn't know what else to say. I had too many thoughts whirring round in my head.

His hand cupped the side of my face, lifting my chin up.

"Don't worry yourself about this. At worst it is a minor inconvenience. Nothing will happen to you, I promise."

I couldn't reply. I was picturing Jason's leering face inches from mine, and feeling the threat of his words. That was a big promise Fraser had made, and I didn't know how he could keep it.

His kiss broke my concentration. I leaned up to him and he pulled me closer. This kiss didn't have the hunger of our kiss by my beach, but it was still full of feeling. Too soon, Fraser pulled back.

"Nothing will happen to you." He smiled at me. This time I managed to smile back.

"Well, I'd better go and meet up with Chris and get the full details." He picked up his coat and headed for the door. "I'll see you tomorrow." He leant down and placed a brief kiss on my head. I was a bit disappointed it wasn't more.

He walked silently along the corridor and out the door. I turned and headed into the living room, to face Lauren's onslaught of questions.

Chapter Fifteen

The dreams were inevitable after being in a car. Noise of an engine; the sound of metal screeching, scrunching; images of origami cars. People screaming, me screaming, Ailsa screaming. Looking across to my dad.

I woke up panting, my hair stuck to my forehead and neck. I sat up, trying to reassure myself it wasn't happening, again. Pulling on my dressing gown, I went and got a drink of water. Then I climbed back into bed. It was only the back of two. I should try to get more sleep.

This time I was running and someone was chasing. I knew I needed to get away. I did not want this person to catch me. Their laughter floated behind me, sometimes close, sometimes farther away, but I knew they were only playing, just giving this glimmer of hope. They could reach out at any time and grab me. I could almost feel their breath on my neck. Their hand would close.

I woke, groggy from my restless sleep. I contemplated rolling over and closing my eyes. I could always copy Cathy's notes. I sighed and swung my feet over the side of the bed. I would feel too guilty to sleep. I was awake now. Might as well make the most of it.

Habit got me through my morning routine more than any alertness. There was a light drizzle that misted my face as I walked outside. I'd gone a full five steps, huddled in my fleece before I sensed someone behind me, standing to the side of the door I'd just walked through. I spun round, lifting my arms in front of me, my heart finally waking up to panicked rhythm.

"Wow, now I realise why Fraser wanted one of us to watch you." Craig moved off the wall and walked towards me.

My hands fell to my sides, my lethargy returning. "Hey, I'm only human."

He grinned and fell in beside me. "You know, you don't look that great this morning. Is that a general morning thing?"

I looked at him with an eyebrow raised. "Some of us are meant to sleep, even if we can't always do it. And it doesn't really help when people start commenting on it."

"Hmm, it's going to be like that, is it? Think I'll just be quiet and fall into bodyguard duties." He gave me a wink, then made his face serious and started checking out the street. I rolled my eyes at him as we cut through the park.

"So what's with the bodyguard thing? Why is Fraser wanting one of you guys with me?"

"Just a precaution, really. I'm kinda hoping this Jason guy sneaks past so I can have a go at him, otherwise Fraser will spoil the fun."

My legs had stopped moving. Craig turned round to look at me. "Steph?"

"You want him to be here?" My voice was high for some reason.

"Ah, no, not like that. Sorry."

He came back and reached for my arm, and we started walking again. "You see, things have been stable here for a long time. We are pretty well established as a group. Even if we go away for a good few years, nobody moves in as they know we will be back. So having someone actually challenging us makes a nice change. I get to do what I do best: strategise and fight."

I couldn't believe the gleam that I could see in his eyes. He was genuinely excited by this.

"Obviously it's not so good when you are involved. But it certainly adds another twist to it."

I could only imagine what my face must look like.

"So, one of us is going to be around most of the time, just to keep an eye out for you. We'll be able to identify the others, and have a chance of getting rid of them if they come near."

"Right." My voice still seemed a bit weak as we walked along the front of the main building.

Craig left me with a wink and a "catch you later" at the door to my lecture theatre. I walked in, still in a bit of a daze. I automatically went to sit with Cathy and Ali without even looking up to pretend to find them.

"Late night, Steph?" Cathy asked as I sat down.

"Yeh, something like that." I pulled out my paper and pen and settled back into my seat. Propping my knees against the row in front, I slouched down. Normally in this position I was in danger of dozing off during a lecture, but this morning I had too much on my mind.

They were convinced this Jason was trying to kill me. I was most definitely a pawn on a giant game of chess. I had bodyguards now, who would be with me all the time.

How far will that go? Will they come everywhere with me?

And then there was Fraser. We had kissed, more than once, but he wasn't the one waiting for me this morning. Had it all been a ploy to get me away for the weekend? The idea stabbed into my chest. I couldn't think that: it hurt too much. After hoping and trying to deny there was anything between us, it seemed a bit too cruel for him to play on my emotions like that. Surely not.

I could hear chairs flipping up as people stood up to leave. I looked around me. The lecture had finished.

"Must have been a late night. You looked as though you slept through most of that lecture. Though you probably weren't the only one," Ali joked as I put my noteless paper into my bag. The only marks on it were doodles.

We left the theatre and walked to the front of the building. Ali and Cathy were chatting but I couldn't tune into the conversation. At the end of the corridor I could see a familiar figure leaning against the marble-finish wall.

Please don't let it have been a ploy.

"Hey, is that Fraser?" Cathy asked in a hushed voice.

Fraser looked up at the sound of his name, even though it would have been too quiet for anyone to hear around us, never mind at the end of the corridor.

Please don't do that to me. I don't think I could stand it.

I met his dark blue eyes and sank into them as I walked along. He looked serious. His hand reached and found mine. He leant forward, planting a kiss on my forehead, and then fell in to walk along beside me, his grip tightening on my hand.

"Morning." His voice was low.

"Morning." I couldn't think of anything else to say.

I could feel the stunned silence behind us from Ali and Cathy. I almost wanted to turn and see their faces but I thought it might make it seem even more unreal to me to see others' disbelief.

As we walked, I began to relax. It felt good to be so close to Fraser, with his hand closed around mine, and it felt as though he was closing his arms around me, protecting me, keeping me safe. I could feel his body brushing against mine as we walked. Eventually Cathy and Ali started talking again, but they kept to the side and didn't invite us in to the conversation.

"I was speaking to Craig this morning," I said. That was one way of saying that his bodyguard turned up.

He squeezed my hand in response. "Ah yes."

"Interesting conversation."

He hesitated in his next step, his eyebrows lowering. "How so?" His voice seemed mild, but I suspected otherwise.

"He seems... enthusiastic. It's slightly disturbing." I could see Cathy glancing over at us and I tried to keep my voice quiet, knowing Fraser would be able to hear me but no one else.

He gave a brief snort and shook his head. "This is the kind of thing that Craig likes. It is not enthusiasm at the whole situation, just enthusiasm for doing what he does best." He was watching me and it was very difficult for me to keep my eyes from his face and focus just to his left.

I didn't want to give in. I didn't want to remind myself of how much I'd fallen for him, wanted him. If this was purely so that he could prove a point to someone else I couldn't imagine the end of it. Having him close to me, pretending to like and want me, and then at the end he turns away, finished. That would hurt, big time. The other option, of course, was that Jason ended it for me. Don't think I would be caring about anything then.

The only plus point was to enjoy the closeness whilst it lasted. But how could I do that if he was only pretending? It wouldn't be real, wouldn't be the same. Plus, it would make the pain at the end all the more penetrating.

We'd reached the maths building. Cathy and Ali moved ahead to the stairs but Fraser slowed and didn't let go of my hand, so I stopped with him. Cathy glanced back.

"We'll get you up there, Steph?" Her voice was unsure.

"Um, yeh, be up in a minute." I gave her a brief smile, then looked back at Fraser's jacket collar, unable to meet his gaze. He continued to stare down at me.

"So now that we are relatively alone, are you going to say what's wrong?" he asked. He didn't sound annoyed, just intrigued.

I eyed the people passing us by. They moved around us, leaving the couple in their own bubble of space.

"Stephanie?"

"There's nothing wrong. I'm just tired. I didn't get a great sleep."

"One part was a lie and one part wasn't. I'm pretty sure which one was which." His voice sounded amused.

I met his eyes briefly and blushed, remembering that he was a human lie detector. He dropped my hand and put his arms around me, leaning his cheek on my head.

"You know you don't need to be worried. I won't let anything happen to you."

Yes, but for what reasons?

My wall was still up so he couldn't hear my argument.

"I'd better go. I'll be late." I tried to move inside his arms.

"Wait." His voice was quiet. He allowed me to move slightly, then his face leant down to mine, and we kissed. It was a gentle kiss but it brought tears to my eyes.

How can he fake this?

I wanted to believe so much that this was real, that he wanted to kiss me. But was I just being naïve? It wasn't as though I was experienced with guys. When we had kissed before I couldn't think of anything else, but now I could because I wasn't sure. I finally pulled away, clearing my throat. "You're going to get me in trouble." I gave his hand a squeeze and headed for the stairs.

I was late for the lecture, and I slipped into a free seat in the front row under the disapproving glare of the professor. Although I pulled out my pen and paper with good intentions, the sheet was as empty at the end of the hour as at the start.

I waited for Cathy and Ali in the corridor as they made their way through the door.

"So, you and Fraser then?" Ali came straight to the point.

I had to smile at his directness. "Yeh. Just a recent thing. Not sure if I really believe it myself, actually."

"Hah! Sarah is going to love this!" He clapped his hands together, anticipating her finding out.

Couldn't say that I would mind her nose being put out a bit. That could be fun, even if a bit mean. But then it wasn't like she would spare my feelings.

"You coming to lunch at the union?" Cathy asked, as if she wasn't sure I would be joining them.

"Yeh. I definitely need something to waken me up."

Chris just happened to be going down the stairs in front of us. He gave a nod and a smile as he turned the corner for the next steps down.

Are they seriously going to be everywhere?

There seemed to be a subdued buzz in the atmosphere as we walked into lunch. People were in big groups around tables and moving between each other to talk to different friends. I didn't pay too much attention to it; just got my lunch, along with a big coffee and a chocolate bar.

"So, have you guys heard the news?" Kev quizzed us as we sat down.

"Is it about the police this morning?" Ali asked back.

Kev nodded in reply, "Yep, found out what they were doing."

"Hang on. Police?" I asked, confused.

"You didn't tell her?" Rachel sounded surprised.

"She's been half asleep all morning and we didn't really get the chance." Ali explained.

"Hello?" I was still waiting on an explanation.

Rachel turned to me with a sigh. "The police were doing door-to-door calls at our halls this morning. We didn't know what it was about because they hadn't reached our block yet, but on the way in there was a big section of the road cordoned off, with loads of police cars and one of those big white tents that they put up to hide things."

"So yeh, as I was saying, we now know what it was about." Kev interrupted, obviously wanting to be the one sharing the news.

My stomach was starting to churn. It couldn't be good – not if they had tents up. That usually meant forensics were involved.

"A student was murdered." His voice was quiet. The seriousness of what he was saying had caught up with his excitement of gossip.

"What?" Cathy's voice sounded shocked.

"Yeh, it's true. Apparently she was a third-year student at the uni, studying psychology, but we don't know for sure."

We were all quiet for a bit as this news sank in.

"So, does anyone know her?" Cathy asked.

Everyone shook their heads.

"Not even sure if the details are right, but I've been in touch with most of the people I know today," Kev continued.

It was quiet after that. I could see people moving around the room between groups, and hear hushed voices, whilst some people seemed oblivious to it.

My food suddenly didn't seem particularly appetising but I picked at it anyway: I needed something for energy. Conversation started again but it was half-hearted, with nobody really making an effort.

I got up to leave when I'd picked everything I could from my wrap.

"I'm going to head off, guys. See you tomorrow."

"Here," Cathy called over, "you can give me them back once you're done." She handed me her notes, and I gave her a grateful smile and put them in my bag.

Downstairs I went to the photocopier, going for the easy option. I reckoned my concentration wasn't going to be good all day. As the machine was scanning the first sheet I saw that Cathy had put in her maths notes too, and I smiled.

She sees more than she lets on.

I stuffed the pages into my bag and left the building. I was down the steps and walking along past the university buildings before I realised there hadn't been anyone to meet me.

May be they're not going to be here all the time.

The thought sent relief and a shudder through me at the same time.

I stopped, pretending to read a flier plastered onto one of the buildings. It wasn't long before I had found my bodyguard. It was Ross this time and he was staying back, maybe trying to give me some space, or maybe he didn't want to talk – who knew? As I turned back to walk home I gave a quick glance in his direction but couldn't see him. Didn't change much, I still knew he was there.

I hovered at the bridge, trying to find some peace, but the trickle of water and the one lonely duck I saw did little to ease my mind. As I unlocked the main door to my building, Ross stayed out of view at the end of the street.

Upstairs I stuck my notes away, put some music on to clear my mind, and tried to read a chapter from one of my textbooks. I didn't get far. My thoughts kept returning to Fraser and Jason, Craig's comments this morning, and the poor unknown girl found.

I came out of my thoughts when I finally realised that I couldn't read the text in my book in the grey light from the window. It was the back of four and starting to get dark already. I flicked on the light, tidied things away, and then went to the kitchen to see if anyone was in.

Natasha was sitting in the living room, flicking through a glossy mag. She tossed it onto the table when I came in.

"Don't know why Lauren gets those – full of rubbish."

I sat down opposite her.

"Yeah."

"So, Lauren was telling me that you came back with Fraser the other night."

I smiled. "She been gossiping already?"

Natasha shrugged. "Think she lives on it." She still looked at me questioningly, but didn't say anything else.

"OK, yeh. I went home for the weekend and Fraser gave me a lift there and back."

"Wow! The whole 'meet the parents' thing."

"It wasn't quite like that. He was going to Perth anyway, so he gave me a lift. He didn't stay with us."

"But he did meet your folks?" she persisted.

"Yeh, he met my mum and Ailsa." I gave in.

She grinned at me and I couldn't help smiling back.

"So things are progressing? Is it more than friends yet?"

"Yeh it is, but…" I struggled to get the right words. "I don't know how long it will last. I feel as though he's not going to stick around long."

"No way. You should have more confidence in yourself. Just because he is absolutely gorgeous does not mean that he is not going to stay. You're good looking, fun, intelligent, and you have the whole martial arts thing in common."

I smiled. "Thanks." I couldn't really believe her though. I still didn't feel on his par. Plus, there was the fact that I was worried he was doing this to almost get back at Jason. It hurt to think that, and I hoped that he was better than that, but I couldn't stop it featuring prominently in my thoughts.

Natasha got up to make her tea and I grabbed the magazine and asked her about her courses and friends. She was just settling down to eat and I was thinking of getting myself something, when Eilidh and Lauren came in together.

"You in, girls?" Eilidh's voice barrelled down the hall.

"Yeh. In the kitchen," I shouted back for the two of us, as Natasha finished off a mouthful of proper lasagne.

They came rushing into the kitchen and flung down a newspaper onto the table, pulling up chairs to sit in.

"Have you heard?" Lauren asked, her voice impatient.

"Heard what?" Natasha asked.

"There's been a murder. Quine from uni. They've just confirmed details of it. Got the evening paper to check it out," Eilidh filled us in.

It was the same as I'd heard at lunch. This time there were a few more things.

"They think the body was moved." Lauren was talking now. "She died because of a stab wound but there was no blood at the scene, so they reckon it happened somewhere else and she was dumped back there. Though why they would dump a body there, I don't know. It's really busy. They would be more likely to get caught."

These words seemed to stand out to me, almost visible in the air. Stab wound but no blood. I got a crawling sensation over my skin, as my brain finally kicked in and formalised thoughts that I'd been running from all day.

Jason had killed her.

That's why there was no blood. That's why I now had bodyguards. He had done it close to where I was and Fraser lived as a clear signal, a clear message. I was responsible for this girl's death. I was the reason that a family was grieving tonight, never able to fully recover. I was the reason.

I stood up and mumbled something, pulling my phone from my pocket as though I needed to call someone. I stumbled through my bedroom door before my horror fully took hold.

I have caused this. I've caused some poor family's misery.

I could feel tears prick my eyes but I couldn't let myself cry.

How can I cry? How can I feel sorry for myself? What have I done? Those poor people.

I knew fine well how it felt to have someone you love taken away from you because of someone else.

Will there be more?

I cried at that. I didn't know what to do. I felt so useless.

How can I fight back?

I spent the evening crying in my room, feeling guilty, feeling ashamed, feeling scared. Old memories and emotions came back and I drowned in my new and old grief.

The nightmares were only to be expected. It started with the familiar: cars driving along a country road, oncoming traffic, horns blaring, tyres screeching, metal scraping and folding. Screaming. Blood.

Then there was the newish chasing dream: someone hunting me, their voice stalking my movements. I run and run but they are always just one step behind. I run uphill, with my legs burning, and just as I see a doorway they reach out.

The newest one of all. The girl looks young. I know she is the girl from university, nameless at this stage. She is being held by a man. He is wrapped around her so that I can only see her face, with the remains of fear on it. Then she is dropped and, for some reason, she is suddenly naked, with a wound at her neck that is mysteriously closing as I watch, and a knife wound on her stomach. She lies there, alone, cold. Her skin is turning grey. Then her face morphs and it is me lying there. I am watching myself. Then it morphs again and it is Ailsa lying on the street.

My scream is cut short as I wake up.

Chapter Sixteen

I woke with a start, suddenly wide awake. I couldn't remember the dream that had forced me to wake but that was probably a good thing. Checking the clock, I saw it was half five and wondered if there was any chance of me getting back to sleep. I decided not, and sat at my desk, trying to find something to distract myself. I pulled open the curtains and watched the people outside, wondering what they did and where they were going at such a time. I played with a stress ball that I hadn't used in years and daydreamed, making up stories for the people walking by.

I went for a shower at a more reasonable hour, and took my time in getting ready for uni. When I walked out my door I knew to expect Craig this time.

"Morning," I called before he had the chance to move away from the wall.

"You're early." His voice was insanely chirpy. I frowned across at him.

"Morning moods still not improved then?" he continued. He was brave – I had to give him that.

I sighed. "No." I wasn't going to complain about my sleep today, not when I was still alive to do so.

"Hmm, oh well then." He fell into step beside me.

I had to admit it was nice to have someone there, so that I could just concentrate on walking and not be searching around me all the time. There was none of the weird tension and excitement of when I walked with Fraser, but it was still reassuring none the less. As we approached my building I came out of my thoughts.

"So, how come Ross was hiding from me yesterday?"

Craig gave a laugh. "I told him! He wanted to see if he could follow you without you noticing. He thinks he has improved, but he is still painfully obvious."

I thought about that. "Well, technically I didn't see him. So that's good, right?"

"Hmm, maybe. He might fool a human, then. But there is no way he would manage it on one of us." He seemed deep in thought at that point.

I said bye as I went in to my lecture, and he gave me a grin and a wink in return. I was in before Ali and Cathy this morning, so chose a seat halfway up, with free chairs on either side. They joined me about five minutes later as I was doodling on my pad. We chatted for a while until the professor turned up.

Fraser was waiting again in the corridor outside. Again Cathy and Ali walked a bit away when they saw him, giving us some privacy. For some reason they didn't want to speak to him. Suppose he'd switched off the charm.

As I drew near his hand cupped my face, his thumb gently running under my eye. There was no hiding my lack of sleep from him. His touch on my skin sent tingles through me, and I took a deep breath to try and calm my reaction.

How can I feel this when someone innocent has died because of me? I shouldn't be feeling this.

I locked into his blue eyes, sinking into them. I didn't have the will-power this morning to try and avoid his gaze. I couldn't fathom out what he was thinking. He just stared back at me, seemingly as lost as I was. I wanted to feel his arms around me, his lips on mine, to feel reassured. But at the same time I knew I didn't deserve that luxury.

"It was him, wasn't it?" I finally managed to speak.

He looked back at me for a second before answering, "Yes."

My eyes moved away from his face and I nodded, letting him confirm what I already knew. Fraser's hand dropped from my face and covered my own hand, wrapping it inside his fingers.

"You are safe. Nothing will happen to you. You do know that, don't you?"

"It's not me I'm worried about," I answered.

"We'll be increasing our patrols," he replied.

"I wasn't meaning that you should – "

He squeezed my hand, cutting me off. "Come on. You're going to be late."

The corridor was deserted around us. I hadn't noticed anyone since I saw Fraser. I hitched my bag on my shoulder as Fraser entwined his fingers in mine and led the way out. Too quickly, we were in the maths building. Fraser didn't kiss me goodbye this time and I frowned at that as I walked in, slightly late again.

I got more of this lecture than yesterday's, but still not everything. Thankfully today's lecturers had their notes on the net, so I could print off copies later. I didn't really notice lunch today. Kev still seemed engrossed in the details of the poor girl's killing, and most people listened with a morbid curiosity. I picked at my food, pushing it round on my plate and not really thinking about anything. Handing back Cathy her notes, I arranged to meet her before our lab in an hour. I went to the computer rooms down one floor and checked my e-mails and surfed the net, clicking on random articles, unable to focus on what they were about.

In the lab I paired up with a nerdy looking guy who was trying to be cool, but should have really been with Matthew. We were allocated our experiment and I let Colin get stuck into the equipment as I tried to read the instructions, and drew up a table for the results. Most of it went OK. It was actually a fairly straightforward process, for a change, but I did manage to spill liquid nitrogen down myself.

Shit!

I brushed at the front of my clothes, hoping most of it had evaporated before reaching them.

Stephanie? What's happening?

Fraser's voice made me melt and my legs folded underneath me, my knees slamming into the floor.

Fuck! That's definitely going to bruise. I'm fine, Fraser. Just being clumsy.

My tone was probably more snippy than I'd meant. I stood up as Colin came over.

"Are you OK?" he asked, a bit unsure what to do.

"Yeh, fine. Just tripped and spilt the canister," I explained, annoyed at myself for spilling it and for falling on my knees.

"Didn't get any on your hands, did you?" His voice didn't sound particularly worried.

"No. Just my clothes, thankfully. Most of it went on the floor."

"Oh. OK. I'll go fill it again, if you want to set up the next bit." He reached for the canister and I let him take it. That was one good thing about working with guys: they didn't make a fuss out of things.

The rest of the day passed without incident. When I came out of the lab, Chris was on the landing at the stairs, chatting to one of the physics postgrads. I stopped on the landing, figuring he was there for me. He said his goodbyes to the guy, and looked across at me.

"So what is it that's going to bruise then?" he asked with a grin.

"You heard that? Thought that had stopped now."

"It's the only thing I've heard in a long time. I'm guessing it was only because your concentration was broken by whatever had happened." He raised his eyebrows, still waiting on an answer.

"I tripped, fell on my knees, and covered myself in liquid nitrogen." I started walking down the stairs again to avoid his face.

"Yep, I'd say that would break most people's concentration." I could hear the laughter in his voice, but thankfully he didn't laugh out loud.

It was after five now, so most things outside were thrown into shadows. Only the harsh white lights illuminating the main building for the city to see, bleached the darkness. Chris walked beside me. He didn't chat as much as Craig but I still felt at ease with him. He left me at the door to my building, and gave a wave as he moved away.

Inside, the girls were all in the living room. Eilidh had another paper spread on the low table in front of her. I dumped my bag on a chair and went into the kitchen to make myself a pot noodle. I knew I couldn't face a proper meal.

As I sat down stirring the flavoured powder into the noodles, the girls continued their discussion about the murder.

"The university are supposed to be putting out safety fliers, taxi phone numbers, and warnings not to go anywhere alone at night – usual advice," Lauren informed us.

"Suppose you could kick their ass, Steph?" Eilidh asked me.

"Yeh, maybe; maybe not. Think that guy is in a league of his own; not just someone trying to grab your purse."

"Did you hear it was a guy on his own? Thought the police were leaning towards a gang thing." Eilidh asked.

Crap!

I was forgetting I knew more than anyone else.

"No, I don't know any more. Just guessing." I tried to change the topic after that, and they followed on to talk about Britney's latest meltdown, as documented by Lauren's favourite magazine.

I knew fine well who had done it but couldn't go to the police. I could just picture that scene: "'Scuse me, Mister Policeman, I know who killed that girl. It was a vampire named Jason. That's why there was no blood, see. He drank it all. But I don't know where he is, or where he lives. In fact, I don't know anything about him except he wants to kill me too." Sure, I could see that going down well. If I was lucky they'd give me enough sedation I wouldn't notice the straightjacket.

The dreams waited for me. Old ones and new, they rotated round, each taking their shot to scare me, guilt me, tear me up. Sleep was once more a chore. It was easier to be awake. At least then you could try to control your emotions.

Chapter Seventeen

The rest of the week passed the same. The new pattern seemed to establish and settle surprisingly quickly. I got used to my escorts. Ross eventually gave up trying to tail me from a distance and would walk with me now as well. I never saw Jonathon though, and I wondered what that meant. They would still mention him so I knew he was around, but I didn't want to ask. Apparently Jason had stopped trying to get close but was still in the area, though they wouldn't give me too many details. Some things were familiar to me – things that I had experienced before. Coping mechanisms that I'd developed over the years flicked back into place. I could smile and make benign chitchat. I finished my work but couldn't really say what it had been about, made myself food and even ate some when people were watching, and went to bed and even slept for a few hours each night. The familiar nightmares were still fresh though. Their edge never faded.

None of guys trained on Thursday. Sarah seemed delighted when I didn't have company and even passed some comment, but I didn't remember it. Her face did fall though when Fraser was waiting in the lobby to walk me home. I couldn't really work myself up about it.

The one thing that still managed to sting was Fraser's distancing. I had been right: he had been close to annoy Jason. He held my hand on occasion but didn't put his arm around me or kiss me any more. It did hurt but I tried not to let those thoughts surface.

The girls in the flat were used to seeing me with one of the guys now. God knows what they thought was going on but they didn't tease me much – not that I noticed anyway.

On Saturday afternoon I was sitting in the living room with Natasha and Eilidh, having done all my work in the morning, and phoned home to check in. Thankfully Mum and Ailsa were getting on better now.

We had the TV on in the background and Eilidh was filling us in on her latest night out and the guys that had been there.

I could feel someone approaching our flat. They were walking down the street. I tuned in and instantly recognised it as Fraser. My eyebrows lowered, wondering why he was coming here. He normally scouted away and left Ross or Craig to watch the street when I was home. Sighing, I tried to listen in to Eilidh's descriptions. Natasha certainly seemed riveted, whether with disbelief or not I didn't know. Someone knocked at the door.

"I'll get it." Eilidh bounced up out her seat. "Never know who it could be!"

She jogged out the room and Natasha looked over at me. "Can you believe what she gets up to?" Her voice said she clearly didn't.

"Sadly, yes I can." I rolled my eyes and she laughed.

Eilidh opened up the door and Natasha looked down the hall to see who it was. Eilidh's surprised and vague voice floating back down confirmed it was Fraser. He followed her into the room and sat down opposite me, his gaze sweeping round, only hesitating on me. My stomach sank a little at that. His eyes seemed a pale blue today.

There was a silence that seemed awkward. I didn't know what to say to him. Eilidh and Natasha were spellbound and so weren't speaking either. He perched on the edge of the low seat, his elbows resting on his knees, his long coat folded and hung down and almost touching the carpet as he sat in the chair. He seemed on edge too, though I couldn't pinpoint anything specific that gave it away.

Clearing his throat, he looked across to me, his eyes meeting mine. "I thought you would like to go out for a walk with me?" It was a question, but one I couldn't really refuse. He would probably just hang around here until I gave in, and I didn't think that I could keep conversation going. Not when I was hurting.

"Sure. I'll go get my shoes." I stood up and escaped into my room. The movement seemed to release Eilidh and Natasha, and I could hear them talking to Fraser through the wall as I grabbed a jacket and stuffed things into a handbag.

Fraser was already in the hall as I closed my door over. We left the flat and walked down the stairs into a cold afternoon in silence. It was a rare dry day for the west coast, with only few wisps of clouds in a clear, washed out blue sky.

Much the colour of Fraser's eyes today.

I pulled a face at myself for thinking like that, and looked round the street to try and distract myself. Fraser hadn't taken my hand but did walk close to me. Whenever his arm brushed against mine there were bittersweet tingles that shot up my arm and into my body. I couldn't help but think of his arms around me, and me having contact with him again. It made tears prick my eyes thinking that I had been close to him but it wouldn't be that way again.

"Stephanie." His voice brought me back to my surroundings. I looked round, seeing that we had stopped on the bridge in the park. I joined him at the wall to look over the edge at the water underneath. We stood for a while. I watched the swirls and even spotted a couple of ducks further down, but it wasn't quite the same as my beach at home.

I was aware of Fraser at my side. Who wouldn't be? He didn't talk though; he just stood looking out over the water with me. He seemed as distracted as me.

"Will you come back to the flat with me?" His voice seemed unsure. It didn't fit his confidence and demeanour.

"Of course." I knew I was safe with him anyway, if not necessarily wanted.

Again we walked in silence. Not speaking never really bothered me though I knew the convention was to make some small talk, but I couldn't think of anything to say. Fraser seemed the same as he didn't speak either. We walked up the stairs to his flat on the top floor. Once inside I was reminded of the last time I was here, discovering I could communicate with thoughts. Possibilities opening up before me, and not just with the communication. Fraser gestured to the sofa and I sat down in the corner, kicking off my shoes and bringing my knees to my chest.

"Where are the rest of the guys?"

"All out. They won't be back for the rest of the day." He hung his coat up and then sat on the other end of the couch. He half turned towards me, his arm along the back of the couch, but his gaze not quite meeting mine.

"I've got a few questions for you, Stephanie." This sounded ominous.

"Questions for me? That's a bit of a reversal, isn't it?" I tried to keep it light and he gave a brief smile in response, but it quickly faded.

"What are you thinking about this whole situation? You haven't said much. It is obviously having an effect on you but you don't say anything." His voice sounded strained. The words came out quickly. His gaze had come up to meet mine and I could have sworn it was concern in his face. Losing myself in his looks, I felt my breath catch.

A second passed before I could break the look between us. I turned my head to look at one of the paintings on the other wall, and took a deep breath to try and phrase this right. Words suddenly seemed jumbled in my head.

"Well, I'm obviously scared. I mean there is no way I can manage to fight this guy off on my own, and that is not a normal situation for me." I took a breath. I could do this. I could voice these things out loud.

"I won't let anything happen to you." His voice was quiet. "What else?"

"Um, the girl that Jason… Well, I'm thinking about her. It's my fault that she is dead, after all. What was she like? What did he do?"

Fraser's voice interrupted me, and it wasn't quiet this time. "It is not your fault, Stephanie. It's Jason's fault. He did this."

"Yeh, to get to me. He was looking for me."

Fraser shook his head. "It is not your fault."

It was, but I could see he wasn't going to give up so I moved on.

"Then feeling scared and thinking about that girl brought up some… old stuff that I haven't really… dealt with." I swallowed, my eyes staying fixed on the picture.

"Your dad." Fraser sighed. "I suppose that me taking you in the car and asking you about it didn't really help."

I tried to smile, but I think it was more of a grimace. My eyes seemed to be fuzzy. He reached over and took my hand, his thumb stroking the back of it. I looked down at it. It was safer than his eyes.

"I'm sorry." His voice was quiet again.

Might as well get it all out.

I took another shaky breath. "And then I'm confused about us." His thumb stopped moving over my hand, but I gripped on anyway to stop him pulling back.

"I thought we were moving on together, but, you seem… distant." Thankfully my voice wasn't too shaky. I kept my attention on his fingers, noticing the fine lines over his knuckles and scars across the back of his hand. "I'm not used to relationships. You have to be straight with me. If you don't want this to go any further, then just say."

OK, that bit was shaky. Better out than in.

I could hear him pull in a breath in the silence that followed. I risked a look up at him. His face was frozen, his mouth open, his expression part surprise, part pain. I didn't know what to make of that. I didn't want to hope and mislead myself.

"I do want us to be together, but only if you want to. I don't want you to be forced into it. I will protect you from Jason whether you are with me or not."

"You think I want to be with you to hide from him?" My voice seemed a bit higher than normal, and I'd definitely found the volume button again.

Fraser frowned at my response. "Well, I hoped not. But I want you to realise that fact."

I let out a snort. "I was thinking you were using me, flaunting me in front of Jason."

Fraser's mouth fell open. "How could you think I would do that?"

"Well I didn't want to, didn't want to think you could, but come on, what else is there about me that would have you interested?"

"Everything else." His voice was soft, almost a whisper. My back tingled with his words.

I was suddenly aware again of how close we were, and how much I wanted him. Excitement grew as I realised I could let myself think about him in that way again. My breathing became shallower. I could hear it. He moved towards me. His lips met mine and he pushed me back till he was lying over me. My hands drifted down from his shoulders to over his chest, feeling the muscles under his top. The pressure on our lips increased and a weak moan escaped me in response. He pulled back despite the hand I'd moved to the back of his neck.

"I can think of a more appropriate place for this." He chuckled and picked me up in his arms with no apparent effort. Our mouths found each other again as he carried me. Then we were on his bed. I completely lost track of time as we kissed, but eventually my hands slipped under his top and were pulling it up. He helped me take it off and my gaze travelled over his torso, my hands following a second behind. I'd known he would be toned but I hadn't expected this. He would have fit amongst any one of the magazines that Lauren drooled over. His body was gorgeous, with hard muscles that weren't overdeveloped like a body-builder's.

He chuckled at my expression, then locked his lips to mine again. The kisses moved to my jaw and then to my neck. His teeth grazed the skin on my neck, but rather than seeming strange, it just sent waves of fire through me and I gasped, my body arching up to his. He moaned. I could feel it vibrate through his chest. Then he moved down again, pulling my top off, kissing all the time.

Where our skin touched it tingled. I just wanted to press myself against him to feel it, though his mouth was doing a damn fine job as well. I couldn't quite understand how it felt as though I was melting and on fire at the same time, but my mind couldn't stay focussed long enough to figure it out.

The rest of the night just merged into one gorgeous memory and sensation. I'd never experienced anything like it, or even imagined any-where close to it.

At some point Fraser lay wrapped around me and I was curled into his chest. I traced patterns on his arm, still enjoying the feel of his skin under my fingers. I couldn't tell what time it was. It was still dark outside but that didn't tell me much. I was sleepy but didn't want to sleep, didn't want to lose a second of this. Fraser was quiet beside me, his fingers stroking the side of my face and my hair.

"I'm so glad we managed to clear that up." I grinned at him.

He laughed. "If that is what comes from misunderstandings between us, then I might have to instigate a few more." He smiled at me, and then kissed me again.

Fraser pulled the covers up over us and I started to feel sleepy, but I didn't want to sleep. I just wanted this moment to last. I must have murmured as much whilst I dozed as the last thing I heard was Fraser's voice saying, "I'll still be here when you wake up." He kissed my forehead and I fell asleep.

I struggled, my arms pumping, my legs aching, running for all I was worth. He was behind me again, his laughter floating forward, his fingertips inches from my back. I was curved away from him, straining forward. The landscape changed around me. I was at home, university, in the park, running up a hill, but he was always there, playing with me, waiting on me falling.

Stephanie!

I woke with a start, sitting bolt upright in the bed. It was dark around me as I sat panting, trying to catch my breath. A hand went on my shoulder and I flinched away till I realised where I was.

"You're OK. It was just a dream." Fraser's voice broke through my panic. I took a long shaky breath and gave him an apologetic smile.

"Sorry."

"No need to apologise." He tried to smile back but I could still see the shadow of a frown on his face now that my eyes had adjusted to the dim light. I sighed, lying back down and pulling the covers around my shoulders. It suddenly felt cold. Fraser lay next to me, pulling me into his arms, and I fell back to sleep with my head on his chest.

Chapter Eighteen

I woke. It was quite a sudden thing. One minute I was asleep, the next my eyes were open, no gradual awareness. I was looking at a well-muscled chest.

Fraser.

I could feel a smile on my face as my gaze travelled up his chest to his face, locking onto his deep blue eyes.

"Good morning." He smiled down at me. My smile got wider in response.

"Morning." I stretched my arms out and rolled onto my back. Our legs were entwined so I didn't get far. His hand went round my waist, pulling me back towards him.

"Did you sleep OK?" he asked.

"Yep, best sleep I've had in ages." He frowned a bit at my response.

"But you had nightmares. You were really restless." He looked at me, confused.

"I only had one nightmare, which is better than normal. Sorry if I was kicking you. Suppose it didn't really keep you awake though."

He laughed at that. "No, you didn't keep me awake. But I'm beginning to understand why you've been looking so tired, if that was a good night's sleep." His hand held the side of my face again, his thumb running under my eyes.

"Trust me, I feel great!" I shifted up in the bed to kiss him, and we both got lost in our kiss for a while. Some minutes later Fraser pulled back from me.

"Suppose you should get some breakfast."

"Hmm, suppose." I didn't make any move to get up from the bed.

Laughing, Fraser got up. "Come on. Let's see what we've got in the kitchen."

"You have food here? Why?"

He smiled over at me whilst he pulled on some jeans. "After you stayed over here last time I thought it would be best if there was something in that you could eat, just in case you started coming around more."

"Oh. Thanks." I was a bit surprised but I suppose I should have known he would think of everything.

"So, what would you like? Think I could cover anything." He stood in the middle of the kitchen, his arms spread.

I laughed. "Could be tempted to test you and ask for something really ridiculous."

He grinned back. "Try me."

"Maybe some other time. I could just do with some toast, actually."

"No problem." He turned and switched on the grill and put some bread in.

"Have you got some juice in the fridge?" I'd grabbed the handle and was pulling the door open as Fraser whirled round, his eyes wide and arm reaching out. Automatically my gaze went to the fridge and its contents.

There, sitting on the top shelf, where most people had yoghurts or packets of food, was a pile of blood bags. I froze, staring at the bags. They were exactly like the ones you would see in a hospital. Fraser was motionless on the other side of the room.

Well, what did I think they would have in their fridge?

"That's quite freaky." I pulled my gaze away from them and looked to see a carton of orange juice on another shelf. I grabbed it and shut the door, turning to face Fraser. His face was set in a look of half horror and half shock. I tried not to let my face show my own shock.

"Quite freaky? That's all you've got to say?" His voice was cautious and he was slowly moving back to a normal standing position, his gaze searching mine.

"Well, you are vampires. What should I expect in your fridge? It's not exactly going to be salad."

He shook his head. "You're so calm." He walked towards me. Bending down, he kissed me and then wrapped his arms around me, resting his chin on the top of my head. "I love that."

My heart broke into a sprint at that. He gave a chuckle.

Suppose you can feel that, right?

Feel it and hear it.

Laughing, he pulled away from me again and grabbed the tray out of the grill without bothering to use gloves. I gasped as he set it down on the worktop, and he flashed a grin at me.

"Hot and cold don't bother us. We can feel them but they can't harm our bodies."

I nodded and finally poured my juice into a glass. Then we went and sat in the living room again. I crunched my toast as Fraser flicked on the TV. Given these few minutes, my brain caught up with everything that had happened. Fraser and I had cleared the air and were now more than friends again. I'd slept with Fraser! My mind was reeling for a few minutes, then memories from last night started to surface, and I was lost in my thoughts.

"What's got your heart rate changing?" Fraser looked across at me, a small frown appearing on his face.

"You." I answered. He smiled and moved across to me, his kiss sending shivers of delight through me.

My phone chose that moment to interrupt us with a shrill chiming announcing a text message. Fraser moved away with a smile whilst I fished my phone out of my pocket.

HEY U OK? DID U COME HOME LAST NIGHT?

"It's Lauren. Looking for gossip whilst checking I'm OK"

Fraser laughed as I texted back that I was fine and would see her later.

"That should keep her stewing for a while." I chuckled as I put my phone back in my pocket and ate the last of my toast.

"When I was in my lab this week and spilt the liquid nitrogen down myself, you talked to me again."

Fraser looked round at me, waiting on the rest.

"When I heard you, it had the same effect it used to have. I thought that had stopped."

He blinked and looked away. "It has to do with emotions. I didn't really think it was happening at first, but after that I could control my emotions. But when I heard you shout I thought Jason had slipped through and found you. My emotions weren't under control."

"Right." I tried to figure out what that meant. "So do any of the rest of the guys experience it? Do I sound like that, so personal, to you?"

He gave a laugh before he answered, "None of us have experienced it before, and no, I do not have that effect on them and you do not have that effect on them." He seemed amused about something. "I don't know if you will have that effect on me, as you send your thoughts out as a broadcast, and not to just one person. It is more personal if you send it to one person."

I was beginning to get an idea of why he had that effect on me, but I didn't want to sound stupid so I kept it to myself.

"Can I practise sending thoughts to just one person? Will I be able to do it?" I asked.

Fraser thought about it before he answered, "I think you probably will be able to do it. You certainly have some form of telepathy. Practice may well help, or it might just be something that will happen with time. Your powers have developed quickly, so it can't be long until you manage to send a thought to just one person."

I sat thinking about how I would actually go about it. I would need to practise it in a room with some of the other guys to see if I just sent the thought to one of them and not broadcast it to them all. There was a tugging at my attention. I was so engrossed in my thoughts it took me a while to realise that Jonathon was coming up the stairs. I told Fraser and he only nodded in reply, which made me frown. He picked up the remote and turned up the TV.

I watched Jonathon open up the door to the flat so I saw his nose wrinkle as he entered the room. His face became smooth though as he looked over to where Fraser and I were sitting on the couch.

"Morning." His voice was definitely neutral, and it made me wonder why it was so flat.

"Jonathon." Fraser nodded in his direction. Goose bumps appeared on my skin at the obvious tension between the two of them. "Anything new?"

"Actually, yes. He got another one last night. Middle-aged guy, close by St Enoch's this time. He's keeping his distance, but details are exactly the same."

My body went cold as I realised what he was talking about. My eyes couldn't move from Jonathon's face. Fraser put his hand over mine as he started to ask Jonathon questions.

"A more public figure? What time? Were there any traces of him? Did you follow his trail?"

I couldn't follow all the questions and the answers. My mind was locked on some faceless man, drained of his blood, killed because of me.

"Stephanie." Fraser voice broke through my thoughts. He squeezed my hand, trying to bring my attention back to him.

"I need to go and check this out. Do you want to stay here or go back to your flat?" I couldn't stop my eyes flickering towards Jonathon.

I cleared my throat. "I'll just go back to my place."

Fraser nodded and I stood and went to his room to collect my things. When I came back out Jonathon was not in view but it didn't take me long to realise he was in his room. Fraser stood at the door. We walked down the stairs in silence. Once outside, Fraser put his arm around my shoulders, pulling me close to him.

"We will catch him. I'll be able to get more information this time if I can get there soon, before the police. He's made a mistake coming back."

I nodded my head mechanically. At the entrance to the park Craig was leaning against one of the gateposts. He looked up when he heard us, giving a nod to Fraser and a grin for me.

"Can you take Stephanie back and keep an eye on the street for me?" Fraser asked Craig.

"Sure. No problem."

Fraser turned round to me. Placing his hands either side of my face, he kissed me gently. "Don't worry." With that he turned and ran out of the park, heading to wherever the body of that poor man was.

Chapter Nineteen

Craig walked me home. I was too distracted to listen to him chatting away. The only thing that caught my attention was when he commented on Fraser and me finally getting together. When I went into the flat no one was around, so I managed to sneak into my room without being ambushed by questions. I spent the afternoon thinking about everything that had happened in the last twenty-four hours. It was a lot.

I came out of my reverie when my stomach growled at me. Checking the clock, I realised it was late for food and I'd only had a bit of toast the whole day. Sighing, I got up and walked through to the kitchen.

"Here she is! Ssooo?" Lauren drew out the word into a question. I had to smile at her persistence. She was determined.

"So what?" I asked, and carried on walking past her seat and into the kitchen.

Eilidh laughed. "She has been fuming about your non-text all day, knowing that you went away with Fraser but not knowing anything else."

"So what is going on between you two?! First you're all lovey dovey, then you seem not interested in him even though you're chatting to all his mates, then you agree to go out a walk with him and don't come back all night! What's the deal?" Lauren voice got louder as she went on, and we were all laughing at her by the end of it.

"So, we're together now." I pulled a meal out from the freezer and chucked it in the microwave.

"How together?" she asked in the next second.

"Together enough that I would be extremely pissed if you made a move on him."

"Yeh! Go, Steph!" Eilidh shouted.

"So, was it a good night?" Lauren's eyebrows rose as she asked the question.

I could feel my face starting to go red. "It was a very good night." Thankfully I was saved by the ping of the microwave, and I turned to sort out my sweet and sour chicken.

Natasha joined us in the kitchen at that point. "What's all the yelling about?"

"Steph finally got it on with Mr Fraser!" Lauren filled Natasha in.

Natasha's mouth dropped open and she looked at me with raised eyebrows, and then quickly changed her expression. "Well, we all knew he was going to make a move at some point. Lucky girl!"

"Thanks." I couldn't help but grin back at them. This was the highlight of uni so far for me. In fact it could be the highlight of my life. Fraser almost said he loved me. I hoped I wasn't having a dippy girly moment, and that he did like me.

"So you gotta tell us details," Eilidh pleaded. "Bet his body is gorgeous."

I nodded, getting red again, and tried to take a mouthful of food so I couldn't answer her properly. The rest of the time was spent with them asking questions, and me avoiding giving the answers. Eventually they got bored of my evasiveness.

"Do you know if any of the other guys are attached?" Eilidh asked.

"Don't think any of them have got girlfriends, but I don't really know."

"Well, find out for me. That Chris is quite a looker as well."

Lauren nodded in agreement with Eilidh. After that we sat and watched the TV for a while. None of the girls were going out tonight. Natasha was actually trying to finish an essay but had given up on it, so she brought it through to the living room so she could at least pretend she was doing it as she watched TV.

My thoughts deviated from the happy part of the last day and I remembered what Fraser went away to do. I shuddered, wondering who the man was that had been killed. What had Jason done to him? I left the girls as my mood suddenly deflated, and went to my room. After getting things ready for uni tomorrow I went to bed early and tried to get some rest.

The dreams were predictable, though when you are asleep they feel fresh each time. I woke several times through the night, either panting from running, choking off a scream of fright and pain, or sweating in fear. It wasn't restful.

Monday morning was the dull grey of Monday mornings everywhere – the dark clouds daring you to go outside without an umbrella. Ross was waiting for me at the door. I was a bit disappointed that it wasn't Fraser, but Ross explained it within the first few minutes.

"They're following a lead. They managed to pick up a trail last night and are seeing where it leads. And seeing as Craig still thinks that I can't follow anything without sticking out like a sore thumb, we swapped. So here I am."

"Oh, thanks." The rain started falling as we walked into uni. I put up my umbrella and Ross pulled his hood over his head. I wondered what it was that they were following. What had they found?

"I'll leave you here, then. Catch you later." Ross gave a smile and walked off, and I trudged up the worn steps into the physics building. I shook off my umbrella, trying not to get soaked in the process, and joined a few people I recognised from the course and walked along to our lecture. Ali and Cathy were sitting with Rachel and someone else I recognised but didn't really know. Ali was telling everyone about his night out on Saturday, which was apparently ace. The lecture passed without much interest, and we trooped over to maths hunched under umbrellas. I didn't see Ross but could feel him following behind us.

Maths passed as normal, and we headed into the union for lunch afterwards. Our group merged with another as we sat around some tables, and I recognised a few faces but didn't know any of them well.

"Did you hear there has apparently been another person killed?" a blonde girl with thick glasses said at the end of the table.

"It wasn't another student though, was it? I heard it was an older guy, and over towards the centre of town rather than round this area."

"Wonder if it was the same person who did it." This time it was a guy with dark spiky hair who spoke.

"What, you mean like a serial killer?" Kev joined in the conversation.

The blonde girl spoke again. "Surely not. That's the kind of thing you hear about on TV."

"But it's not as though Glasgow has got that much crime. It is a bit odd that in just over a week two people have been killed, and apparently in the same way." Kevin replied.

I concentrated on my food and tried not to make eye contact with anyone. I just knew the questions I would see in their faces, and knew that even if they did have the answers they still wouldn't happy. I certainly wasn't.

Cathy left the same time as me as we were both going to the uni shop for some supplies of paper and pens. The rain had stopped, thankfully, but the few trees were still dripping, the water running down the street into drains. I couldn't see or feel Ross around so I hesitated for a second before walking onto the street, and pretended to sort my jacket. At the end of the street I spotted a moody figure leaning against a building, oblivious to the damp. It was Jonathon, looking extremely bored. He didn't look over and I didn't try to acknowledge him.

I smiled at Cathy. "Let's go. Hopefully the rain will stay off."

We hurried along the street towards the shop, and almost bumped straight into Eilidh.

"Steph! Fit like?" She didn't seem fazed by the weather and still looked full of energy.

"Hey, Eilidh. You remember Cathy, right?"

"Yeh, sure. How you doing?"

They smiled at each other. Then Eilidh focussed back on me, "So, where you in such a rush to go? Going back to spend the night with Fraser again?"

I blushed and saw Cathy's mouth drop open as she looked at me.

"I might be seeing him later, but that's not where I'm going right now."

Eilidh snorted, "Yeh. Oh well, I'll see you when I see you. Enjoy!" She grinned at me, and then trotted away towards the library.

Cathy was looking at me with her eyebrows raised. "Steph?"

I couldn't help but give a laugh that probably sounded more like a giggle.

"No way! How come you didn't tell me?" she demanded.

"Well, it was only at the weekend, and there were other people around this morning. I'm not like Kev and willing to share all with everyone," I replied defensively..

She laughed and linked her arm through mine and started walking again. "So… Fraser! I thought you two were together but then you weren't saying much about it, so Ali and I had kinda given up trying to figure it out."

I just laughed. "Yeh. It was a bit confusing for a while, but we're definitely together now."

We got our bits and pieces at the shop and stood chatting for a while before Cathy went back to halls to start on her tutorial work. I hung about at the door, pretending to find my umbrella in my shoulder bag whilst I was really trying to figure out who and where my shadow was. It was still Jonathon and he was again brooding further up the street. He obviously had some issues with me to the extent that he didn't even want to be near me. Sighing, I stepped out into the rain, pushing up my umbrella, and headed for home.

The only people in the park had their heads down and were walking quickly, and I followed their example, trying to get back to the flat and out the rain as soon as possible. The cars passing in the street made a whooshing noise as their wheels sent sprays of water onto the pavement. I was looking up to try and judge when to pass the puddles as the cars were passing, when I spotted two very out-of-place cars further along the street. They were two big black four-by-four type vans with blacked out windows and silver bars across the grills. The bonnets of the vans were at the same level as the top of the small city cars parked around them. The stood out like sore thumbs. For some reason I couldn't tear my gaze away from the two cars sitting one behind the other, almost looking like one of those long stretch limos. My feet seemed to keep moving of their own accord. I searched out and found Jonathon still behind me, just coming out of the park now. I felt his hesitation, and could imagine one foot still raised as he froze.

"Steph, stop." His voice whipped around me, and by a miracle my feet stopped. At the same time the doors of the black cars opened in front of me. Out piled a mixture of eight guys. Most were young, but there were a few older ones as well. They all had a look of the unwashed, and there, at the back of the group, hanging back like a nervous dog, was a grinning Jason. He looked exactly the same, with too-long stubble, and lank hair pulled back. He stayed behind the others as though it was possible that I wouldn't see him, but he was bouncing on his toes, with excitement no doubt.

One man walked to the front. He was one of the older ones – possibly late thirties. He was clean – at least he had on clean clothes – and appeared to have washed, unlike some of the others, but there was an air around him that could only be described as sleazy: an oily smile with movements too smooth.

"Steph, I believe?" His voice was oily as well. Slightly too high pitched, with no distinguishable accent.

I was frozen to the spot. Jonathon hadn't moved behind me. Jason was still bobbing at the back of the guys spread out in front of me.

"My name is Vincent. I was hoping you would let me have the pleasure of your company for a while." He smiled at me and I could feel my stomach roll. For some reason my body was already trying to move towards him.

What is going on? I know he is with Jason. I know he is probably more dangerous than Jason. And yet I'm wanting to go with him!

At least my mind didn't seem to be affected, and I tried to understand what was happening. Vincent's eyes slid beyond me and focussed on Jonathon, the creepy smile spreading further.

"Ah yes, you will definitely be coming too." With that he turned around to walk back to the vans, jerking his head back to us whilst looking at the men by the cars. They stepped forward as a group, and Jonathon's growl behind me helped me to wake up out of my stupor.

Fraser? Fraser!

Stephanie, what is it?

I tried to send a picture of what I was seeing, but I had no idea if that would work. There wasn't much time.

Jason, and several friends, and a guy called Vincent.

I could feel the vibration of Fraser's growl in my mind.

"Someone knock her out! She's projecting!" Vincent's voice didn't sound so calm now.

The cronies' heads turned away from Jonathon and towards me, with looks of surprise on their faces. They hadn't moved yet so I started to back away, slowly, still trying to send pictures to Fraser, but my mind wouldn't work properly. I just ended up shouting his name as a huge brute strode towards me, his arm pulled back. Then he moved, and I just saw black.

The first thing I noticed was the background noise – a humming. Then it was the vibration. Vibration. Noise. My eyes sprang open and I sat up from my previously slumped position against a cold window. My memories came flooding back and my breathing was already panicked by the time I was fully upright.

I was in a car. In a car with not-so-friendly vampires.

Fraser?

Stephanie!

His voice sounded full of relief.

Are you OK?

I'm in a car!

A hand grabbed my throat and pushed me back against the seat.

"Sit back!" a voice snarled at me. The hand left my neck and I immediately sat forward to try and grab the handle of the door. I could hear an exasperated chuckle but couldn't tell if it was from someone in the car, or Fraser in my head. Hands closed round my wrists, crushing my hands, and pushed me back against the seat. I brought my feet up and swivelled to try and kick at the guy who was holding me, but I only caught the third person in the back seat on his jaw. He swore and tried to grab my flailing legs. Adrenaline was making them move quicker than I would have imagined. Eventually he caught them and I knew I was going to have bruises where his fingers gripped.

Where are you?

I twisted my head back in my now horizontal position to look out the window. It was difficult to tell where I was. Everything was moving so quickly. I could hear passing cars, and see sandstone buildings and then newer grey buildings. Then we joined what looked like a motorway.

On a motorway.

Which one?

LIKE I KNOW! I'm stuck in a car with oversized monkeys, who won't let me go!

I'm sorry. I'm coming to get you.

His voice did sound sorry but I couldn't really register it. Someone moved in the front and I couldn't help but turn my head to look at him. It was the sleaze, but he wasn't focussed on me. He was looking at the guy next to me.

"If you can't control her, you really have no chance. Now knock her the fuck out, and it better be for longer this time."

I caught a glimpse of an elbow, and then everything was dark again.

Chapter Twenty

I was screaming but no one could hear me. I was running, but I might as well have been on a treadmill. I was trying to hide in an empty room. They had found me.

I woke when I heard my ragged breath being pulled in through my too dry throat. My face ached. I could feel the pressure in it, like hay fever gone to the extreme. I tried to open my eyes but my eyelids wanted to stick together. After a few attempts they finally opened, but not very far. I was staring at a brick, my nose just a couple of inches from it. It took me a second to focus, it was so close. I hadn't been expecting a brick, and it took my befuddled brain a few moments to catch up. In the meantime I just breathed.

So Jason, and his friends, had caught me. But instead of killing me, as I'd expected, they'd kidnapped me.

Why?

I didn't know why, so I moved on. I'd been in a car, so I could be anywhere now, especially as they had knocked me out and I had no way to know how long I'd been out for. Was I alone? I tried to quiet my ragged breathing and listen. The only thing I could hear was a steady drip somewhere behind me. Then again, if there was a vampire in the room, I wouldn't know: they didn't need to breathe. The only way to be sure was to look, and that meant moving, so if anyone was in the room they would know I was awake as soon as I moved. Would it be better to just wait and see if anyone made a noise?

I blinked a few times, feeling my eyelids stick together, and wondered if there was blood on my face. I scrunched my nose up and could feel my skin tightening, and guessed there probably was blood on my face. Next, I tried to move my fingers, only now becoming aware that I was lying on my front with my arms underneath me. They twitched but it made my forearms ache. I must have had bruises from where that guy in the car grabbed me. Next came the toes. They were the important digits. If I could wiggle them then my legs were working and I had a chance of getting away from wherever here was. I smiled when they responded.

"Everything still working?" The sarcastic voice wiped my grin away, and I froze, not even breathing. I rolled over slowly, not sure what to expect. I was in a rectangular room – all orange bricks with sloppy mortar between them, which supported a variety of mosses and mould. There was a bare bulb swinging from a metal chain from the ceiling of the room, throwing animated shadows as it swung. The walls were marked by the water running down them, the steady drip coming from a corner of the ceiling that looked crumbled, and landing on bare cement and dribbling away to a drain in a different corner.

A figure was sitting on the floor, hunched over at the other side of the room. As he lifted his head the light from the weak bulb above us hit his face and I realised it was Jonathon. My body relaxed slightly, but not all the way. Why hadn't he got us out of here? Why had his voice seemed so callous?

"How long we been here?" The dry throat didn't help my voice.

"A few hours. I was beginning to wonder if you would ever wake up." He didn't sound concerned either way.

"So what's happening?"

Jonathon snorted and looked away from me. "Pretty much what I guessed would happen when Fraser got you tangled in our lives. The shit has hit the fan."

So I wasn't his favourite person right now – that much I could gather. Unfortunately it doesn't do much for my attitude when people are giving me attitude.

"That doesn't really give me much to work with." Despite my dry throat I still managed to inject some sarcasm. Jonathon obviously felt it as his gaze swung back to mine, his eyes narrowing in the process.

"It turns out this Vincent knows Fraser from way back. Vincent wasn't too specific, but I get the feeling they're not friends. Vincent was content to come and challenge Fraser for this area, humiliate him, possibly kill him, but then they discovered you. When Fraser stopped Jason he just made it a bigger game. Now they realise you're some kind of toy for Fraser and they want to have some fun of their own."

Toy. Fun. I tried not to flinch as he said it.

"So they've already been through me. I tried not to give them too much to work with, but I don't really know why I bothered. As soon as they start with you they'll learn what they want. There's no way you'll be able to stop them."

His words sent a chill along my spine and down the rest of my body. What did he mean by 'through him'? Torture?

"So what's stopping us getting up and leaving?" I looked at the misfit-ting door that had huge gaps around the edges, and no obvious lock. Jonathon again just snorted.

"There are more of them than the few that caught us. Even if I could take care of the vampires there are a few human followers that would be enough to stop you. No, we don't leave until they let us."

"Have you been able to contact Fraser?" I asked. His face screwed up in what I guessed to be chagrin.

"No, I'm not able to yet. And I can't hear him. It's the reason I've been waiting on you waking."

I wondered what he would have done if I wasn't the one who was able to contact his friends. I shifted round, sitting up, leaning against the wall behind me. I wrapped my arms around my legs, hugging them to my chest. It wasn't particularly warm here. I rested my chin on my knees and wondered how bad my face looked. It certainly felt sore enough.

I lifted my head up, shut my eyes and tried to locate Fraser. I felt a faint tugging on my mind, away to my right and in front of me. Frowning, I tried to concentrate but things didn't get any clearer. Normally I could tell you exactly the position anyone was in, but I only had a hazy idea now.

"How long did we drive for?" I asked Jonathon, opening my eyes up.

"At least an hour, but we could have been doubling back. I couldn't see outside the car."

Pity he didn't have my sense of direction. At least he had been awake for the journey.

"Right. I'll try and reach Fraser."

"Remember that you project. As soon as you start they will be able to hear you."

I nodded. I only had limited time before they came to stop me.

Fraser? Fraser, can you hear me?

Stephanie! Are you all right?

I gasped, melting, my head dropping back against the bricks behind me and giving me another bruise, but I didn't care. My hands thumped to the floor.

I'm fine. Well, a few bruises, but fine.

I could almost hear a growl and my eyes flew open to check there wasn't anyone else in the room.

Where are you? We're coming to get you.

It's a trap. There are lots of them.

Yes, but that doesn't mean I'm going to leave you. We can easily deal with them.

Fraser, it seems one of them knows you.

I know. You managed to tell me the name before. I tried to call you but you didn't answer me.

They knocked me out.

Another growl.

Where am I in relation to you?

I concentrated.

To my right and front, but you're hazy. I can't pinpoint you.

That's OK. Keep concentrating on me, and tell me which direction I'm moving.

I frowned. That didn't seem to make sense but I did as he asked.

Stephanie? Which way am I moving?

I could hear footsteps pounding on some stairs, they were getting closer. There was some shouting but I couldn't make out what it was.

You've moved to the right more and further away from me, I think. You're getting more fuzzy.

Which direction did I move more in – the right or further away?

The door to our prison banged open, hitting off the wall and showering the floor with bits of cement mortar and rust off the door. Three men piled in through the door.

The right.

"You!"Vincent strode towards me. Jason followed behind one shoulder, and some guy I'd never seen behind the other, effectively blocking out the light, so I could only see silhouettes. I'd stood up as they approached but it didn't make one blind bit of difference; my legs felt weak and my head spun as I tried to stand. There was no way to defend myself.

"Well, you are an interesting pet. But right now I don't need you talking to everyone." He pulled his arm across his body and backhanded me. I saw the light again, then the approaching wall, then darkness.

Something gritty was against my face. I could feel small hard things digging into my cheek.

God, my head hurts.

It ached – the whole thing. The front, my temples, the back of it – it all throbbed with my pulse. As though my body was coming back to me bit by bit, I felt my shoulders next. One of them was twisted underneath me, straining my neck. I tried to roll so that my weight wasn't on it, and emitted a grunt as my head rolled on the hard floor.

"Looks like that one is waking up." A voice reached me. I didn't know it.

"Hmm, maybe it's time she had a turn." This voice I recognised. It was Vincent.

I pulled in a breath and tried to open my eyes, but the lids were stuck together again and I had to rely on my ears instead. Several pairs of feet moved across the floor. A set of hands grabbed my arms just below the shoulders and hauled me up, and then set me on my feet. This time my eyes flew open, just needing the right incentive.

There was a guy in front of me only a little bit taller than me. He was holding me upright but I could see beyond him. Vincent was walking over to me. Two other vampires behind him were holding Jonathon. His arms were spread out to either side and held against the wall. Jonathon's head hung down, his chin against his chest, which was covered in slashes which bled a dark red.

I felt my eyes trying to widen despite the puffy lids, and my heart kicked into action. Unfortunately my brain was still too befuddled to hit the adrenaline, and my limbs still remained floppy and feeling extremely weak. That they could inflict these wounds on Jonathon, Jonathon who so easily beat me at sparring, Jonathon who I knew could move so fast and was so strong, was just unbelievable. My body was cold, and the hairs on my arms stood on end. The only heat was in my head, where it throbbed.

"So you're finally awake. I'd forgotten how flimsy humans are." He smiled down at me. I wasn't sure if it was supposed to be friendly but it certainly didn't seem it. I didn't answer. My gaze was transfixed to the blood spreading across Jonathon's chest. The patches were joining together, soaking his shirt. I was in shock. I hadn't even known that vampires could bleed.

A pair of fingers snapped an inch from my face and I jerked back, looking round to Vincent. He smiled again.

"Don't worry about your friend. He will recover. We just needed some answers. So how about you? Will you give us some answers too?" His smile sent shivers down me. I tried to swallow but instead choked on my dry throat. "Nothing to worry about, my dear. Just answer truthfully."

"How long has Fraser stayed here in Glasgow?" he started.

"I don't know." Pain exploded in my stomach and I gasped, trying to fold over, but the guy holding my arms kept me upright. He had moved round the side, giving both Vincent and another one clear access to me. When my vision returned both of them were standing still, watching me. I couldn't tell which one of them had punched me but I was guessing it wasn't Vincent.

"This could get quite tedious. How long have you known Fraser?"

I couldn't see any harm in answering this one. "A few months."

His eyes narrowed and I tensed for the blow, but none came.

"How many are in Fraser's group?"

"I don't know." Lightening struck my side, resulting in an audible crack. I panted, and was held upright by the one behind me. Each breath hurt. Tears stung my eyes, making my vision even more blurry. It was only at this point that I remembered Fraser telling me that vampires were just as good as lie detectors.

Shit!

There was a muttered conversation which I only heard parts of as I struggled to breathe: "barely touched", "weak bodies", "can't take". It didn't need a genius to work out that they were annoyed at how little punishment my body could withstand. Can't say that I was disappointed: sooner they decided I'd had enough, the better.

"Since your pathetic body can't handle very much, you force me to take other measures." Vincent's face swam into my vision. He gripped either side of my head in his hands and looked down at me. I realised what he was about to do just in time. It was a miracle that I did realise. Fraser had never needed to touch me to read my thoughts. I desperately flung up my wall, building the bricks high and bracing the inside.

I felt a slight pressure on the outside. A crease appeared on Vincent's forehead and the pressure increased. I pictured myself on the inside of the wall. My shoulder pressed against it, holding it up, willing it to stay in place. There was no way I wanted him inside my head. Just the thought of it sent shivers of revulsion through me.

Vincent's face wore a frown and was becoming darker by the second. I didn't care. He could do whatever to me; he wasn't getting in my head though.

"Bitch!" He flung his hands down. He reached round to the one next to him and grabbed the knife I hadn't seen out of his hand, and whirled back to face me.

"This will make it easier, and certainly more interesting for that one over there." There was an evil grin on his face as he tossed his head in Jonathon's general direction. He was on the floor now. There wasn't any more blood but he still didn't look great.

"Everyone out!" he snapped. "They are no threat to me." He kept his eyes on mine and I was suddenly even more nervous. I hadn't thought that possible. The other vampires left the room, one giving Jonathon a hefty kick in the passing, producing a grunt which I was grateful to hear.

Vincent spoke to me now. "The weaker you are, the easier it will be. All I want to know is: who does he hold close, where does he get his money, and how many are with him. It is really simple. I just want him to suffer. I want him to come here, but at a time of my choosing. I want him to sweat first and not arrive before we are ready." There was a sadistic grin on his face. "You will give me the answers and, even better than I expected, it seems *you* will probably be the bait, not that one." He pointed to where Jonathon had rolled onto his back on the other side of the room.

The door to the room creaked open on rusty hinges and my eyes darted to it, searching for any distraction or possible escape. My stomach sank when all I saw was Jason in the doorway.

"Do you want me to do anything?" His voice almost seemed respectful. It sounded weird. He sent me a leer before Vincent turned round.

"I told them to get out for their own good. Do you think I need help?" He spat the question across the room.

Jason's face paled. "No, no, that's not what I meant." He took a step back towards the door. I have to admit I did enjoy the sight of his discomfort. Vincent's eyes narrowed as he hesitated.

"Actually, I've thought of a use for you. We need to bleed her." He waved the knife in my direction. "Let's test your control."

Jason licked his lips as he stepped towards me. I felt the colour draining from my face and I started to pant, my ribs sending me regular stabs of pain. I backed away a step and hit the wall. My eyes darted round but the only way to the door was past either one of them. My body tensed, ready to run, but I couldn't see a clear way through.

Jason was level with Vincent now and I couldn't bear it any longer. I darted to the left, hoping to go around Jason and reach the door. I was nowhere near fast enough. Vincent stepped behind Jason and grabbed me, throwing me against the wall. He pressed his hand against my sore ribs and I couldn't move. I could hear my gasping breath as Jason moved up and grabbed my arm and held it out from my body. His face lowered to my forearm and my breathing escalated. I heard a whimper but surely it wasn't me.

"Don't use your teeth, you idiot." Vincent's voice dripped with derision. "She won't feel any pain that way. Use the knife. I want her to suffer, so that when Fraser appears he will suffer too." His smile was just plain creepy.

Jason hovered over my arm, and then grabbed the knife Vincent held out to him. He looked back at me then and I don't know what was in my eyes, but it made him grin.

Damn it, Steph, you're giving them everything they want! Where has your backbone gone?

I argued with myself but it seemed my backbone had broken along with my ribs. I couldn't keep the fear off my face, so I turned away. At least that way he wouldn't have the satisfaction of seeing it. Jason dug the knife into the soft flesh inside my forearm and I gasped, sucking in breath, and then gritted my teeth. I managed to not scream. That was as much backbone as I could muster. The pain at the cut was sharp, and I could feel warm blood on the outside of my skin running down my arm.

It was Jason's ragged breathing that made me face him, not any morbid fascination to see the wound. His eyes were wide and transfixed on my arm. I realised he was battling to not grab me and drink, and keep drinking until there was no more. Vincent deliberately drew in a deep breath, closing his eyes in the process, and then sighed, smiling.

"Delicious." He smiled at me. I could only stare back with frightened eyes as I watched them both. "Well, we'll let that take effect, and leave you in peace." His eyes flickered towards Jonathon. "Come now, Jason. You can get your fill elsewhere." He grabbed Jason's shoulders and steered him towards the door.

Once it creaked shut behind them I stared down at my arm. The cut was deep – a dark line slashing across the width of my arm. Bright red blood was streaming out of it. It seemed too crimson compared to the patches on Jonathon's shirt, but I couldn't think about that now. I tried to flex my fingers. They moved, and I gave a sigh of relief.

At least they haven't gone deep enough to cut the tendons.

I was making a bit of a puddle on the floor. The blood was running off my fingers. I pulled my arm close, wrapping it around myself, and put the other arm on top, pressing it to my stomach. I hoped it wouldn't be long till the bleeding stopped.

With my arm safely tucked in, I looked up at Jonathon. He was no longer lying on the floor but crouched low, facing me. His mouth was open and his eyes were wide, and entirely too focussed on me.

"Jonathon?" My voice shook.

He slowly stood up. His eyes were still fixed on my arm. I tried to press it closer to me. His shirt was black with blood but it didn't look as though there was any more coming out.

"Bastards." He spat the word out.

I didn't know what to say, but my face must have been enough to ask for an explanation.

"They bled me. I need to feed, and soon. My wounds will heal but I can't replenish the blood. Then they go and cut you. If I kill you I do them a favour, and Fraser will end up killing me. If I don't kill you, I'll be too weak to fight them and I die anyway." He backed up to the wall and sank to the floor.

I mirrored his actions, moving to the opposite wall, but I didn't sit down. The hairs on my neck stood on end. Now I realised what Vincent had meant when he said it would be more interesting. My muscles were tense. I tried not to move too much. I didn't want the scent of my blood to fill the room. I kept my arm tight against me.

I watched Jonathon. He finally managed to tear his gaze away from me, and focussed on the wall opposite him. "I can't guarantee that I will be able to refrain. It's a question of time." His voice was quiet.

Realising he wasn't about to charge me, I sank down to the damp floor. Sighing, I shook my head, trying to clear it to think of a way out. I tried to consider options. Fraser said he was coming, but I didn't know where he was, when he would arrive, and how he would manage to get us out. Eventually Jonathon was going to charge across the room and drink my blood. The only question was time. We could try to get out of here together, but he was weak and so was I after all the bumps to my head. Jonathon said there were more than we originally saw. I tried to count how many I had seen but gave up after ten. There was no way the two of us could beat ten.

I pulled my knees up in front of me to keep my arms pressed against my stomach. My back scratched the wall behind me. I could ask Fraser some questions but everyone would hear me. I wanted to talk to Jonathon but I didn't entirely trust him. He was disapproving of Fraser and me. He didn't like me, and blamed me for this whole situation. I also didn't want to break whatever concentration kept him on the other side of the room from me. His eyes showed the effort it took, his nostrils flared, and his knuckles were white as he clenched his hands. Considering that he didn't like me, I wondered why he went to the effort to restrain himself.

I closed my eyes and tried to ignore the warmth spreading across my stomach, and think of a way to get out of this situation. I concentrated on Fraser, wondering how close he was. I scanned the area around me, picking up Jonathon first, and then another vampire in the corridor outside our room. The next ones I could pick out were above us, and there were several of them. Next to them, away to the side, were a couple of humans. I frowned, wondering why they were here, but couldn't spend too long thinking about it. Judging from the position of everyone, I guessed we were being held in the basement of the building. I then moved outward, trying to find who was close to the building, but couldn't find anyone: vampire or human.

I sighed and prepared to wait, wait on me thinking of a way out of this. I put my forehead on my knees and closed my eyes, trying to think. I had no way to measure time, and I lost track as I muddled through my thoughts.

Stephanie?

I pulled in a breath, my ribs screaming in the process. My head fell back onto the wall behind me and my eyes flew open.

Don't respond if you can hear me, as they will know.

I listened, my heart pounding, waiting to hear Fraser's voice again.

I think we should be closer to your position now. We are in an area of deserted woollen mills and warehouses. I don't know how to confirm this with you without them knowing we are near. I don't even know if you can hear me.

His voice sounded frustrated.

My eyes stung. He was so close. I'd managed to locate him as he was talking and he was only a few blocks away. Chris, Craig and Ross were with him as well. They were spread out over a few different buildings but were still fairly close together. I focussed on him, trying to picture him in more detail, seeing where he was exactly, just like Craig had tried to get me to do when I was sparring. I had to try.

Can you hear me?

I could feel his shock. It was really weird to explain. He didn't say anything, but I could feel his shock, almost see his stunned expression. I looked across to Jonathon and he hadn't moved. His expression was still strained. I couldn't tell if he had heard me or not, and I didn't want to disturb him.

Stephanie, you just spoke directly to me. You didn't project!

Does speaking directly to you have the same effect for you, as when you speak to me?

He laughed. *Yes! I'm currently holding onto a wall to stay upright.*

His voice sounded ridiculously happy at the situation, but I didn't waste time puzzling over it.

You are close. Right now Craig is the closest. Jonathon and I are in a basement.

I hesitated, not sure what to say. I didn't want to tell him to hurry as I knew what was waiting for him upstairs. At the same time Jonathon didn't look too great either.

Be careful. They know you are coming.

Of course. You will be safe soon.

I swallowed and looked across to Jonathon, trying to pick up the courage to speak.

"They are near. They are coming for us." My voice wasn't very strong but it was enough for him to turn his eyes towards me. He snorted in response. I didn't know what to say so I just shut up and wondered what we could do to help.

"We could try and cause a bit of a distraction, when they are near. I'm guessing it would help."

"What kind of distraction would you suggest?" His voice wasn't friendly, and goose bumps appeared on my arms at his harsh tone.

"Well, there is only one of them outside this room. Surely between the two of us we could take him?"

He just snorted in response again, and I could feel anger starting to build up in me, washing away my nervousness and tiredness. He wasn't being particularly helpful. It was almost as if he was resigned to this.

"I won't be able to take him on my own, not like this." He gestured down to his blood-soaked shirt. "You have now lost so much blood you won't be much use either." He sounded angry but defeated at the same time. This just annoyed me even more. Surely he could use that anger to get out of here?

"Well, you can barely stand the smell of me right now, correct?" He nodded jerkily. "So could we not use that? I could go out the door and the smell of me will distract the guy so much you could jump him when he isn't prepared."

This time Jonathon turned his head as well as his eyes to me. "That might work. But what about after. You're not planning on going upstairs and fighting your way out of here, are you?"

"No. I just thought one less could help. And if some of them turn around with their attention focussed on us, then the rest of the guys will be able to get close unnoticed." My voice was stronger now. The plan seemed to make sense to me.

"Right. So we wait on them coming close, then get out this room and get rid of that guy out there." I nodded to myself, feeling better for having a plan and not just being the bait. I shivered. It must be night-time. It was feeling colder – either that or the damp in this place was getting to me. I pulled my knees closer, and felt my wet top move against my skin. It was cooling down, which wasn't helping me feel warm. I didn't really want to look down at it. I didn't want to see the bloodstain. Jonathon had said I'd lost a fair bit of blood and I suppose he should know about these things. Looking would only make me feel worse, and blood on clothing always looked worse than it was. I settled down to wait.

Stephanie. We've found the building you're in. We are approaching now. You will soon be safe.

I opened my eyes, not realising I'd dozed off. Jonathon sat frozen in the same position as before.

"Time for us to move; they are just about here."

Jonathon stood up in one smooth motion, whilst I struggled to stretch out my stiff legs and put my arm down to lean on the ground. When I did I heard Jonathon suck air in between his teeth, and I quickly looked up at him, freezing where I was. His eyes were staring at my T-shirt.

"Let's get this done quickly." His voice was strained. I stole a glance at myself as I stood up but didn't manage to see anything as I swayed and lost my vision. I groped out and felt the wall, leaning into it, panting. My vision slowly returned. Jonathon still stood on the other side of the room.

"Like I said, you're not going to be much use."

"Thanks, but I'll still try."

He shrugged and gestured me towards the door, I noticed he didn't move any closer. My legs were shaky as I walked, but I managed to reach the door in a fairly straight line and I was still upright, with no loss of vision, so I was quite proud.

Maybe this will work.

It had to be of some help. Four against nine was better odds than four against ten. At least I might distract some of them, hopefully not the ones on my side.

I pulled on the door and the hinges protested, loosing some rust in the process. A shadow moved across, blocking the doorway. He was bigger than me, but that wasn't a surprise, he wasn't huge though. He looked to be in his early twenties, though that was no indication of what age he really was. His clothes were up to date – jeans and a long-sleeved jumper. He looked down at me with a bored expression.

"Hey, is there a toilet around here somewhere?" As I spoke his face changed. His eyes dropped from mine and saw the T-shirt. His pupils dilated and his focus shifted to my arm. Having just moved it, I could feel the cut had pulled open. I tried not to concentrate on it too much or I would puke. The guy stepped forward, staring at my arm. I'm sure he wasn't aware of anything else. I stepped back, leading him into the room.

From my peripheral vision I could see Jonathon moving round behind him, now blocking the exit for the guy. He then stopped, hesitating. The other vampire was still moving towards me and I shot a panicked look at Jonathon. This was only going to work if he helped. There was no way I could fight this guy off on my own.

Why is he hesitating?

I could feel my heart rate increase. I started to breathe quicker, my ribs sending little stabbing sensations across my side. Adrenaline finally kicked in. I was beginning to wonder if I had run out of it. My arms and legs tingled as it shot through my veins. My arm was starting to feel warm on the outside, and I guessed the blood had started flowing out of the cut again.

Jonathon sent a cold smile over the other vampire's shoulder at me, "This will solve quite a few problems." With a nod to me, he turned and left.

I froze. He'd left me. Now I was stuck in the room with a vampire drooling over my blood and standing between me and the only exit.

Shit!

He lunged straight at me and I spun round, elbowing him in the ribs as he passed me. He stopped quickly and I faced him. I tried to move slowly back to the door, which I was now closer to, but he lunged in again. He tried to grab my cut arm but I pulled it away and used the heel of my other hand to smack his jaw and push his head back, twisting as I did it. He staggered back a step but that was all. Then he turned and faced me again.

My breathing was loud but the pounding in my ears from my rapid pulse was louder. I quickly tried to reassess this guy. I hadn't been sizing him up before, thinking that Jonathon was going to do the hard bit.

Bastard!

He'd left me. There was not liking me, but then there was assisting in my murder.

Focus, Steph. Don't get distracted.

Pep talk over, I looked back at the vampire in front of me. He was still focussed on my arm and not really registering the person it was attached to. If his focus stayed like that I would have a better chance. He didn't seem to be any great strategist as he'd only managed wild lunges so far. There was really no point in looking at his build. As a vampire he was way stronger than me, no matter how he was built.

I had to get out of the door, away from this dead end. Hopefully I might meet one of the vampires on my side.

I started to sidestep towards the door, and the vampire mirrored me, stepping closer at the same time. His mouth was open, body hunched in a half-crouch. His arms were out to the side, like he was trying to shoo me into the corner. With his next step he lunged again, this time reaching straight out for my bleeding arm. I blocked across my body with my other arm, and then twisted, backhanding him with my fist as I straightened. I heard the crack as my knuckles connected with his cheekbone but it took a couple of seconds before the pain registered. Then I yelled out, which just spurred him on again.

I wasn't prepared; I was too distracted by the shooting pain going up my hand. I just kept back-peddling frantically through the doorway until I hit a wall behind me. My arms were definitely out of action so I brought a foot up, thrusting out at the rapidly approaching vampire. It connected just below his ribs, which would have winded and floored anyone else but this guy just paused long enough to grab my ankle and swing my leg aside.

The movement of my leg twisted me round, and my back ended up to him. In a blink he was there to my side, hands fastened either side of my bleeding forearm. I tried to twist my arm but there was no way I could break his grip. Panicking, I brought my leg up and stomped down on his knee joint. The adrenaline must have given me an extra boost as his knee gave way and he fell to the floor. Unfortunately he still had a hold of my arm, so I staggered forward as well.

I felt a blur behind me. I had an awareness that we were no longer alone, and my heart plunged. I was struggling enough with one of them. Two, and I had no chance. I felt my body go limp, adrenaline leaving as I realised there really was no hope. My legs gave way and I barely registered my knees smacking the concrete floor. I looked round at the face that was centimetres away from my arm, his mouth stretching open, his lips pulling back from his teeth. A hand appeared on his face, grabbing his jaw. Then the head yanked out of view.

I frowned, confused, still kneeling on the floor. I felt myself falling forward, with a random thought floating through my head.

Wonder if they don't like sharing?

Chapter Twenty-One

I was bouncing. Could feel the motion of the top half of my body flopping. Next thing I registered was the pain. Pain in my stomach and enough pain in my ribs to make me scream if there had been any air left in my lungs from the bouncing. Someone was carrying me in a fireman's lift.

God, I hate this lift!

Apart from it being really painful to have someone's shoulder in your stomach it had to be the most undignified way to be carried ever, with your bum on view to the world.

I retched, but couldn't bring much up. The motion and soreness was making me feel extremely nauseous. I finished coughing, and became aware of noise around me. Banging, yelling. I couldn't make anything out other than it was noisy.

I was unceremoniously dumped on the floor, where I tried to retch again, without much success. I panted into the concrete and tried to see what was surrounding me. My sore arm was lifted up by someone, but my body remained on the floor.

"Fraser!" A voice yelled the challenge above me.

All other noise seemed to die out. The drumbeat of footsteps signalled someone's fast approach. The footsteps stopped and I turned my head to try and see who it was. Feet were the only thing in focus.

Stephanie!

I sucked air in.

Fraser!

Someone waved my arm above me, wiggling my wrist as though I was waving to them.

"Here she is." An oily voice spoke above me. "Who would have thought you would go to these lengths for a human?" The tone was definitely mocking.

"Hand her over." Fraser's voice was torn. I couldn't decide if it was cold or desperate.

Vincent just laughed, "You know, you've really made this more fun than I imagined. I came here to hassle you, destroy your life like you did to me. Instead I've managed to attract the attention of several groups, inspire some youngsters, and enjoy a bit of freedom. All of these will cause you trouble on their own. But I really did not think to find you matched; that would be too sweet a revenge. And with a human!" He laughed.

"You know fine well why you got the punishment you had. This has nothing to do with that. Now hand her over!" I'd never heard Fraser's voice raised. The power in it was clear and it sounded scary, even though he was fighting for me.

I lay still, trying to understand what was going on. I could see Fraser now. He was about ten metres in front of me, with Chris and Craig to either side and Ross further back. The building was dark, with some light coming from the side. There must have been a room lit up over there. Everything was in shades of grey and brown, only the light on clothing revealing some colour.

Wonder what my top looks like?

Awful, but you're going to be OK.

I hadn't actually meant to project that thought but my concentration was a bit off.

"Uh uh, no talking now! It seems you've forgotten a few things, Fraser." Vincent raised his arm, holding onto my wrist, and my torso lifted up off the floor. I couldn't stop a pathetic squeal in the process, which I immediately regretted when Fraser's face tightened.

There were sounds of a scuffle coming from behind some crates piled to one side. Chris and Craig turned their heads to see what it was, though they didn't move from where they stood. Fraser continued staring at Vincent, who had let me back down to the floor but still had one hand encasing my wrist.

"Finally caught up with him, Boss!" Jason appeared around the crate, followed by two others on either arm of a snarling Jonathon. Jason had a smug grin on his face, which just widened as his gaze dropped from Vincent towards me.

"Good! Now he's stopped running he can add to the confusion by finally choosing a side." Vincent's head turned back to Fraser, and I could just imagine the evil grin on his face.

Craig was frowning as he watched Jonathon and his guards, who let go of Jonathon's arms as they propelled him forward to the middle ground between the two groups. Jonathon's head swung between Fraser and Vincent. Fraser didn't even acknowledge him, and kept focussed on Vincent.

"Fraser, I had to take the chance to get out. I thought I could find you, show you where we were, and help you get Steph out of this." Jonathon's voice sounded pleading but then I had been there when he'd abandoned me, so I knew it should be pleading.

I could feel my mouth opening. He had run at his first opportunity, leaving me in a situation I was very lucky to get out of. He'd already known that Fraser was coming. I'd told him! The only thing he had in his favour was that he didn't kill me himself.

Despite feeling as though I'd run a marathon (which would be some achievement for me), been ten rounds with a heavyweight boxer, and as weak as a newborn pup, I could feel my outrage growing, fuelling me.

How dare he!

I didn't care if they all heard me. It wasn't just old familiar adrenaline running back through my veins now. It was anger. Heat spread down my limbs, and my arm was trembling in Vincent's grip. He glanced down and then laughed, clearly taking it as fear. Fraser's eyes dropped to me as well, but his face was unreadable. His eyes seemed grey rather than blue.

I just wanted to hit something. My muscles were trembling with the effort of holding still, not with fear. I looked round, analysing the layout of everyone for the first time, knowing I was going to fight my way out of here, not be carried out. It didn't seem as dark any more. The colours on clothes stood out, edges sharper, as though my vision had just swapped to 3D. I could read the body language of those who had brought Jonathon. Jason seemed the most eager. One other looked capable but the last one didn't look confident at all.

"Ah, just in time. I thought they were going to miss the fun." My jailer lifted a hand and gestured to his left. Three more of his group came through a doorway, one holding some contraption at his side which I couldn't make out.

Nerves came back to me but I was still eager to get up and hit something. Now there was just a cautionary edge to my enthusiasm to hit something. There were four vampires and an injured human of Fraser's side – who knew where Jonathon stood? – and seven vampires, including Vincent, against us. Jason clearly had enough brain cells to be able to count, as his grin just kept getting wider.

"Come now, Fraser. Surely you have faced worse odds before? Or can you not do it without an enforcer by your side?" Vincent taunted.

I had no clue what an enforcer was, and all the conversation between these two definitely hinted at a past which I was *so* going to find out about later. But right now I couldn't care. I just wanted to get started, and then get the hell out of here.

"Hand her over and this will be quick. Last chance," Fraser's voice warned, one foot slipping back to balance out his body more.

"No." Vincent's voice was final and gloating. "Peter?" His hand gestured to those on the left again, and the one with the contraption lifted it up and aimed. It took a while to realise what it was. I'd never seen one in real life – only in films. It was an old-fashioned crossbow.

By the time I realised this, it had been fired and my head snapped round to find out who had given the ragged gasp. Jonathon stood in no man's land, staring down at the wooden bolt sticking out of his chest, presumably in his heart. As his head lifted up there was a roar, and suddenly Ross was on the guy who had fired the cross bolt. Chris quickly followed after him as he disappeared between the three vampires.

Craig took the distraction and leapt at Jason and his friends. A snarl bought my attention back to those closest to me. As I looked back a blur streaked above my head, knocking Vincent to the floor behind me. Two bodies rolled over each other, with vicious snarls and growls emanating from the tangle. Just as quickly they pulled apart. Vincent and Fraser stood a few metres apart and paced around each other, looking for an opening.

I was still on the floor, and had barely taken a breath since the explosion of action. I was jolted out of this when a hand closed round my ankle and dragged me across the floor. Kicking out with my ankle, I looked down towards my feet to see who had me. I should have really known before I looked. Jason.

"Now, just like I said before, I always get what I want!" He dropped my leg and reached for my arms. I kicked his knee, and then rolled to the side, getting up in the process. He looked at me in disbelief as I settled into a wide stance and brought my hands up.

"You can't fight me. I would have beaten you flat as a human, never mind now!" He looked amused, which wasn't exactly what I was aiming for but I suppose I didn't look much of a threat right now. "Suppose there is nothing to stop me playing with my food!" He gave a laugh and lunged in with a punch aimed for my head, which I dodged and then gave him a roundhouse kick to his stomach as I moved.

He continued testing me, coming in with attacks that were getting quicker and quicker. I tried to retaliate when I could, but opportunities were getting fewer as he picked up speed. Dodging wasn't as easy when he moved quicker, and I was having to use my arms to block his attacks, and retaliate with side kicks or knees.

The inevitable happened. His punch landed. Having not moved quick enough, it landed on my cheek instead of nose, but was still enough for me to lose my sight as my head rang with the collection of blows I'd had today.

I sensed movement and managed to drop to all fours as something whistled over me. Jason's grunt made me smile. He'd missed. This reminded me of Craig's tips on fighting a vampire. Keeping my eyes shut, I focussed on the position of Jason. It was confusing, with so many people around me. Ones that I cared about stood out more in my mind, so narrowing on Jason took a bit of concentration.

Eventually he came into focus: the rough outline of a body with no details – just an outline, a shape. I had to read the body language. His weight was on his back foot, but his arms were down and his head was forward, leaning towards me. He was curious, wondering what I was doing.

Standing up, I kept my eyes closed, concentrating. Jason decided to take advantage, and moved forward. Looking at him this way, in my head, he seemed to move slower than before. It was just as Craig had said: my human reflexes weren't fast enough to keep up, whereas my new talents could.

I easily dodged Jason's punch, and grabbed his wrist, twisting his arm and smashing through it with my elbow. His breath shot out in a grunt and he yanked his arm back out of my grasp, which nearly sent me toppling as I still didn't have the vampire's strength. Eyes squeezed shut. I watched his reaction. His arm hung down straight and he didn't try to bend it. It should have been broken but I had no idea what it would take to break his arm.

He lunged forward, this time with his hand open, trying to grab me. I sidestepped again, except he reacted quicker now and moved his hand to grab the top of my arm. I overlapped his hand with mine, not that I needed to reinforce his grip, and then stepped into him and twisted my hips, my leg shooting out behind his, and he fell over.

It was a great view for me – one I could play over and over again as his legs went flying up in the air, the arm not holding me spread out trying to grab anything. His grip tightening on me was enough to leave bruises and make me yell, but it was still a great sight. So the move wasn't textbook but I was quickly learning that fighting in real life wasn't textbook. As he landed I heard his breath leave in an almighty whoosh and he lay still for a second, which I took advantage of and wrestled my arm free from his hand. As I moved back a step a familiar shape jumped into view between Jason and myself.

I opened my eyes, wincing at the sudden influx of light. Craig's back was to me and he leant over the winded Jason, blocking my view. Although I couldn't see what he was doing, I did hear the sickening crack as Craig's shoulders moved. It was as though someone had plunged me in ice.

Craig stood up and turned to me. "You were doing all right there! See you were trying out the whole second sight thing." He paused. I suppose he was expecting an answer but I couldn't take my eyes off the legs lying still behind him.

"Oh, sorry. I forget. He's dead, Steph, properly dead. He won't bother you again." He walked towards me and so revealed the prone figure on the floor. Jason looked exactly the same, yet smaller somehow. As Craig moved beside me, Jason started to change. His skin quickly turned grey, and then almost black. It tightened against his bones as though all the fat was being sucked out of him. Eventually it was so tight it seemed to disintegrate, exposing muscles and tendons underneath. They were a dark grey as well, and looked like charcoal – all dry and shrivelled. Eventually the few bones and tissues that were left collapsed under their own weight, and all that was left of Jason was a pile of dust on the floor.

I stood frozen, horrified by what I'd seen. If ever I'd thought that vampires were like me I'd been wrong. You could forget what they were when you chatted with them, but this brought it home. No matter how different people are in life, they are all the same in death. With vampires: for all they seem the same in life, they are totally different in death.

My eyes swung round to the middle of the room, where Jonathon had been shot. He wasn't there. Only a pile of dust on the floor showed that he had ever been there. Quickly my eyes sought out the others. Ross stood with Chris, not far from the pile of ashes in the middle of the room. Ross was looking at the ashes. Chris stood looking further into the room. My eyes followed his gaze to the side of the room and to Fraser. He stood with his back to us. Beyond him I could just make out my captor, his back against the wall.

Vincent was stringing a volley of abuse at Fraser. I didn't have a clue what was being said as it was no language I'd heard of. Keeping my eyes on them, I asked Craig, "You got any idea what they're saying?"

"Nope, but I'm guessing they're not exchanging niceties." He sounded calm.

"Shouldn't you guys go and help him?" My voice had a shake again. Well, my bravado couldn't last for ever.

Craig snorted. "Nah, we'd just get in the road. Fraser won't have any trouble. Vincy boy was relying on us being outnumbered and surprised, but you foiled the surprise."

"Oh." I stayed focussed on the other side of the room. Vincent's face was contorted up, his hands were clawed, and there was spit flying from his mouth as he hurled abuse. I couldn't help but be nervous for Fraser. The other vampire was cornered and that's when animals were at their most dangerous.

I couldn't tell who moved first; they were just suddenly on each other.

Their movements blurred together and I couldn't follow the attack with my eyes but I should be able to see them in my head. It took a whole lot of willpower but eventually I was able to close my eyes.

Fraser was crystal clear, but Vincent was an indistinct figure. Just like before, everything seemed to slow down, and I could see the block and attacks that Fraser and Vincent were using on each other. Vincent's arm snaked out and struck Fraser's jaw. Fraser's head went flying back and he staggered back a couple of steps. There was a strangled shout, which I think came from me, and I stepped forward automatically, my eyes pinging open. A pair of hands grabbed my shoulders and held me in place.

"You can't help, Steph. Believe me, Fraser can handle this." Craig's voice was right beside me.

It was difficult to close my eyes again, so counter-intuitive – to see something you normally keep your eyes open. Even with them shut, things started to speed up. Vincent was making mistakes though, over-reaching and leaving openings. When a big gap appeared Fraser stepped in, grabbing Vincent's throat and slamming him against the wall behind. Vincent's head rebounded a couple of times. Fraser's mouth moved as though he was whispering to him. Then he leaned back and brought his other hand up.

The snap of Vincent's neck could be heard throughout the old factory as there was no one else making any noise.

Except for my overly loud breathing.

Fraser stepped away from the body as it fell to the floor. He turned around as it faded to grey then black. Once he was facing me I couldn't look away from his face, not even to watch Vincent finally dying. Fraser's expression was tight, angry almost, as he looked up to where I was standing. It made me freeze for a moment until his eyes met mine, and then the tension left his face. He blurred, and then reappeared, standing so close to me that I started to stagger back. His arms shot round my back, catching me before I'd moved a step.

"Stephanie." His whisper was full of relief. He pulled me close, kissing my forehead as his arms tightened around me. I leaned into his chest, emotions whirling through me. I could feel tears start to sting my eyes. As Fraser's arms tightened I couldn't help wincing as a stab of pain shot through my ribs. Of course Fraser immediately noticed. Releasing his grip on me and taking a half-step back, he looked me over as though for the first time. His mouth thinned into a line.

"We need to get you to a doctor." His voice was back, sounding tight again. "Craig, can you bring the car to the door?"

"Of course."

Craig shot away, the sudden movement making me stagger. Fraser leaned down, his arms moving to lift me up.

"No." My voice was sharper than I meant it to be and he froze, frowning down at me. I tried to carry on a bit softer. "I swore I was going to walk out of this, not be carried."

He gave a half-smile and shook his head. "You can at least take my arm before you pass out." He held his arm out, which I leant on gratefully. The room was starting to spin.

He led me away from where the fight had been, and out through an empty doorway. We stopped once we were outside as I scrunched my eyes up against the sudden blinding brightness. A thin white covering lay on the ground, leaving only the outlines of close objects visible. Thick white flakes were falling from the sky, making the brickwork on the buildings next to us indistinct. I shivered, the cold seeming much more intense than it should have been.

A car pulled up next to us. It wasn't Fraser's Audi but a silver four-by-four. I didn't know what make it was and I didn't care as long as there was heating inside. Craig jumped out, leaving the door open, and walked towards us. The cold seemed to be sinking into me, and I could feel my eyelids wanting to close. I gripped onto Fraser's arm as I took a step towards the car, but my foot didn't land right and I started to fall. Strong arms caught me and lifted me up. I didn't feel any movement but I could hear the hum of an engine and, for once, I didn't care – I was just too tired.

Chapter Twenty-Two

I was warm. Moving my legs, I could feel the starchy sheets that covered me. Only my arm felt cool as it was on top of them. My nose stung with the antiseptic that was in the air. Light shone through my eyelids. It must have been bright as my eyelids seemed red. I was in a hospital. I'd been in enough of them with Ailsa to recognise the key parts.

I opened my eyes and looked up at a ceiling that seemed really far away. Blinking a few times, I remembered everything that had happened and noted that my eyelids didn't seem as puffy any more. I wrinkled my nose, partly due to the smell, and also to see if the movement hurt my face. I could hear a rustling next to me and I turned my head round to see who was there. I smiled when I saw Fraser.

"How are you feeling?" he asked, his eyes scanning my face.

"Don't really know yet. I don't want to move." I gave a half-smile at my cowardice, and he smiled back.

"You lost quite a lot of blood. They had to do a few transfusions, so it is normal to feel weak." He continued staring at me as I tried to read his face.

I heard the door opening to the room and I turned, looking round the room for the first time. It was a private room with lots of space. A cot was set up on the other side next to a sink and a few cupboards, and there was a huge bay window with blinds tilted over it. As I took in the shape and dimensions I frowned. This wasn't a normal hospital. If it was, then it was in a really old building. I looked back to the opening door to see who was coming in.

A middle-aged guy with a heavy stomach and greying hair walked in, wearing a white coat and the standard stethoscope around his neck. He peered over his glasses and smiled when he saw me looking back at him.

"Good afternoon. I'm glad to see you awake." He smiled at me in what seemed like an overindulgent grandfather sort of way. I was just waiting on the Wether's Originals appearing from his pocket.

He reached for my wrist and started taking my pulse. "How are you feeling?" he asked, whilst still staring at his watch.

"Tired." I didn't really know what else to say. I seemed to ache everywhere but I suppose that was to be expected. I'd had a fight with some vampires, after all.

He checked my pupil responses and looked at my chart, which was over by the cupboards, and then stood at the foot of the bed, letting his glasses dangle on the cord around his neck, to give his prognosis.

"Well, you seem to be recovering fine. The wound on your arm appears to be clean. Your other hand will have to stay in a brace until the knuckles fully heal. I'm afraid there is not much to be done for broken ribs apart from taping you up and lots of rest. The swelling on your face has gone down considerably, and there was no real damage done there. I want to keep you in for another day, just to be sure you don't have any side effects from your head injuries. After that you will be free to go." There was a small frown on his face as he tried to smile at me again, and I wondered what he thought had caused all of this.

Fraser spoke next to the bed. "Thank you, Malcolm; I'm very grateful for this."

"Yes, yes. Well get some rest, and I'll see you later in the day." He tapped his pen against the chart for a moment longer. Then he seemed to come out of his thoughts, and went back out the door.

I looked back to Fraser. "What did you tell him?"

"Nothing," he replied. "Malcolm and I have known each other for quite a while. I've helped him in a few tricky spots and he provides some medical care if ever we need it, and gets paid well for not asking questions."

"Oh." I took that in. "You didn't have to bring me here. You could have just taken me to A & E. I hit my head, so I wouldn't be expected to remember anything."

Fraser just shook his head and smiled down at me. "You weren't going anywhere without me, and only to doctors who I knew were good."

"Oh." My vocab seemed to be a bit limited with all the knocks to my head.

He sat on the edge of the bed and stroked my hair, "Sleep, Stephanie. You're safe now and I'll be here when you wake."

My eyes closed over, even though I didn't really want them to.

I could hear the murmur of low voices. The room didn't seem as bright through my eyelids this time. The voices stopped as I rolled over towards them and opened my eyes. Chris and Fraser sat in a couple of chairs next to the bed, looking back at me. They both smiled as I focussed on them.

"Good to see you looking better," Chris commented.

"Good to feel better," I smiled back.

There was a pause. "So what were you guys talking about?"

"Vincent, you, and how this whole situation came about," Chris replied.

I froze where I lay, looking back and forward between them.

Is this it? Is this where they decide I'm too much hassle? Just like Jonathon, they are not going to want me in their lives?

"Relax, Stephanie. Nothing will change between us." Fraser gave Chris an exasperated look.

"Sorry. I wasn't meaning it in that way. Just that we were talking over everything that has happened." Chris looked apologetic and I finally exhaled. "Once you are better we'd be keen to hear what happened to you."

"Well, it would pass some time just now," I replied, getting myself more comfy in the bed.

"You don't have to talk about it just now, Stephanie. It can wait." Fraser sat up, looking concerned.

"No, it's better to talk about it now. It's over anyway. Nothing else is going to happen."

So I told my version of events. It was awkward to talk about Jonathon, especially the part where he left the room without me. He had been their companion for years, but I remember Fraser once saying that he didn't consider him a friend. Chris did not look impressed with this news, and Fraser's hands tightened on the armrest of the chair until there was an audible crack. By the time I'd finished, my throat was dry. Fraser handed me a glass of water from the side table.

"That fills in some of the blanks," Chris said.

"Yes it does," Fraser replied.

We sat in silence for a while, and I felt my eyes begin to get heavy again.

When I next woke it was bright again, and judging by the noise of traffic outside it was daytime. My head was clear, and some of the aches were easing. I pulled myself up in the bed and everything didn't spin in the process.

Fraser looked over from the window and smiled at me, moving over to sit on the bed.

"Feeling better?"

"Much better." I smiled back. "When can I get out of here?"

He laughed. "Malcolm is coming round again in a few hours. Then, if he is happy, I'll take you back to the flat."

I sat there without saying anything, just happy to be awake and feeling almost normal. Fraser sat on the edge of the bed and held my hand. My thoughts drifted over everything that had happened but I wasn't panicked about it. It was as though I was floating above it all and could look down on it, separate from me.

"So how did you know Vincent?" I asked Fraser.

He looked round at my face, searching my eyes.

"I think I've got a right to know." I kept eye contact with him and he sighed, looking away.

"Yes you do have a right to know. I only met him once before, a long time ago." He stared out of the open blinds on the window. "I was turned, against my will. My maker was not being discreet about his activities, and so orders came for him to be killed. The top enforcer came to carry out the deed."

He must have seen my confusion as he explained, "an enforcer is like the police for the vampire world, except there aren't any trials. If you've broken rules or brought attention to yourself, then an enforcer is sent to kill you.

"Sankataharana is the most feared enforcer. He is the best at what he does, partly because his talent is killing – even his name means 'remover of difficulties' – but also because he is so old he predates most modern calendar systems. There is not much known about him by younger vampires, except that you don't cross him.

"San was sent to kill my maker. He killed him, along with most of the group, as young ones are not to be left alone. He found my communication skills useful and so kept me around. I travelled with him for a long time – around a hundred and forty years. I learnt a lot about survival and fighting from him."

I stayed as still and quiet as I could. This was the most information I had got about Fraser's past, and I didn't want to distract him.

"One of San's jobs was to stop a vampire who was using his talent to make people do what he wanted, and so was becoming conspicuous. It was Vincent. He had turned people against their will. The same as happened to me. He killed humans, which is allowed, but he was excessive. He used his talent to influence politics, royalty, and to gain extensive power and wealth. His talent is, was, slight persuasion. You were more open to his ideas. That is why you wanted to move towards him even though you knew you shouldn't. The powers-that-be in the vampire world decided he had to go.

"San needed my help in the job, as Vincent had gathered a lot of followers. We destroyed the coven, including his closest friends and lovers. Vincent himself managed to escape though. He ordered his followers to stop us at any cost, so they all died covering his exit.

"The constant dealing of death to all those vampires and humans turned me away from that life. I was still new to being a vampire, and the human belief in the sanctity of life hadn't left me. San continued working as an enforcer and hunted Vincent as he was the only one ever to escape him. Vincent's talent made him difficult to catch. Last I heard he was hiding in Russia. It seems that he decided to get back at us for all he had lost, and I was the much easier target rather than San."

He continued to stare out of the window once he had finished. I could imagine him replaying scenes from his past. How Fraser could ever be considered a much easier target was beyond my imagination. He blinked, coming back out of his reverie, and then looked at me.

"I'm sorry my past put you in danger. You should never have been in that situation." His voice was quiet.

"Well, it's not exactly your fault. You don't need to apologise for Vincent's psycho behaviour. And besides, if being in a little bit of danger means I get to be with you, then I think I'll cope." I tried to give him a cheeky grin to lift the mood, and he gave a small smile back. He leant down closer and kissed me. His lips were light on mine, as though he was trying not to hurt me, and he pulled back far too soon for my liking.

"Hopefully we'll get to carry that on soon?" I asked once I got my bearings again, and he gave a laugh in reply, smiling properly at me.

Doctor Grandad pronounced me fit to go home as long as I was looked after and took it easy. He piled clean dressings and bandages on us for my arm, and warned that with the first sign of infection I was to come back.

I stepped outside and pulled in a huge lungful of cold air, lifting my head up to look at the light grey clouds above us. The bare branches of trees opposite were swaying in a steady breeze, adding their rustling sound to the drone of traffic a few streets over.

"God, I'm glad to be out of there. I hate hospitals." I started to walk down the steps at the front of the sandstone building.

"That wasn't technically a hospital," Fraser pointed out.

"Close enough."

Fraser took my unbraced hand, giving it a light squeeze, and steered me along the pavement. He carried a bag filled with toiletries and spare clothes he had brought for me. I hadn't asked how he had got into my flat and picked out the clothes without anyone noticing him. Figured it was just better to appreciate it rather than puzzling over it.

His Audi was parked along the road and I eased myself in, my ribs protesting a bit at the movement. Soon we were back at Park Circus and it wasn't until we were out of the car and walking up the stairs to his flat that I realised that I hadn't been panicked at all by being in the car. I froze between two steps when this realisation hit, and Fraser turned back to me, concern on his face,

"Are you OK? Is it too sore? Do you want me to carry you up the stairs?" He walked back down two steps to my side.

"No, it's not that;" – though I was out of breath from climbing the stairs – "I just realised I've been in a car and not freaked out. Not even noticed. I wasn't bothered at all." I looked up at him, excited and confused at the same time.

"Does this mean you trust my driving, or have you got over your fear of cars?" He smiled back at me.

"I don't know, but either way, it's good. Maybe it's just a reality check. You know; face bad things and suddenly the smaller stuff doesn't seem so bad any more."

Fraser nodded and put his hand under my elbow, guiding me back up the steps. "Well at least that's one good thing: you don't need to rely on public transport any more."

I laughed and we moved up the stairs again. Once in the flat Fraser insisted that I call my mum and flatmates so that they knew I was OK. It took a while to decide what to tell them. For my mum, who only knew that I hadn't called for a few days, she got the lost phone charger story, which seemed plausible, and we chatted fine. I hadn't missed anything with them. For my flatmates I decided to say that I'd been staying at Fraser's. I phoned Lauren, who completely bought that story. Why wouldn't I stay with the hunk of a boyfriend? I deliberately didn't call Natasha as she would have been more suspicious about the sudden sleepover, with no texts from me.

Fraser cooked me a meal and watched me eat it all, saying that I had to eat properly to get my strength back. After that I was knackered, so tired after what were only a few simple tasks. I flaked out on the couch.

Fraser carried me through to his room and put me in his bed. As he straightened, I woke up more. "Don't go." I grabbed his wrist, stopping him moving away.

"It's OK. I'm not going anywhere." He walked round to the other side of the bed and climbed in, pulling me close to him. I curled up to his chest, feeling the heat from his body warm me. His hand traced patterns on my back and I started to drift off to sleep again, when I remembered a question from earlier.

"Vincent said that we were matched. What did he mean by that?" Fraser's hand stopped moving for a second on my back, and then he started tracing patterns again.

"It's difficult to explain," he avoided.

"Try me." My voice was stronger as my curiosity was aroused.

He gave a snort and I could imagine him smiling though I couldn't see his face as I was still curled up to his chest. His chin rested on the top of my head.

"Do you remember when you asked why when I spoke to you it had such an effect?" I nodded, not wanting to interrupt him. "I said it had to do with emotions. My emotions. If I controlled them when I was talking to you, then they wouldn't have that effect."

I nodded again, wanting him to get on with explaining it. "I remember."

"Well, when a vampire is matched, he cares for that person deeply. It's as though there is no one else, only them. Kind of like the idea of a soul mate, but stronger. If that happens, then as they get older their psychic connection gets stronger as well, and eventually when they can talk to each other telepathically, this connection can project their emotions to each other. So if you love someone enough, this love will come through the psychic connection. I'm told it can be quite something in certain situations."

I hadn't moved as he spoke – just listened to the sound of his voice, hearing it through his chest.

He loves me? Is that what he is saying?

"I didn't want to explain it earlier as I didn't know how you felt. I didn't want to scare you. But then when I was trying to find you a few days ago, you managed to speak to me directly and not just project. It had the same effect on me. I'd never felt it before. The emotions were so strong." His voice was quieter but I knew there was a smile on his face. "You love me. I don't know why you would fall in love with a vampire but you have, and I'm not complaining."

He shifted me to the side and looked at me, searching my face. I was in shock. I knew that I loved Fraser but hadn't properly admitted it to myself, never mind voice it aloud to him. I looked back up at his blue eyes. They were a darker colour than normal, looking back at me. I moved up to him and kissed him.

Soul mates, matched. My vampire. Fraser loves me, and is my vampire.

Acknowledgements

The biggest thank you goes to my husband for not laughing when I first said, "I want to write a book." He should also be praised for his patience with me when I was glued to my laptop and couldn't think about anything else.

A massive thank you to Claire, Gill and Christine for being my first readers. Your encouragement is the reason *Wake* is published.

Lastly, thank you to Melrose books for taking on this new author.

About the Author

Susan Reid was born and raised in Scotland. Her passion for reading books was evident from a young age and she started writing during her teens. This was also when she discovered her natural talent for martial arts.

After graduating from the University of Glasgow, Susan moved to Aberdeenshire where she lives with her husband and lazy greyhound. When not working, Susan is usually found within easy reach of both books and chocolate.